The Criminal Mastermind of Baker Street

Rob Nunn

Paperback ISBN978-1-78705-174-4
ePub ISBN978-1-78705-175-1
PDF ISBN978-1-78705-176-8

Published in the UK by MX Publishing
335 Princess Park Manor, Royal Drive,
London, N11 3GX
www.mxpublishing.co.uk

Cover design by Brian Belanger

Introduction

In "The Adventure of the Speckled Band," Sherlock Holmes said, "when a clever man turns his brains to crime it is the worst of all." What if one of the cleverest men in London had in fact turned his brains to crime instead of detection? Sherlock Holmes believed that crime was common, but logic rare. How would Victorian London have looked if Holmes had decided to combine the common crime element in London with his superior logic to create a great criminal empire? Criminal organizations have operated under a less impressive mind many times. How would Doctor Watson fit into a world where Sherlock Holmes was a criminal mastermind? Would Professor Moriarty be Holmes' friend or foe? If Sherlock Holmes decided to pursue crime instead of thwarting it, what would that London look like?

The following book is an examination into this hypothetical situation. All of the original players are still here: Doctor Watson, Mycroft Holmes, Scotland Yard, and the others. Using William Baring-Gould's chronology of the Sherlock Holmes cases, I have attempted to reimagine how all of the events from the Canon would look if Sherlock Holmes were not trying to prevent these crimes, but were behind many of the crimes himself. Some of the original cases would not be of any interest to him; sometimes Holmes' involvement would remain similar to how he behaved as a consulting detective, and sometimes his responses to events would be wildly different. Let us investigate how Sherlock Holmes, Doctor Watson and London would have been affected by Holmes' decision to become the criminal mastermind of Baker Street.

Chapter 1: Begin at the Beginning

"Dr. Watson, meet Mr. Sherlock Holmes," young Stamford said as he introduced the two strangers in the laboratory at St. Bart's Hospital one January day in 1881.

The young man looked up from his chemical research and greeted them. "How are you?" Sherlock Holmes asked cordially, gripping Watson's hand with strength that surprised the doctor. His sharp and piercing eyes took in the doctor at a glance. "You have been in Afghanistan, I perceive."

Suspicious, Watson asked the tall, gaunt man, "How on earth did you know that?"

A smile crossed Holmes' thin, eager face. "When I saw you, I thought 'Here is a gentleman of a medical type, but with the air of a military man. Clearly an army doctor then. He has just come from the tropics, for his face is dark, and that is not the natural tint of his skin, for his wrists are fair. He has undergone hardship and sickness, as his haggard face says clearly. His left arm has been injured. He holds it in a stiff and unnatural manner. Where in the tropics could an English army doctor have much hardship and got his arm wounded? Clearly in Afghanistan.'"

"Interesting," Watson remarked.

"Never mind. The whole train of thought did not occupy a second," remarked Sherlock Holmes. He pricked a finger on one of his hands that were blotted with ink and stained with chemicals to draw a drop of blood and then placing a small piece of plaster over the prick. "I have to be careful," he continued, noting Watson's look, "for I dabble with poisons a good deal."

"We came here on business," said Stamford, sitting down on a three-legged stool. "My friend here wants to take diggings and is looking for employment, but is slightly embittered at how the great cesspool of London is treating a wounded war veteran. I thought that I had better bring you together."

"A veteran," Holmes mused. "You are not of active duty."

"No," Watson continued. "I was an assistant surgeon for the Fifth Northumberland Fusiliers, but I was struck in the shoulder by a Jezail bullet. After regaining my strength at the base hospital, I suffered an attack of enteric fever, leaving me laid up until I was discharged and sent back to here to London where I have no kith or kin. I mentioned all this to Stamford over lunch and he said that you seem to know of most things in London and might be able to point me in the direction of employment and a place to call home."

Stamford was correct that Holmes knew of most things in London. Sherlock Holmes loved to lie in the very center of the five millions of people in London, with his filaments stretching out and running through the city, a city he considered *his* city. Holmes was attentive to every little rumor, suspicion or opportunity that came his way, and this strongly built doctor who had just been introduced to him presented a definite opportunity.

"I might know something about employment in a few days, but as for lodgings, you may start and end here," Holmes stated. "I have been looking for someone to go halves on a suite in Baker Street. You don't mind strong tobacco, I hope?"

Happily surprised at the possibility of finding decent lodgings, Watson answered, "I always smoke 'ships' myself."

"That's good enough. I generally have chemicals about, and occasionally do experiments. Would that annoy you?"

"By no means."

"Let me see – what are my other shortcomings. I get in the dumps at times, and don't open my mouth for days on end. You must not think I am sulky when I do that. Just let me alone, and I'll soon be right. What have you to confess now? It's just as well for two fellows to know the worst of one another before they begin to live together."

Watson laughed at the cross-examination. "I object to rows, because my nerves are shaken, and I get up at all sorts of ungodly hours, and I am extremely lazy. I have another set of vices when I'm well, but those are the principal ones at present."

Seeing beyond Watson's initial assessment of himself, Holmes asked, "Do you include violin playing in your category of rows?"

"It depends on the player. A well-played violin is a treat for the gods – a badly-played one…"

"Oh, that's all right," Holmes laughed. "I think we may consider the thing as settled – that is, if the rooms are agreeable to you. Call here at noon tomorrow, and we'll go together and settle everything."

"All right – noon exactly," said Watson, shaking Holmes' hand.

Watson and Stamford left Sherlock Holmes working among his chemicals. Once out of the room, Watson turned to Stamford, "Was he really able to deduce so quickly that I had come from Afghanistan? Did you tell him about me?"

Stamford smiled. "No, no. That's just his little peculiarity. A good many people have wanted to know how he finds things out. You mustn't blame me if you don't get on with him."

Watson stopped and looked hard at his companion. "It seems to me, Stamford, that you have some reason for washing your hands of the matter. What is it? Don't be so mealy-mouthed about it."

"Nothing so serious," Stamford replied. "It is not easy to express the inexpressible. Holmes is a little too scientific for most people's tastes – some would say that it approaches cold-bloodedness. He appears to have a passion for definite and exact knowledge."

"Very right too."

"Yes, but it may be pushed to excess. When it comes to beating the subjects in the dissecting rooms with a stick, it is certainly taking rather a bizarre shape."

"Beating the subjects!" Watson ejaculated.

"Yes, to verify how far bruises may be produced after death. I saw him at it with my own eyes. But as far as I know, he is a decent fellow enough."

"After my time in Afghanistan, I don't find myself too picky of company. He is a medical student, I suppose?" Watson asked.

"No – I have no idea what is his actual employ. I believe he is well up in anatomy, and he is a first-class chemist; but, as far as I know, he has never taken any systematic medical classes. His studies are very desultory and eccentric, but he has amassed a lot of out-of-the-way knowledge which would astonish professors. At times, he seems to be a walking calendar of crime, always talking of police news of the past. He is not a man that is easy to draw out, though he can be communicative enough when the fancy seizes him."

"Oh! A mystery is it? This is very piquant. I am much obliged to you for bringing us together. The proper study of mankind is man, you know."

"You must study him, then," Stamford said, as he bade Watson goodbye. "You'll find him a knotty problem, though. I'll wager he learns more about you than you about him."

Holmes and Watson met at noon the next day and inspected the rooms at 221B Baker Street. They consisted of a couple of comfortable bedrooms and a single large airy sitting-room, cheerfully furnished, and illuminated by two broad windows. The two men found the rooms and the rates so desirable that they closed the deal on the spot.

During their first few weeks together, Watson made good on his word to Stamford that he would make a study of Sherlock Holmes. Watson noted that Holmes would sometimes spend his days at the chemical laboratory, sometimes in the dissecting room, and occasionally in long walks, which appeared to take him to the lowest portions of the city. His zeal for certain studies was remarkable, and within eccentric limits, his knowledge was so extraordinarily ample and minute that his observations would astound Watson.

While Watson was making a study of Holmes, Holmes was of course studying Watson in turn. After their first week together, Holmes knew that Watson was a solid and reliable man and felt comfortable enough to receive callers in their new home. Watson found himself confused by Holmes' many acquaintances from all different classes of society. One morning, a fashionably dressed young girl called and stayed for a half hour. Later that day, a gray-headed, seedy visitor came by. Other visitors included an old, white-haired gentleman, a slipshod elderly woman and a railway porter in his velveteen uniform. Anytime one of these visitors came by, Holmes would beg for use of the sitting-room. He would apologize to Watson for the inconvenience, telling him that he had to use that room as a place of business and those people were his clients. Watson simply took himself to another room and never seemed to be bothered by these clients, no matter their social class, which pleased Holmes and solidified his judgment of the doctor's character.

Two months after they had moved into Baker Street, Watson rose early one morning and found Holmes already seated at the breakfast table, reading a French book on graphology. Watson picked up a magazine and his eyes fell upon an article titled *The Book of Life*. As he read the article, he became more and more astounded by the claims in it. The author of the article claimed that by a momentary expression, a twitch of a muscle or a glance of an eye, to fathom a man's innermost thought. Deceit, according to him, was impossible in the case of one trained to observation and analysis. The article went on to proclaim that the practitioner of deduction could meet a fellow mortal, learn at a glance to distinguish the history of the man and the profession to which he belongs.

"What ineffable twaddle!" Watson cried, slapping the magazine down on the table. "I've never read such rubbish in my life."

"What is it?" Holmes asked innocently.

"This article. I see that you have read it since you have marked it. I don't deny that it is smartly written. It irritates me though. It is evidently the theory of some armchair lounger who evolves all these neat little paradoxes in the seclusion of his own study. It is not practical. I should like to see him clapped down in a third-class carriage on the Underground, and asked to give the trades of all his fellow-travelers. I would lay a thousand to one against him."

"You would lose your money," Holmes remarked. "As for the article, I wrote it myself."

"You!"

"Yes; I have a turn both for observation and for deduction. The theories which I have expressed there, and which appear to you to be so chimerical, are really extremely practical – so practical that I depend upon them for my bread and cheese."

"And how?" Watson asked.

After a methodical study of John Watson, Holmes had decided that he was an intelligent, trustworthy and adventurous man whose time in Afghanistan and return to London had allowed his morals to be less rigid than many other Victorian gentlemen. Now that Holmes felt confident in his assessment of the former army doctor, he had had this article published to spark such a conversation, to make it seem as though Holmes' line of work had come up in conversation organically.

"Well, I have a trade of my own. Yes, it has been done before, but not to the level of which I aspire. To the average person, my persona is that of a gentleman with eccentric interests who then turns those studies into monographs and articles. I have published writings on subjects as far-ranging as differences in cigar ashes to the origin of tattoo marks. But in reality, my specialty is planning and executing crimes so perfect that they are untraceable. You might call me a consulting criminal."

Surprised, Watson sat back in his chair.

"Before you object, Doctor, my plans are, almost without exception, devoid of violence. What would be served by a circle of misery, violence and fear? Nothing. I take the view that a when a man embarks upon a crime, he is morally guilty of any other crime which may spring from it. You see, I strive to elevate criminal activity to a gentlemanly fashion. Society can never do away with crime completely, so why not civilize and organize the practice? My methods will greatly reduce dangerous criminals acting with malice towards their victims, for violence does recoil upon the violent. I also strive to eliminate poorly planned crimes resulting in harm coming to people when it can be avoided. You said that Stamford called me a walking calendar of crime, and he had no idea how close to the truth he really was. I have made a study of past crimes, and endeavored to learn from them. Take, for example, the Worthington bank robbery in 1875. The gang's bumbling led to one murder and five prison terms. It was only luck that a guard was not present during the robbery, or surely more blood would have been shed. If I had a hand in the planning of that case, no one would have been harmed, hanged or even caught.

"Look out the window to the fog that permeates London," Holmes continued. "A thief or murderer could roam London on such a day as the tiger does the jungle, unseen until he pounces and then he is evident only to the victim. But if there is a great, controlling force that oversaw all crime in London, petty thugs would know not to accost citizens, and that working under my tutelage would benefit them more than acting on their own ideals. But I am also happy to consult on other's plans for a fee and to help those in need. Those people you have seen in our rooms are my clients. They are mostly sent on by my private inquiry network of agents. They are all people who are in trouble about something, and want a little enlightening. I listen to their story, they listen to my comments, and then I pocket my fee."

Intrigued, Watson asked, "Do you mean to say, that without leaving your room you can unravel some knot which other men can make nothing of, although they have seen every detail for themselves?"

"Quite so. I have a kind of intuition that way. Now and again, a case turns up which is a little more complex. Then I have to bustle about and see things with my own eyes. You see I have a lot of special knowledge which I apply to the problem, and which facilitates matters wonderfully. Those rules of deduction laid down in that article which aroused your scorn are invaluable to me in practical work. Observation with me is second nature, such as when I deduced that you had come from Afghanistan. This trait benefits my organization's planning greatly."

Watson sat quietly, and Holmes poured him a cup of tea from his favorite plantation in India.

"But how could you have created such a profession? And why has no one before you done so?" Watson questioned, stunned but intrigued.

"When I attended university, I realized how great my capabilities were. One afternoon, I was sharing my talent with my friend's father, and he pointed me in my line of work. I had only thought of this as a hobby until that day."

"And why did you never use your abilities to solve crimes instead of committing them?"

"I had intended to do so in my own capacity, and even helped Scotland Yard solve the Tarleton murders in '78, but when another university acquaintance hired me to solve a mystery at his estate, my course changed that day. His butler had solved an old, peculiar family ceremony that led to the finding of the ancient crown of the kings of England. The butler's intellect solved what had gone unnoticed for generations, but in the end, he was undone and ultimately died because of poor planning on his part. I was able to solve the same problem, but the treasure was turned over to the one who had hired me.

"Instead of solving other people's puzzles for an affordable fee, why couldn't I build my own puzzles that would benefit me while being unsolvable to others? Over time, my plans grew and allowed me to be the head of a well-hidden crime syndicate right here in London. Which brings me to you, my good doctor.

"Before you and I met, I had been plying young Stamford for information on reliable men that he knew, and he eventually delivered you. My original interest was that of a discreet doctor, one that I could call on when one of my employees needed mending, and their injuries might arouse suspicion from a more traditional medical service. But after first meeting you, I saw a hint of your nature and wanted to give you further inspection. You immediately struck me as a man who was not happy with how the world had treated him and yearned for adventure. You, no doubt, have been studying me as well."

Watson chuckled, embarrassed to be found out.

"Never mind our prying natures. Over the past few weeks, I have found you to be a most reliable and trustworthy companion. You have not been taken aback by some of my visitors and seem tolerant of my curious habits and hours. If you object to what I have to say, we may part on amicable terms, and no word of this need be spoken again. But if you are, as I suspect, a man of adventure, then I believe you will be interested in my proposal."

Watson sipped his tea and took a moment to respond. "It is true that I have found London to be rather dull and unwelcome since my return. I wouldn't object to hearing what you have to offer."

Holmes smiled with delight. "Excellent! Your medical knowledge will, of course, be of use to my organization. But more importantly, I would like to offer you to be a colleague. I prefer to keep my hands clean of the actual business that brings in my earnings, but sitting and dispatching orders can become so tiresome when it is done alone. I would like you to be present and available while I am doing so. And while you may not see every nuance and detail of my plans, I feel that a man of your nature would be a welcome addition to my operation. A trusty comrade is always of use. Please take your time in considering this proposal, but I would be thrilled if you joined me."

Before Watson could reply, there came the pattering of many steps in the hall and on the stairs, accompanied by audible expressions of dismay from the landlady, Mrs. Hudson. The sitting room was soon overrun by half a dozen of the dirtiest and most ragged street Arabs that anyone had ever seen.

"It's the Baker Street division of my organization," said Holmes to Watson, and then turned to the young scoundrels. "'Tention!"

The boys lined up like six disreputable statues.

"In the future, you shall send up Wiggins alone to report, and the rest of you must wait in the street. Wiggins, do you have my replies?"

"Yessir. Here you are," replied one of the youths.

"Good, good." Holmes took the scraps of paper from the boy and took three others out of his blue dressing gown pocket. "See that these are to be delivered immediately. The first is for the band of gypsies in Surrey. You will need to talk to our man about transportation. The second will go to Beddington, and the third is for Detective Gregson at the Yard. Now, off you go, and come back with replies once you have delivered your messages."

The boys scampered away downstairs and Holmes and Watson could hear their shrill voices the next moment on the street. Holmes turned back to Watson. "I prefer to stay removed from most of my associates, so I employ the Baker Street Irregulars to deliver messages. Many of my employees would arise suspicion from the authorities if they were to be seen frequenting my door."

"But you delivered a message to a detective at Scotland Yard," Watson observed.

"Of course. As I said, my aim is to conduct crime in a professional and gentlemanly way. When dastardly instances such as yesterday's murder in Lauriston Gardens happen, I want them stopped just as much as the force. London's inhabitants should feel safe. And the safer they feel, the easier my plans become. I only help a few of the detectives, though. Most are not worthy of my time. Gregson is the smartest of the Scotland Yarders; he and Detective Lestrade are the pick of a bad lot. They are both quick and energetic, but conventional – shockingly so. They have their knives into one another, too. They are as jealous as a pair of professional beauties and are happy to use my suggestions to gain a step up on each other. I also find it useful to hear their thoughts as they track down criminals. Lestrade got himself into a fog recently over a forgery case, and hearing his methods helped me to know what steps the force would follow in my future plans. No, I don't worry about the Scotland Yard detectives picking up my scent any time soon. I am well-hidden right in front of them."

Watson finished his tea, and cleared his throat. "Your offer is quite an appealing one. It seems to me that you endeavor to bring crime to as near an exact science as it ever will be brought in this world. I would be happy to join you."

Holmes clapped Watson on the shoulder and welcomed him to the organization. Soon, their conversation drifted away from matters of work, and Holmes, in the best of spirits, prattled away about Cremonas and the difference between a Stradivarius and an Amati. Watson listened attentively, expecting to learn much from his new employer, and Holmes was happy to talk with the man that would quickly become his most trusted friend and associate.

Chapter 2: Everything In Due Order

With Watson by his side, Holmes' empire grew. He acquired new employees and nurtured their talents until they were at the top of their professions. One such employee that Holmes took special pride in was Victor Lynch, an up-and-coming forger. Lynch had been performing small jobs for another criminal, Reginald Matthews, when Holmes became aware of his talents. Holmes always preferred to handle incidents without violence when possible, and his hiring of Victor Lynch put this philosophy to the test.

Holmes had been watching Lynch for three weeks, when he finally had his chance to meet with the man without his employer around. After getting into a fight with a neighbor, Lynch was being tended to at Charing Cross Hospital. Holmes and Watson visited the man, looking to anyone else as typical well-wishers, but when they entered his room, Holmes handed Lynch his business card.

Lynch read the card out loud. "Sherlock Holmes. Consultant. What's consultin' got to do with me?" he asked suspiciously.

"Mr. Lynch, I have been aware of your talents in forgery for some weeks now," Holmes replied.

"Oy! You can't come in here accusin' me-"

Holmes held up his hands. "Please, Mr. Lynch. I am not the police. Scotland Yard and the constabulary have no idea of your gift. And I would like to keep it that way. You are currently working for Reginald Matthews, correct?"

"Maybe."

Holmes looked to Watson. "A man who does not readily answer questions about his employer is a good man to have on staff, wouldn't you say?"

"Indeed. It is a sign of character," Watson agreed.

Turning back to Lynch, Holmes continued, "You have a chance to be the top forger in London and I am in need of someone with your capabilities. Judging by your reaction to my card, you've never heard of me. And that makes me happy, for I strive to keep my name away from crime. But if you ask around, Mr. Lynch, you will find that many people in your line of work, are not only aware of who I am, but are employees of mine. Simply mention the phrase 'Vatican cameos' and you will find that the organization I would like to employ you in is one that is subtle but very effective. All jobs are planned by me. If you choose to be in my employ, you will no longer work by your own motives, but neither will you work at your own risk. My employees follow my orders, and because they do, they are protected and very well cared for. Am I making myself clear, Mr. Lynch?"

"You want me an' my scribbles to come work for you, but if I does, I can only do what you tell me to?" Lynch asked.

"That is correct. I don't expect an answer today, but when you are discharged from here, please make a few inquiries using the given phrase. If my proposition is one that would suit you, please dress appropriately, and call on me at the address on the card. If not, make sure that your work never interferes with mine."

With that, Holmes and Watson nodded goodbye to Victor Lynch and left his room. As they walked down the hall, Holmes assured Watson that they would hear from Mr. Lynch very soon. When they entered the hospital waiting room, a ruddy-faced man stepped in front of Holmes.

"I shoulda known you'd show up sooner or later," the man growled.

Holmes sighed as he looked at the man confronting him. "I had hoped I could conduct my business quietly. Please keep your voice down and don't make a scene, Mr. Matthews."

"Don't you go poachin' my boys. You stay up there in your little apartment, and let me do my business," Matthews said, shaking a fist in Holmes' face.

Watson tried to step between the two men, his hand on the service revolver in his coat pocket. But Holmes held out a hand to stop him, his quiet, self-confident manner allowing the situation to play out how he knew it must.

"No need, Watson." Turning back to the petty crime boss, Holmes continued, "We were just visiting Mr. Lynch to make sure that his needs were being met. His future plans are his alone. Not yours or mine to make."

"He works for me and he knows that if he tries to work for a dandy like you, he'll get a rough go of it. And so will you!"

Matthews threw a hard right fist into Holmes' cheek, knocking out his left canine. Holmes, seemingly unfazed by the whole display, demurely spit the tooth into his palm, placed it in his pocket, and then looked at Matthews, who was more than surprised to see his rival so unshaken.

Holmes' cocked an eyebrow as his grey eyes looked at the man coldly. "You will never lay a hand on me or any of my associates ever again. If you do, you will be the one to get 'a rough go of it.'" He brushed by Matthews, and out the door of the hospital and into a cab waiting for him in the street.

The following evening, Mrs. Hudson knocked on the door at 221B and announced that a Mr. Lynch was there to see Mr. Holmes. Holmes, clapped his hands together, looked knowingly at Watson, and told Mrs. Hudson to see Mr. Lynch up. The man that appeared in the doorway was a cleaner version of the one in the hospital room from the day before, and his demeanor was much more subservient.

"Mr. Holmes, sir. Thank you for seeing me," Victor Lynch said.

"Welcome to my home, Mr. Lynch. Please, have a seat."

Lynch sat in a wicker chair. "I asked aroun', and what you said was true about your organization, Mr. Holmes. But, right after you left, Matthews came in to see me and tol' me he knocked one o' your teeth out. I don't like workin' for a man like that, and I'd rather work for you. But Mr. Holmes, that Matthews is a rough man…"

"True, Mr. Matthews and I did meet last night," Holmes conceded. "I also promised him that if he ever touched one of my employees, of which I now view you, that it would not end well for him. I will handle Mr. Matthews. As for the matter of employment, are we in agreement on my terms?"

"I think so, Mr. Holmes. But how will I know when you want me to do a job for ya? And how will I live between jobs if I'm not doin' my own work?" Lynch asked.

Holmes nodded to Watson, who gave a handful of bank notes to the forger. "This is your starting bonus," Watson said. "You will receive a monthly payment and extra for certain jobs. All other communication with Mr. Holmes will be done through our messenger service, the Irregulars. Any street Arab will know how you can get in touch with Mr. Holmes. This will also be your last visit to Baker Street. All other communications will be done by messenger."

Lynch nodded, impressed by the money in his hand and the separation between the employer and empoyees.

"I will be in touch with you shortly, Mr. Lynch. I believe your services will be of use in the next week or so," Holmes smiled.

Just as Lynch was rising to leave, the door from the stairs burst open, and Reginald Matthews stared at the men inside. "I knew you'd turn tail and come work for this toff!" he roared at Lynch, who flinched at the intruder's words.

Matthews strode into the room. "I'll give you one chance to come back and work for me. If not...," he grabbed the fireplace poker and bent it between his large hands and dropped it to the floor, never taking his eyes off Lynch.

Watson cleared his throat, and only then did Matthews notice the gun trained on him that the doctor was holding.

Holmes stood to his full height of over six feet and quietly picked up the bent poker. "Mr. Matthews, Mr. Lynch and I have just completed an employment agreement." Without straining, Holmes bent the poker back to its original shape, much to the surprise of his uninvited guest. "I believe I made myself clear at the hospital yesterday. But," he sighed, "You chose not to heed my advice."

Holmes stepped closer to Matthews, his words and demeanor turning to ice. "You are done in London. You are clearly not aware of my reach. Not only do I have the upper hand on you in this room, but I have the upper hand on you in this city. I have tolerated your bumbling crimes long enough. You are becoming a thorn in my side, and I will not tolerate it, Mr. Matthews. You have until tomorrow morning to leave my city. If not, you can expect a visit from Scotland Yard. And when the detectives bring you into their cells," Holmes tilted his head and paused for effect, "some of my friends inside may find other things to discuss with you."

Up until this point, Matthews had only heard rumors of the busybody living on Baker Street who liked to think of himself as a crime boss, but had dismissed them as just stories. Suddenly, he realized that Sherlock Holmes was not a man to be trifled with. A man that could possess such self-discipline had to be a man with enough resources to back up what he was saying. "A day won't be enough time to get my things."

"I don't care," Holmes stated flatly. "You are wasting your time here. Get out."

Matthews turned and quietly walked out of the room, closing the door behind him. Holmes turned back to Victor Lynch. "You see, Mr. Lynch, as long as you are in my employ, you are under my protection. All I ask of you is your loyalty and to use the utmost discretion when dealing with others outside of our organization, and you will be rewarded. You are never to speak my name yourself, and you may only discuss business with those who know our passwords." Holmes stuck out his hand. "Do we have a deal?"

Lynch jumped from the chair and shook Holmes' hand. "Yessir. We have a deal!"

Watson cleared his throat. "Not to rush you, Holmes, but Mortimer Maberly has sent ahead and asked to meet you at seven. Perhaps we should prepare for your meeting."

Holmes nodded and thanked Lynch for his time. "We will be in touch soon."

Although Holmes' self-control was unsurpassed, he knew that not every would-be competitor could be scared off as easily as Reginald Matthews. So Holmes decided that he would become not only an intellectual force, but a physical one as well. Strength had always come easily to him, but his refined tastes dictated that he have an effective and gentlemanly way of using is. Holmes dove into boxing, Baritsu and singlestick. One evening in the autumn of 1884, Holmes told Watson to dress for a night out.

"Where are we off to tonight, Holmes? The de Sarasate night at Covent Garden was yesterday."

Holmes picked up a small bag. "Tonight, we will be taking in the fine art of pugilism. And we must be on time, for I am appearing in the fourth match!"

"Holmes, this is preposterous! You can't mean to set foot in a seedy den after all this time of distancing yourself from the criminal class. Surely, word of you appearing in a backroom match will make its way back to –"

Holmes held up his hand. "Of course not, Watson. We will be attending a benefit at Alison's rooms tonight. The fee to the benefit is ten pounds, so we will hardly be rubbing elbows with London's lesser ranked citizens. Come along, Doctor!"

Holmes and Watson arrived just as the first round was beginning. Watson nodded hello to a few acquaintances from his social club as he read the match card for the evening, planning on placing a few bets as the night went on. Holmes, on the other hand, found a vantage point at the back of the crowd, where he could observe those in attendance as well as the fighters in the ring. Always on the lookout for business opportunities, he made a study of those in the room, and once the fights started paid close attention to the fighters and how they maneuvered, possibly to pick up any tips that would help him in his match.

When the fourth match began, Holmes stared across the ring at his opponent, McMurdo: a short, deep-chested man. The referee invited the two men to meet in the middle and reviewed the Queensberry rules before beginning the match. When the match started, McMurdo pounded his gloves together, bobbing and weaving like a ship at sea, while Holmes moved in calmly and coolly. McMurdo barreled towards his opponent and tested a few punches to Holmes' stomach, and Holmes retaliated with a right feint followed by a short jab to McMurdo's protruding face, forcing the smaller man to take a step back as he shook his head.

The crowd cheered for more, and McMurdo waded back in with a combination to Holmes' midsection, expecting his taller opponent to move away. Instead, Holmes blocked and absorbed the brunt, returning a wicked two-punch volley to McMurdo's chin. McMurdo clipped back and forth on the canvas while Holmes stood his ground. McMurdo delivered short punches to Holmes' midsection again and Holmes whipped a right uppercut to his chin. The two opposing styles continued for the remaining minutes of the round, McMurdo's frenzied body blows countered by Holmes' carefully placed punches until the first round ended.

In the intermission, gambling picked up in the crowd surrounding the ring and Watson shouldered his way to Holmes' corner. "Holmes, McMurdo is favored two to one after this round. Can you last five rounds with his energy?"

"*He* will not last five rounds with his energy. He is already beginning to lag. I'm afraid we will not make it past three rounds. Wait until the end of the next round to place your bets," Holmes warned before being called back into the ring.

Round two started with McMurdo charging into Holmes, punching hard with both hands with a barrage of punches that would have downed most men. Holmes staggered back from the attacks and regrouped as the crowd roared for McMurdo to attack again. Holmes tentatively moved back into the fight, and swung a left as the short man came in, only to catch two more high hard hits to his head. Holmes tried to retaliate by throwing out a few tentative punches that were quickly batted away and returned with strong blows by McMurdo. The two men circled each other and Holmes feinted suddenly and threw a roundhouse swing that McMurdo easily went under, smashing a right to Holmes' ribs, knocking him back. Counting down the seconds to intermission in his mind, Holmes staggered back towards his opponent, only to be met with a strong left hook. He reeled back on his heels, and the crowd cheered as they expected him to fall, but the referee called time for the round and Holmes staggered back to his corner.

Instead of going back to consult with Holmes during this intermission, Watson worked the room for odds against his friend. Placing as many bets as he could at 7 to 1 odds, he turned back to the ring to watch what Holmes had promised would be the final round.

When the third round started, McMurdo smelled blood in the water. Although his energy was waning, he was encouraged by Holmes' poor showing in the second round and expected to end the match quickly. The opponent he met in the ring this round was hardly the same man. Standing tall and confident, his eyes staring coolly at McMurdo, Holmes blocked his initial volley and returned a strong cross to McMurdo's mouth and a right to his chin to back the shorter man off. When he barreled back in again, McMurdo was met with a combination that caught him by surprise. McMurdo waded back in and landed a hard right to Holmes' ribs while Holmes delivered another hard right to his opponent's mouth. The two men circled each other, McMurdo's ragged breathing contrasting sharply with Holmes' cool demeanor. They moved back in at the same time, Holmes jabbing with his right, followed by a left cross and then moving back out. McMurdo shot out two tentative jabs that landed, but with little force. This back and forth continued until McMurdo noticed Holmes drop his left arm. McMurdo moved in again and landed a solid hit to Holmes' ribs only to have his breath knocked out of him by Holmes' right. He staggered back, and Holmes moved in with a cross-hit to McMurdo's jaw that spun the man around and knocked him to the mat.

The crowd cheered and groaned as the referee held Holmes' gloved hand up to name him the winner of the match while Watson moved around the crowd to collect his winnings. After Holmes had changed back into his evening wear, he met up with Watson just as the next match was beginning.

"How did we do?" Holmes asked.

"A very nice take for less than fifteen minutes of work," Watson chuckled. "And, Lord Backwater has asked for a meeting with you to discuss a delicate matter."

Holmes smiled. "A man's work is never done, Watson. Please have Lord Backwater meet me in the side room."

Watson retrieved the man and brought him to meet with Holmes. "Lord Backwater, very nice to see you this evening," Holmes greeted.

"The pleasure is mine, Mr. Holmes. And may I congratulate you on your victory, though it cost me," he chuckled. "I should have known better than to bet against a man with such a reputation as yours."

Holmes smiled in response. "And what reputation is that?"

"You have the reputation as a man who is able to handle discreet situations, and that is what I would like to speak with you about tonight," Backwater said, glancing towards Watson.

"Doctor Watson is a trusted colleague and anything you say in front of him will be treated with the same discretion as I would," Holmes stated.

Nodding, Backwater continued. "I have a business opportunity with a gentleman in the States that would be frowned upon if my name were to be attached to it, and I am looking for someone to facilitate safe passage from America. I thought that you might be the man to handle such a situation."

"I welcome exchanges with our American cousins, predicting that our children will someday be citizens of the same worldwide country. I am hesitant to extend too far into that country due to the resourcefulness of the Pinkerton Agency. Their tenacity surpasses anything we see here in England. I must warn you that unless a well thought out plan is in place, I am not interested in tangling with the Pinkertons unless I must. What sort of business opportunity and passage would you need?"

Backwater pursed his lips. "I am not at liberty to say the business proposition and had hoped that you would provide the arrangements for passage."

Holmes nodded gravely. "Lord Backwater, while I admire your industrious spirit, I am accustomed to having mystery at one end of my cases, but to have it at both ends is too confusing, I fear."

"I must insist upon this level of secrecy, Mr. Holmes."

"Then I must decline the offer, Lord Backwater. Plus, I am currently working with a certain circus belle and fishmonger, so I would not be able to give your little problem the proper attention that I feel it would require. But you may rely upon my discretion on our conversation, and no others will know of it."

Disappointed, Lord Backwater said goodbye and left Holmes and Watson alone in the room.

"Holmes!" Watson called out, "Lord Backwater is a leading man in London. Why wouldn't you listen to his offer? Imagine extending your reach to America!"

"I meant what I said, my dear Watson. The Pinkertons in America are a force to be reckoned with. And, while I agree that I am more than up to that challenge, it would divert my attention away from dealings here in London and I am not yet completely satisfied with my position in our criminal world."

"But why on earth would you mention a fishmonger to his lordship when you've just finished working with the King of Scandinavia?"

Holmes smiled wryly. "I didn't want Lord Backwater to feel that I was above his class. And anyway, the humbler of my works are usually the more interesting," he smiled as they stepped back out to enjoy the rest of their evening.

Chapter 3: This Great International Affair

After spending an entire night out in the wind and rain, Watson returned to Baker Street early one morning in October of 1886. Bedraggled, weary, and the Jezail bullet throbbing in one of his limbs, he found Holmes already at the breakfast table.

"Welcome home, Doctor. I presume that you have tended to our man in Grosvenor Square appropriately?"

"Yes," Watson sighed as he settled into his chair. "Mister Monken is mending and well-hidden. There is no reason to fear for him. He's told me the story over and over, and I still don't understand how he ended up under a furniture van."

"No need to worry, Watson. Now that you have our man on the mend, everything is quite cleared up."

"That is good to hear. Now, if I can just stay awake through my breakfast, I plan to spend the rest of the day in bed."

Appreciative of his friend's work to mend one of his employees, Holmes meant to entertain Watson while he ate.

"Have I ever told you of my early times in Montague Street before the time in our current rooms?"

After five years of association, Watson had rarely been able to elicit from Holmes what had first turned his mind to crime other than their first conversation on the day that Holmes had hired him. Finding his friend in a communicative humor, Watson immediately perked up. "No! You arouse my curiosity, Holmes."

Sitting forward, Holmes lit his pipe. "I told you of my first encounter with deduction with Victor Trevor's father?"

"Your friend from college? Only that he was the man that put your life on a course towards deduction as a livelihood."

"That was only part of a larger story. I was an awkward and unsociable fellow while at university. I was more interested in working out my own little methods of thought than mixing with the other men of my year. Other than fencing, I had few athletic tastes, and my line of study was so distinct from that of the other men, that we hardly had any points of contact. In fact, Victor Trevor was the only friend I made during the time that I was at college. While we were visiting his father, he fell under a blackmailer, which ultimately led to his death. Victor was understandably heartbroken and did not return to university. He took to India and became a successful tea planter, but rumors of his familial affairs and my involvement followed me back to the university.

"After some time of introspection and the loss of my only friend, I had learned that emotional qualities are antagonistic to clear reasoning. This was convenient as my aloof manner and rumors surrounding my involvement with the tragedy at the Trevor estate had caused my peers to distance themselves from me, although they still remained interested in my keen abilities.

"Upon graduating, I took rooms on Montague Street, just around the corner from the British museum. I set up as a consultant of all kinds, dealing with whatever clients I could find, from confounded detectives to old Russian women. But I spent my too abundant leisure time studying all branches of science which could make me more efficient in my line of work. These days were immeasurably useful, but extremely solitary.

"During this time came the Musgrave ritual problem, that in which the butler found the ancient crown but died due to poor planning. This was a watershed moment for me, as I have told you. For two years after that, I dedicated myself to my studies, reading up on subjects of all natures, spending time in the lab at St. Bart's and with a taxidermist in Lambeth. At the museum of London, I immersed myself in law, anatomy, botany, geology and chemistry. But most of all, I studied crime.

"I pored over every police report and article on criminal activity that I could find, assessing the risk against the reward from the crime. I dissected every criminal report and would then map out the crime in my own mind. What were the possibilities of capture? How could the crime have been hidden or its discovery delayed?"

"But where did your employees come from? Surely you couldn't have formed your empire from a library and a laboratory?" Watson asked, all thought of exhaustion gone by now.

"Of course not. I began to make associations with the more active participants in London's underworld. I built up these associations into a form of trust, where the criminals felt that they could share their stories with me. I was always an eager audience to hear of their jobs. These new allies discussed ideas for future activities, and I would readily give feedback, making their heists all that much better. Once I gained a reputation among the criminal class as someone who could devise fool-proof plans, I was able to start charging a small commission on each planning session, building my business without getting my own hands dirty. Ironically, many of London's lawbreakers came to trust me more once they saw that I was making a profit off of their work and my clientele picked up steadily.

"After a particularly successful case where my men were able to relieve a lady of a valuable opal tiara, I knew that my organization had hit its stride. I had established a chain of command and was now planning and orchestrating crimes of my own crimes, and many of the criminal class saw the benefits of working under my leadership. At this point, I had decided to move to a more respectable room and distance myself from the more suspicious members of my organization. This was also the time that I felt having a doctor on staff would be useful, and our partnership began."

"Fantastic, Holmes! I am amazed at your rare ability at crime," Watson smiled.

"Crime is common, doctor. Logic is rare."

The next day, the Secretary of State, Trelawney Hope, entered Holmes' rooms, looking despondent, and laid out a case that could lead to dire circumstances for Europe, if not all-out war. A document had been stolen from Hope's dispatch box, written by a foreign potentate. If this letter were shared with other countries, disastrous results would occur. Hope confided that a source from inside the government recommended that he seek out help from Holmes. It was said that he was discreet and that his nationalistic pride would encourage him to help his queen and country.

Knowing there would be little if any financial gain to this endeavor, Holmes still agreed to take the case. Watson was surprised to see his friend's patriotism outweigh his greed.

"Now, Mr. Hope, I should be much obliged if you would tell me exactly the circumstances under which this document disappeared," Holmes said.

"That can be done in a very few words, Mr. Holmes. The letter was received six days ago. It was of such importance that I have never left it in my safe, but I have taken it across each evening to my house in Whitehall Terrace, and kept it in my bedroom in a locked dispatch-box. It was there last night. Of that I am certain. I actually opened the box while I was dressing for dinner, and saw the document inside. This morning it was gone. The dispatch-box had stood beside the glass upon my dressing table all night. I am a light sleeper, and so is my wife. We are both prepared to swear that no one could have entered the room during the night. And yet I repeat that the paper is gone."

"What time did you dine?"

"Half-past seven."

"How long was it before you went to bed?"

"My wife had gone to the theater. I waited up for her. It was half-past eleven before we went to our room."

"Then for four hours the dispatch-box had lain unguarded?"

"No one is ever permitted to enter that room save the housemaid in the morning, and my valet, or my wife's maid, during the rest of the day. They are both trusty servants who have been with us

33

for some time. Besides, neither of them could possibly have known that there was anything more valuable than the ordinary departmental papers in my dispatch-box."

"Who did know of the existence of that letter?"

"No one in the house."

"Surely, your wife knew?"

"No sir; I had said nothing to my wife until I missed the paper this morning. Until this morning, I have never breathed one word to my wife upon this matter."

"Could she have guessed?"

"No, Mr. Holmes, she could not have guessed – nor could anyone have guessed."

"Who is there in England who did know of this existence of this letter?"

"Each member of the Cabinet was informed of it yesterday; but the pledge of secrecy which attends every Cabinet meeting was increased by the solemn warning which was given by the Prime Minister. Good heaves, to think that within a few hours I should myself have lost it! Besides the members of the Cabinet there are two, or possibly three, departmental officials who know of the letter. No one else in England, Mr. Holmes, I assure you."

"But abroad?"

"I believe that no one abroad has seen it save the man who wrote it. I am well-convinced that his ministers – that the usual official channels have not been employed."

Holmes leaned back in his chair, tenting his fingers in front of him and sat quietly for some time. After some minutes, he leaned forward and said, "Now, sir, I must ask you more particularly what this document is, and why its disappearance should have such momentous consequences?"

"Mr. Holmes, the envelope is a long, thin one of pale blue color. There is a seal of red wax stamped with a crouching lion. It is addressed in large, bold handwriting to-"

"I fear that my inquiries must go more to the root of things. What *was* the letter?"

The Secretary of State hesitated.

"If you cannot share that information with me, then any continuation of this interview would be a waste of time. I have a good many calls upon me and you are a busy man," Holmes replied.

Sighing in resignation, Hope continued. "The letter, then, is from a certain foreign potentate who has been ruffled by some recent colonial developments of this country. It had been written hurriedly and upon his own responsibility entirely. Inquiries have shown that his ministers know nothing of the matter. At the same time it is couched in so unfortunate a manner, and certain phrases in it are of so provocative a character, that its publication would undoubtedly lead to a most dangerous state of feeling in this country. There would be such a ferment, sir, that I do not hesitate to say that within a week of the publication of that letter this country would be involved in a great war."

Holmes, understanding the gravity of this situation, continued. "Have you informed the sender?"

"Yes, sir, a cipher telegram has been dispatched, and we have strong reason to believe that he already understands that he has acted in an indiscreet and hot-headed manner. It would be a greater blow to him and to his country than to us if this letter were to come out."

"If this is so, whose interest is it that the letter should come out? Why should anyone desire to steal it or to publish it?"

"There, Mr. Holmes, you take me into regions of high international politics. But if you consider the European situation you will have no difficulty in perceiving the motive. The whole of Europe is an armed camp. There is a double league which makes a fair balance of military power. Great Britain holds the scales. If Britain were driven into war with one confederacy, it would assure the supremacy of the other confederacy, whether they joined in the war or not. Do you follow?"

"Very clearly. And to whom would this document be sent if it fell into the hands of an enemy?"

"To any of the great chancelleries of Europe. It is probably speeding on its way thither at the present instant as fast as steam can take it."

Holmes promised to do what he could, although he admitted that matters may already be past his means. The Secretary of State nodded and walked gravely from the room.

Holmes lit his pipe and sat in silence for some time, lost in deep thought. Watson, knowing not to break in upon Holmes before he roused himself from his reverie, opened the morning's paper and began to read about a sensational crime committed the night before.

"The situation is desperate, but not hopeless," Holmes stated from his chair. "Even now, if we could be sure which of the international spies and secret agents have taken it, it is just possible that it has not yet passed out of his hands. After all, it is a question of money with these fellows, and I have the British Treasury behind me. If it's on the market I'll buy it – if it means another penny on the income tax. It is conceivable that the fellow might hold it back to see what bids come from this side before he tries his luck on the other. There are only three capable of playing so bold a game; there are Oberstein, La Rothiere, and Eduardo Lucas." Holmes' mouth twisted in disgust. "I will see each of them."

"Is that Eduardo Lucas of Godolphin Street?" Watson asked from his newspaper.

"Yes."

"You will not see him. He was murdered in his house last night."

Holmes jumped to his feet and stared down his thin, hawk like nose at the newspaper report that Watson indicated. "Well, Watson, what do you make of this?"

"It is an amazing coincidence."

"A coincidence! Here is one of the three despicable men whom we had named as possible actors in this drama, and he meets a violent death during the very hours when we know that that drama was being enacted. The odds are enormous against its being a coincidence. No figures could express them. No, my dear Watson, the two events are connected – *must* be connected. It is for us to find the connection."

"But now the official police must know all."

Holmes chuckled. "The police rarely know all. They know all they see at Godolphin Street. They know – and shall know – nothing of Whitehall Terrace. Only *we* know both events, and can trace the relation between then them."

"Then you have an idea?"

"It is a capital mistake to theorize in the advance of the facts. We must spend time at Godolphin Street, but must be aware of the regular establishment already there. With Eduardo Lucas lies the solution of our problem, though I must admit that I have not an inkling as to what form it may take. I will while away the morning at Godolphin Street, seeing who is on the case. Perhaps one of the detectives I have helped out in the past. Do stay on guard, my good Watson, and receive any fresh visitors. I'll join you at lunch if I am able."

Lunch came and went, and Holmes returned as the lamplighters were working their way down the street. "Did anyone call while I was gone, Watson?" he asked, bursting through the door.

"Only a message from Monty Wolder declaring the Margate job to be a success, and an update that Lynch is nearly finished with his latest assignment. But what have you found out for the Secretary?"

Holmes smiled. "I spent some time observing the scene from afar, when who should I see in charge but our old friend, Lestrade. Appearing to walk by on other casual business, I greeted him and asked what his matters were of late.

"'A bad case here, Mr. Holmes. Shaping up to be a lover's quarrel gone wrong,' he told me

"'An open and shut case then? Hardly a case to drag you from your perch?' I ventured.

"'Hardly. This one is an international incident. Seems this Lucas fellow got a surprise visit from his wife, only she didn't know that he had a secret life here in London. See, he kept his life in watertight compartments. She told him how she had traced him, reproached him, one thing led to another, and then with a dagger, the end came. Our friends on the Paris force picked her up just now, stark raving mad as she entered back into the country. Before they could get her calm, she told them the whole story. I just now found out about her, though. Was investigating a curious stain on the floor. But now that the mystery is solved, it doesn't bear much interest.'

"I cajoled him into telling me about the stain of interest, playing up my interest in queer incidents. The carpet had a blood stain on it that did not match where the blood on the floor had been. Seeing that the case was solved as far as he was concerned, I convinced him to letting me have a look at the stains. Now that it was not an active crime scene, Lestrade called his men off and sent them away, saying he would call on them later for reports.

"I entered the house, Lestrade giving me only a few minutes before he would lock the doors and shoo me off. Once alone in the room, I saw the aforementioned stains. I tore back the corner of the carpet to find a hidden compartment in the floor that the inspectors would have seen if they looked closely. Thank heavens they didn't! But to my dismay, the space was empty. I quickly concealed it and bid Lestrade good day."

Watson deflated. "So you have not found the missing letter then? I had such high hopes."

"My story is hardly finished. I worked my way back through the problem. If Lucas *had* known of the letter, how would he have gotten it out of the Secretary's house, I pondered. Do you remember how the Secretary described his wife's despair at hearing of the loss of the letter?"

Watson paused. "I can't say that I do."

"Exactly. A man as shaken as he was would most likely have described his wife's concern along with his. While she undoubtedly would have worried for her husband, he did not say that she was shocked by the theft. Come, friend Watson, the curtain rings up for the last act."

"You have solved it!"

"Hardly that, Watson, there are some points which are as dark as ever. But we have so much that it will be our own fault if we cannot get the rest. We will go straight to Whitehall Terrace and bring the matter to a head."

Arriving at the residence of the European Secretary, Holmes asked for the lady of the house, who appeared momentarily.

"May I help you, gentlemen?" she inquired.

"I know, madam, that you are aware of the missing paper from your husband's dispatch-box. Unfortunately, I have no possible alternative but to make an unsolicited call upon you. I have been commissioned to recover this immensely important paper. I must therefore ask you, madam, to be kind enough to place it in my hands," Holmes stated.

Looking shocked, the lady responded, "You insult me, sir!"

"Come, come, madam, it is useless. Give up the letter. I am endeavoring to avoid a scandal for the good of the nation, and you are only frustrating my efforts. Give up the letter, and all will be set right. If you will work with me, I can arrange everything. If you work against me, I must expose you."

The lady paused, clearly considering her options.

"I know that Eduardo Lucas had the document, and that Lucas was murdered last night. The letter is now missing. It is my belief that you gave the man the letter, and then thinking better of it, returned to his house, found him dead, and retrieved the letter for yourself. If I am correct, the matter may still be adjusted. I have no desire to bring trouble to you. My duty ends when I have returned the lost letter to your husband. Take my advice and be frank with me. It is your only chance."

Seeing that she had been found out, Mrs. Hope quickly told her story to the two men seated in front of her. Eduardo Lucas had compromising letters of hers and used them for blackmail. Lucas knew of the potentate's letter and had Mrs. Hope take it to him. The rest of the story was as Holmes had stated. Deciding she would rather be shamed than her husband put at risk, she returned to Lucas, only to find him dead, and pulled out the blue envelope he had only recently put into his floorboards. She then fled home, unsure of her next step. Holmes told her to place the letter back into the dispatch-box among her husband's other papers and bid her good day, asking her not to speak of his visit to anyone, especially her husband.

Once he returned to Baker Street, Holmes dispatched a message to Trelwaney Hope: "All inquiries have turned up dead ends. I encourage you to retrace your steps and search through your papers once more. SH"

Of course, the Secretary found his missing letter and crisis was averted. When Watson asked him why he took the case on when no mention of a reward was given, Holmes looked out the window. "Sometimes, it is best to use your abilities for good, Watson. The problem was an interesting one, and if I am able to deal a blow to traitorous men such as Lucas, I am not only helping my country, but I can sleep easier at night. Plus," he added, "it could be useful to have a member of the Cabinet in our debt."

Chapter 4: The Affair is a Tangled One

As 1886 turned into 1887, Holmes' empire faced a grave threat from a competitor named Baron Maupertuis. Maupertuis, a dashing figure, had evaded authorities in Paris and Berlin before setting his sights on London and all it had to offer him. After succeeding in political and financial schemes abroad, the Baron intended to organize and lord over the criminal class in London. Maupertuis created a shell organization called the Netherland-Sumatra company, stating that it was an international shipping company, and used it to cover his criminal dealings.

Arrogant and cocksure, the Baron did nothing to hide his ambition from the public, almost reveling in the international reputation as a master schemer that the London papers had painted him with upon his arrival to London society. The press reported breathlessly of his nightly engagements at balls and musical performances, speculating wildly which society belle would be seen on his arm next. Although many were aware of his sullied reputation abroad, the younger members of society were caught up in his debonair manner and disregarded his past as he entertained them each night.

With his public persona garnering attention and the Netherland-Sumatra Company in place, Maupertuis began his rise in the underworld, moving swiftly from street-level crimes to financial swindling and political blackmail. Every criminal activity was handled so deftly that no paper trail existed to connect him back to any wrongdoing. Only whispers of his involvement lingered, adding to his already dangerous and romantic reputation.

As he had shown with Reginald Matthews, Holmes did not actively seek out confrontation with other criminal organizations. Knowing that many operators created their own downfall, Holmes often allowed events to play out. In other cases, the time would come when the operators would have to be dealt with or absorbed into his own. Holmes was well aware of the Netherland-Sumatra Company, following it through the newspapers and continuous reports from his agents in the underworld, but did not engage with it during its meteoric rise. Maupertuis' rise through the criminal underworld of London was so quick and easy, that he did not take into account the possibility of another organizing force in criminal London. Within months of his arrival in the city, Maupertuis' cavalier actions showed that he felt that he was the only organizing force behind London's criminal enterprises.

Holmes' and Maupertuis' two forces finally crossed paths on a day when Holmes and Watson were off in Trincomalee, clearing up a mess made by two brothers in his employ. While out of town, Holmes had some of his most trusted employees substituting a forged painting at Darlington Castle so that the original could be sold to an unscrupulous art dealer. Unbeknownst to Holmes, Maupertuis' agents were on their way to Darlington Castle that same night to demand payment in a current blackmail scheme.

The lady of the house refused to pay and ordered her servants to block Maupertuis' agents from leaving the property. The whole estate lit into an uproar, and Holmes' employees were barely able to escape with the stolen painting in time. The local police were called in and an investigation was launched, which of course did not lead back to the Baron. But Holmes knew that it was finally time to deal with his rival.

It was a cold morning of the early spring, and Holmes and Watson sat after breakfast on either side of a cheery fire in Baker Street. A thick fog rolled down between the lines of houses, through which the opposing windows loomed like dark, shapeless blurs through the heavy yellow wreaths. Holmes had been silent all morning, dipping continuously into the advertisement columns of a succession of papers until at last he emerged in no very sweet temper to discuss the previous night's near catastrophe.

"Watson, I am afraid that I will have to suspend any further projects for the time being. Let the employees know that their regular payments will continue and that I will need their talents in the future, but for a foreseeable time, I will have a larger matter which will require all of my attention," Holmes gravely stated.

Watson lowered his newspaper. "The Netherland-Sumatra Company finally has to be dealt with, doesn't it?"

Holmes sighed. "I'm afraid it does. I had hoped that the Baron's colossal schemes would lead to his capture by the authorities, but his brazen behavior is matched by his ability to distance himself from his crimes. The matter at Darlington Castle proved that the time has come to act. We were not caught in our work, but knowing that he and I had targeted the same estate only proves that his crimes interfere with mine. Luckily, his egocentric behavior hasn't allowed him to look closely enough to know of my organization, which is to my advantage."

"I am amazed that Maupertuis is unaware of our agency."

"To someone like the Baron, there is nothing more deceptive than an obvious fact."

"I am happy to help, Holmes. You only need to give me my orders."

"This is a path I must take alone, Watson. I don't doubt your willingness to help, but I will need to become a student once again and learn a new trade. Your position will be to keep the wheels turning in our little family. Take care of any correspondence and payments due. If any opportunities arise, assess if they are worth discussing when I am ready. Although business will stop for now, I will still need a steady hand at the tiller."

Puffing out his chest slightly, Watson replied, "Or course. But how will you become a student again? Surely you don't mean returning to university?"

"Hardly," Holmes said as he scratched off a note. "I will also need you to deliver this to Mr. Michael Sasanoff. He will be staying at Grand Hotel."

"Sasanoff, the actor?"

"Yes. It has long been an axiom of mine that education never ends. And now it is time that I learned the art of disguises."

Swayed by Holmes' generous payments, Sasanoff tutored Holmes day and night on acting for the following weeks.

Surprised by his student's quick learning, Sasanoff was able to begin discussing costuming and posture with Holmes, who soaked up every bit of information like a sponge. Once his crash course was complete, Sasanoff offered Holmes a position in his touring company, but Holmes declined, citing more pressing matters in London. So great was Holmes' new ability Sasanoff mused that the stage truly lost a great actor that day.

Over the next two months, Holmes took on many different personalities, all while gathering incriminating evidence against Baron Maupertuis. From a common loafer and a sailor to a gentleman of leisure and even an old woman, Holmes toiled away every day with this fresh weapon in his arsenal. Working at least fifteen hours a day, and sometimes for five days at a stretch, Holmes methodically built up his case against Maupertuis, right under the Baron's nose, slowly linking known criminals to the Baron, and twice even finding documentation that incriminated him in schemes.

Unbeknownst to Maupertuis, his employees were quietly disappearing from London. Holmes had arranged for them to be hidden away in hamlets throughout the countryside until he was ready to strike. Confessions were collected in these men's and women's handwriting, while Holmes investigated the Baron's crime scenes, looking for evidence that could be traced back to him. Using his special knowledge of tobacco ashes, Holmes was able to pronounce the ash found at one scene to be that of an Indian cigar favored by a well-known associate of the Baron. And zinc and copper filings found at another spot were used to run down a coiner who was easily persuaded to confess his employment by Maupertuis.

Finally, after his immense exertions, Holmes disappeared from London and a large parcel was delivered to Scotland Yard. Within hours of its delivery, a swarm of officers rounded up Baron Maupertuis and his lead associates. Maupteruis' hidden agents were returned to London and confessed their crimes, making sure to incriminate the Baron in everything they spoke of. The European press rang with praise for the anonymous man who single-handedly brought down the most accomplished swindler in Europe.

But the task had taken its toll on Holmes. After the Netherland-Sumatra Company had been dissolved, Watson waited for days to hear from his friend. After a week of patience, on April 14, Watson received a telegram from Lyons, France, calling him to the Hotel Dulong. Within twenty-four hours, Watson was beside his friend and was relieved to find nothing serious in Holmes' symptoms, although his iron constitution had broken down under the strain of his crusade against Maupertuis. He found Holmes prey to the blackest depression. Even knowing that he had succeeded where the police of three countries had failed, and that he had outmaneuvered Maupertuis at every point, was insufficient to rouse Holmes from his nervous prostration.

Watson poured his friend a glass of brandy and water. "Surely, you must understand what you have accomplished, Holmes," he ventured. "Not only have you put a stop to a criminal force that would impede your own, but you have done England, and all of Europe a great favor."

"What you say is true, my friend, but knowing that such an upstart could force my work to stop in such a drastic manner and for such a long period is insufferable to me. I confess that my arrogance allowed the Baron's schemes to exist for too long, but it is better to learn wisdom late than never learn it at all. I know that I must return to London and resume activity, but the strain of the past two months has been a great one."

After three days of convalescence in France, Watson and Holmes returned to Baker Street. To regain his ambition for work, Holmes took to cocaine, restoring his fierce energy for bouts of time. After two days of furious notes and messages returning his organization to working order, it was evident to Watson that his friend could not continue at this pace; he simply wasn't restored yet. Even though he had observed Holmes' energy return, Watson could see that the stimulant would eventually drag his friend back into a black depression once again.

Colonel Hayter, who had come under Watson's professional care in Afghanistan, had a house near Reigate in Surrey, and had frequently asked his old friend to come down for a visit. With a little diplomacy, informing Holmes that the establishment was a bachelor one and that he would be allowed the fullest freedom, Holmes fell in with Watson's plans, and a week after their return from Lyons, Holmes and Watson were under the colonel's roof.

Holmes and Watson spent their first few days with the colonel fishing and reading, but Holmes was unable to relax for very long. He began work on a monograph on the art of acting and disguise until a new puzzle presented itself. After demonstrating his extraordinary skill at analyzing handwritings to solve a local problem, he completed his monograph and stated to Watson, "I think our quiet rest in the country has been a distinct success. It has been a charming stay, and I shall certainly return, much invigorated, to Baker Street tomorrow."

When they arrived back in London, Holmes encouraged Watson to set up his own medical practice, citing that if any authorities investigated them, Watson would need to show a source of income. Agreeing with this logic, Watson dedicated the next few weeks to building up a practice in Holborn and spent the evenings hearing Holmes tell of his exploits such as a burglary at Arnsworth Castle, before he had to spend some time in Odessa on a matter of business.

On the evening May 20th, Watson returned home to find Holmes in front of the fire.

"Welcome home, Holmes!" Watson greeted his friend.

"Thank you, Watson. It is good to be back in London. I fear that Russia lacks the creature comforts of home." Holmes waved Watson to his armchair, threw across his case of cigars, and indicated a spirit case and gasogene in the corner.

"Your business is taken care of then?" Watson asked after he had made them both a drink.

"Yes, the Trepoff murder has been dealt with. I made a stop on my way back and procured our next client." Holmes indicated a sheet of thick note paper.

Watson read the note. "There will call upon you tonight, at a quarter to eight o'clock a gentleman who desires to consult you upon a matter of the very deepest moment. Your past services to one of the Royal Houses of Europe have shown that you are one who may safely be trusted with matters which are of an importance which can hardly be exaggerated. This account of you we have from all quarters received. Be in your chamber then at that hour, and do not take it amiss if your visitor wear a mask."

Looking up from the paper, Watson asked, "You said you procured this client?"

"Perhaps I speak too freely. I made myself known in certain circles, aware that this gentleman is looking for someone to handle a delicate problem. What can you deduce from the note itself?"

Watson carefully examined the writing and the paper. "The man who wrote it was presumably well-to-do," he remarked, endeavoring to imitate Holmes' process that he had witnessed over the years. "Such paper could not be bought under half a crown a packet. It is peculiarly strong and stiff."

"Peculiar – that is the very word. It is not an English paper at all. The man who wrote the note is a German. Do you note the peculiar construction of the sentence – 'This account of you we have from all quarters received.' A Frenchman or a Russian could not have written that. It is the German who is so uncourteous to his verbs. It only remains, therefore, to meet with this German who writes upon Bohemian paper, and prefers to wear a mask. And here he comes, if I am not mistaken."

A slow and heavy step was heard upon the stairs and in the passage. It paused outside the door and then there was a loud and authoritative tap.

"Come in!" said Holmes.

The man who entered was six feet six inches in height, with large chest and limbs. His dress had a richness which would have been looked upon as bad taste in England. His hand had just finished adjusting a black vizard mask, which extended down past the cheek bones.

"You had my note?" he asked in a deep, harsh German voice. "I told you that I would call."

"I did," said Holmes. "Pray take a seat. This is my friend and colleague, Dr. Watson. Whom have I the honor to address?"

"You may address me as the Count von Kramm, a Bohemian nobleman. I understand that this gentleman, your friend, is a man of honor and discretion, whom I may trust with a matter of the most extreme importance. If not, I should much prefer to communicate with you alone."

"It is both or none," Holmes replied flatly. "You may say before this gentleman anything which you may say to me."

The count shrugged his broad shoulders. "Then I must begin by binding you both to absolute secrecy for two years, at the end of that time the matter will be of no importance. At present it is not too much to say that it is of such weight that it may have an influence upon European history."

Holmes and Watson both agreed to the terms.

"And you will excuse this mask. The august person who employs me wishes his agent to be unknown to you, and I may confess at once that the title by which I have just called myself is not exactly my own."

"I was aware of it," Holmes said dryly, settling himself down in his armchair and closing his eyes. "If your majesty would condescend to state your case, I should be better able to advise you."

The visitor sprang from his chair, and paced up and down the room in uncontrollable agitation. Then, with a gesture of desperation, he tore the mask from his face and hurled it to the ground. "You are right," he cried, "I am the King. Why should I attempt to conceal it?"

"Why, indeed?" murmured Holmes. "Your majesty had not spoken before I was aware that I was addressing Wilhelm Gottsreich Sigismond von Ormstein, Grand Duke of Cassel-Falstein, and hereditary King of Bohemia."

"You can understand," said the King, sitting back down and passing his hand over his forehead, "that I am not accustomed to doing business in my own person. Yet the matter was so delicate that I could not confide it to an agent without putting myself in his power. You have just only been recommended from one of my advisors and I have come incognito from Prague for the purpose of consulting you."

"Then, pray, consult," said Holmes, shutting his eyes again.

"The facts are briefly these: Some five years ago, during a lengthy visit to Warsaw, I made the acquaintance of the well-known adventuress Irene Adler. The name is no doubt familiar to you."

"Kindly look her up in my index, Doctor," murmured Holmes, without opening his eyes.

Finding her biography in between that of a Hebrew rabbi and one of a staff-commander who had written a monograph upon deep sea fishes, Watson handed Holmes the filing system.

"Let me see," said Holmes. "Hum! Born in New Jersey in the year 1858. Contralto, La Scala. Retired from operatic stage. Living in London. Your Majesty, as I understand, became entangled with this young person, wrote her some compromising letters, and is now desirous of getting those letters back."

"Precisely so. But how – "

"Was there a secret marriage?"

"None."

"No legal papers or certificates?"

"None."

"Then I fail to follow Your Majesty. If this young person should produce her letters for blackmailing or other purposes, how is she to prove their authenticity?"

"There is the writing."

"Pooh, pooh! Forgery."

"My private notepaper."

"Stolen."

"My own seal."

"Imitated."

"My photograph."

"Bought."

"We were both in the photograph."

"Oh, dear! That is very bad! Your Majesty has indeed committed an indiscretion. You have compromised yourself seriously."

"I was only Crown Prince then. I was young. I am but thirty now."

"It must be recovered," Holmes stated.

"We have tried and failed. She will not sell it."

"Stolen, then."

"Five attempts have been made. Twice burglars in my pay ransacked her house. Once we diverted her luggage when she travelled. Twice she has been waylaid. There has been no result."

Holmes laughed. "It is quite a pretty little problem."

"But a very serious one to me," reproached the King. "I am to be married and she means to ruin me. A shadow of doubt as to my conduct would bring the matter to an end. Irene Adler threatens to send them the photograph. You do not know her, but she has a soul of steel. She has the face of the most beautiful of women, and the mind of the most resolute of men. Rather than I should marry another woman, there are no lengths to which she would not go – none. She said that she would send it on the day when the betrothal was publicly proclaimed. That will be next Monday."

"Oh then, we have three days yet," said Holmes, yawning. "That is very fortunate. I have one or two matters of importance to look into. I shall drop you a line to let you know how we progress. And, as to money?"

"You have *carte blanche*. I tell you that I would give one of the provinces of my kingdom to have that photograph."

Smiling, Holmes continued, "And for present expenses?"

The King took a heavy leather bag from under his cloak, and laid it on the table. "There are three hundred pounds in gold, and seven hundred in notes," he said, handing Holmes a slip of paper with Miss Adler's address written on it.

"Then, goodnight, Your Majesty, and I trust that we shall have some good news for you."

As the wheels of the royal brougham rolled down the street, Holmes turned to Watson. "I first heard rumors of the King's dalliance with an American woman while I was in Odessa. Having some familiarity with women of the sort, I knew that the King would be most anxious to have the matter handled discreetly. I have made some inquiries into Miss Adler, but was not able to find out much more than the index told you. Tomorrow, I will look into the matter myself."

"Surely you could send agents out, Holmes."

"If all the King's horses and all the King's men could not get his photograph back again, it is a serious matter indeed. Plus, a client such as ours will appreciate a personal touch to this matter. I'm sure he will show his gratitude in the end. Now, if you would be good enough to end your work day and return here by three o'clock tomorrow, I should like to chat this little matter over with you."

With that, Watson retired for the night, and left Holmes to his pipe in front of the fireplace.

Watson returned to Baker Street at three o'clock from practice the next day, only to find the rooms empty. Just before four o'clock, the door opened, and a drunken-looking groom, ill-kempt and with an inflamed face and disreputable clothes walked in. At first, Watson thought the man to be one of Holmes employees, and was startled to see that it was actually Sherlock Holmes in disguise! Holmes nodded to Watson and vanished into his bedroom, emerging minutes later in respectable clothes. Holmes stretched his legs out to the fire and laughed heartily. "Pour me a glass of Montrachet, Watson, and I will lay out my activities for the day."

Holmes had left Baker Street that morning dressed as an out-of-work groom. After finding Irene Adler's home in St. John's Wood, he lounged down the street and helped Adler's employees rub down her horses, receiving a small payment, a drink, some tobacco, and plenty of information.

"She has turned all the men's heads down in that part," Holmes said. "She is the daintiest thing under a bonnet on this planet.

She lives quietly, sings at concerts, drives out at five every day, and returns at seven sharp for dinner. Seldom goes out at other times, except when she sings. Has only one male visitor, but a good deal of him. He never calls less than once a day, and often twice. He is Godfrey Norton, a lawyer. That sounded ominous. Was she his client, friend, or mistress? Before I could balance this new information and what it meant for the photograph, a hansom cab drove up to Briony Lodge, and a handsome gentleman sprang out. Evidently this was the man of whom I had heard. He was in a great hurry and rushed into the house with the air of a man who was thoroughly at home.

"He stayed in the house for half an hour, and I could catch glimpses of him through the windows, pacing up and down, talking excitedly and waving his arms. Of her I could see nothing. Presently he emerged, looking even more flurried than before. As he stepped up to the cab, he pulled a gold watch from his pocket and looked at it earnestly. 'Drive like the devil,' he shouted, 'to the Church of St. Monica in the Edgware Road. Half a guinea if you do it in twenty minutes!'

"I was just wondering whether I should follow them, when up the lane came a neat little landau. It hadn't pulled up before she shot out of the hall door and into it, rushing off to the Church of St. Monica also. I was just about to perch on the back of her landau when a cab came along. The driver looked twice at such a shabby fare, but I jumped in before he could object. Off to the church we sped after them. It was twenty-five minutes to twelve, and of course it was clear enough what was in the wind. I hurried into the church when I arrived, only to find that it was completely empty except for the clergymen and the two people I had followed. Norton saw me and exalted, 'Thank God! You'll do! Come! Come! Only three minutes or it won't be legal.'

"I was half-dragged up to the altar, and before I knew where I was I found myself mumbling responses which were whispered in my ear, and vouching for things of which I knew nothing, and generally assisting in the secure tying up of Irene Adler, spinster, to Godfrey Norton, bachelor. It was done in an instant, and there was the gentleman thanking me on the one side and the lady on the other. It seems that there had been some informality about their license, that the clergyman absolutely refused to marry them without a witness of some sort, and that my lucky appearance saved them. The bride gave me a sovereign, and I mean to wear it on my watch-chain in memory of the occasion."

"This is a very unexpected turn of affairs," said Watson. "And what then?"

"It looked as if the pair might take an immediate departure, and so necessitate very prompt and energetic measures on my part. At the church door, however, they separated, and she told him that she would drive to the park at five as usual. I was left to make my own arrangements."

"Which are?"

"Some cold beef and a glass of beer," Holmes answered. "I have been too busy to think of food and I am likely …"

Holmes was interrupted by a ringing of the bell.

"Do you think that is the King calling to see about our progress?" Watson asked.

"It is doubtful. He is too proud to make more than one visit here on his own accord. No, this will be someone else."

A slim youth in an ulster was ushered into the room. "Good afternoon, Mister Sherlock Holmes," he stated. The youth hurried across the room and seated himself with his back to the window.

Holmes looked quizzically at the newcomer. "I've heard this voice before. Now, I wonder who the deuce you are."

The youth tipped back the bowler that was pulled low to reveal the face of the most beautiful woman. "You will forgive the imprudent nature of my visit, but a certain nobleman has sent the most cunning agent to my doorstep recently."

"Well, really!" Holmes cried, and then laughed again until he was obliged to lie back, helpless in his chair.

"What is it?" Watson demanded, looking between Holmes and the lovely woman dressed as a young man.

"A touch, an undeniable touch! It's quite too funny. Dr. Watson, may I introduce to you Mrs. Irene Norton, nee Adler."

Stunned, Watson stared at their visitor.

Irene Norton smiled gracefully at Watson and then turned her attention back to Holmes. "I have been warned against you months ago, Mr. Holmes. I have been told that if the King employed an agent, it would most certainly be you. When my coachman alerted me of a suspicious man around the stables making inquiries this morning, I immediately called for Mr. Norton. When he arrived, we both thought this would be the best recourse. We must lure you out and make sure that the new arrival was the great Sherlock Holmes. I have been trained as an actress myself. Male costume is nothing new to me. After I left the church, I returned home and got into my walking clothes, as I call them, rushed to Baker Street, as your address had been given to me previously, and observed the same ill-dressed groom from the stables and the church enter the front door of this very house.

"You really did it very well," she continued. "You would have taken me in completely had I not been on guard against you specifically. And now I am here to appeal to your competitive nature, Mr. Holmes."

Holmes took up a glowing cinder with the tongs and lit his long cherry-wood pipe. "Pray, continue, Mrs. Norton. But I must warn you that I have already been employed by your adversary, and am unlikely to go against his wishes."

"That will not be necessary. For what I propose will benefit us both."

Holmes waved a hand, indicating for her to continue.

"Mr. Norton and I feel that the best resource is flight while pursued by so formidable an antagonist. But I know that my absence will not appease the King. As to the photograph, he may rest in peace. The King may do what he will without hindrance from one whom he has cruelly wronged. I wish to keep the photograph only to safeguard myself, and to preserve a weapon which will always secure me from any steps which he might take in the future."

"I cannot guarantee that the King will take your word on this matter, madam."

Irene Norton leaned forward. "That is why I came to hire you, Mr. Holmes."

Holmes cocked an eyebrow and she continued. "I do not wish you to go against the King's wishes. In fact, I am counting on you to carry them out. You no doubt have a plan to burgle my house to obtain the photograph. It has all been done before, but not by one so skilled as you. I trust that you will follow that line of inquiry. I only ask that I be allowed to consult on the outcome. And for that allowance, I am willing to pay you a second income for the same problem on which you are already working.."

"A double cross!" Watson ejaculated.

"You may call it that, sir," Mrs. Norton smiled. Turning back to Homes, she continued. "By all means, go about your business, but I ask only that you allow me to keep the photograph as a token of security against future acts of the King. In its place, I will leave a different photograph which he might care to possess along with a note explaining my actions to him. I am confident that the King will take me at my word. I have no doubt that you would be able to follow my movements. If the King is not willing to believe me, I will give up the original photograph and you may keep my payment."

"This is an intriguing offer, Mrs. Norton," Holmes said from behind his pipe, "but why come to me at all in the first place?"

"Because I am tired of this man, Mr. Holmes. It is true that I originally said that I would use the photograph against him, but my life has moved on. I do not wish to be harassed by him or his agents any further, but I do wish to leave some safeguard in place against him."

Holmes puffed on his pipe and watched the blue smokerings as they chased each other up to the ceiling as he contemplated for a few moments.

"Alright then, Mrs. Norton, I agree. I will be injured tonight on your doorstep, dressed as an elderly clergyman. You will bring me in to be bandaged, and while doing so, you will open the window to allow me fresh air. Dr. Watson will throw a plumber's smoke rocket through the window, and after that, I will disappear. I will call on you tomorrow morning with the King to show him where you have hidden the photograph, and you must be gone by then."

Holmes' newest client smiled. "It is very clever, Mr. Holmes. I agree."

"One other thing, you must not show any pretense of leaving the country until after I have departed from your home tonight, or some suspicion may arise. Leave your note and photograph for the King at your house and send your payment to me in two days' time to allow the King and his agents to depart from London."

Mrs. Norton agreed to Holmes' terms. Pulling the hat back down over her face, she rose. "Until tonight, Mr. Holmes."

After Mrs. Norton had left, Watson smiled at Holmes. "A most remarkable woman, indeed! It's a shame she married earlier today, for I think she might have matched you suitably."

Holmes chuckled. "You add too much romance to the situation, Watson. I should never marry myself, lest I bias my judgement."

"But you cannot deny the woman's merits," Watson persisted.

"Hardly not. From what I have observed, Mrs. Norton eclipses and predominates the whole of her sex, but you put me in a false position placing me as a lover. For the trained reasoner such as myself, admitting such an intrusion would introduce a distracting factor which might throw a doubt upon all my mental results."

Watson chuckled at his friend's cold and precise manner. "I trust your judgement."

"A very sensible reply, doctor."

The night went according to Holmes' plans, and the next morning, Holmes and Watson sat at the breakfast table when the King of Bohemia burst into the room.

"You have really got it!" he cried, grasping Holmes by the shoulder, and looking eagerly into his face.

"Not yet, but I have hopes."

"Then, come. I am all impatience to be gone. My brougham is waiting."

When the men arrived at Briony Lodge, the front door stood open, and an elderly woman stood on the steps.

"My mistress told me that you were likely to call. She left this morning with her husband by the train from Charing Cross for the Continent, never to return," she announced as Holmes looked on with a convincingly startled gaze.

"And the papers?" asked the King hoarsely. "All is lost!"

Holmes pushed back the servant and moved into the sitting-room, and pulled out a photograph and a letter from a small sliding shutter. The photograph was of Irene Adler in evening dress and the letter was addressed "To my mysterious clergyman. To be left until called for." The note read:

"My dear guest, You really did it very well. You took me in completely. Until after the alarm of fire, I had not a suspicion. But then, when I found how I had betrayed myself, I began to think. I had been warned against an agent in London months ago that the King could employ. Yet, with all this, you made me reveal what you wanted to know. Even after I became suspicious, I found it hard to think evil of such a dear, kind, old clergyman. But you know, I have been trained as an actress myself. I immediately started to see my husband.

"We both thought the best resource was flight, so you will find the nest empty when you call. As to the photograph, your client may rest in peace. I love and am loved by a better man than he. The King may do what he will without hindrance from one whom he has cruelly wronged. I keep it only to safeguard myself, and to preserve a weapon which will always secure me from any steps which he might take in the future. I hope that you can respect my wishes, and take me at my word. I remain very truly yours,

"Irene Norton, *nee* Adler."

"What a woman, what a woman!" cried the King of Bohemia. "Did I not tell you how quick and resolute she was? Would she not have made an admirable queen? Is it not a pity she was not on my level?"

"From what I have seen of the lady, she seems, indeed, to be on a very different level to Your Majesty," said Holmes coldly.

"I know that her word is inviolate. The photograph is now as safe as if it were in the fire. I am immensely indebted to you. Pray tell me in what way I can reward you! You have to name it."

"This photograph of Miss Adler," Holmes pointed.

The King stared at him in amazement. "Certainly, if you wish it." Thinking that his business with Holmes had concluded, the King took a step towards the door.

"And would you prefer to discuss the rest of your payment here or back at Baker Street?" Holmes asked.

Chapter 5: We Can But Try

The year 1887 continued to be a busy one for Sherlock Holmes. After toppling Baron Maupertuis and the Irene Adler incident, Holmes turned back to his work with an energy Watson had never seen before. Within weeks of the Adler business, Holmes had taken control of a luxurious secret club, The Amateur Mendicant Society, who held meetings in the lower vault of a furniture warehouse. Holmes' stealthy ownership was known to only one member of the society, and its funds were used to finance Holmes' other operations. During this time he also arranged for two men to escape from their jealous wives and rigid families by sailing on the *Sophy Anderson* which Holmes arranged to disappear from all knowledge. That masterful work was quickly followed by a heist from the Grice-Pattersons off the coast of Scotland, of which Holmes was especially proud. The year also found Holmes assisting Scotland Yard in his special way with capturing the villain behind the Camberwell poisoning case.

But all of Holmes' activities during this year were not well-thought out successes. One such instance was the problem of the Bar of Gold opium den. Holmes' syndicate not only planned out criminal activities, but also operated and provided protection for places such as this seedy den. While reading through the papers one morning, Holmes saw that the Bar of Gold was a focal point in a missing man investigation. While walking home the previous day, a lady had seen her businessman husband's face in one of the den's upstairs windows. But when she forced her way in, he was nowhere to be found; only her husband's clothes and a local beggar were in the room. The beggar had been arrested by the police on suspicion of murder.

Enraged that he had not been notified of this problem before the police and newspapers became involved, Holmes planned to infiltrate the den without arousing suspicion from police in the area. He meant to solve the disappearance before Scotland Yard and make the problem go away. The opium den was a steady source of income for Holmes' operation, and he despised any interference from the authorities or attention being called to it by the newspapers.

With police still around, Holmes was unable to address the lascar who operated the Bar of Gold. Taking the disguise of a wrinkled and bent old opium addict, Holmes left the next day to collect his information.

"Holmes," Watson reacted, "Surely you cannot be thinking of going to that vile den!"

"Ay, Watson. I hope to find some clues in the incoherent ramblings of the sots who frequent the establishment. Do not fear, though. I have no intention of adding opium smoking to cocaine injections and all the other little weaknesses on which you have favored me with your medical views."

"But what of the police investigation?"

"It is my hope that they are off on the wrong scent. The Yarders' temptation to form premature theories upon insufficient data is a boon to our profession."

So, dressed as an old addict, Holmes spent the day with an opium pipe dangling down between his knees, as though in sheer lassitude. Holmes listened to the gossip among those sober enough to discuss yesterday's events and caught bits of conversations from the officers passing through. When the opportunity arose, he sneaked up to the second floor and investigated a trap door that the police suspected was where the missing man had been dropped into the Thames to his death.

Holmes found no evidence of a struggle, but the police had not done a thorough enough search of the room and he found a letter addressed to the missing man's wife wedged behind a loose board in the wall. Pocketing his evidence, Holmes slipped out of the opium den and returned to Baker Street. The letter he found contained the man's signet ring and was dated from that morning. It read:

"Dearest, do not be frightened. All will come well. There is a huge error which it may take some little time to rectify. Wait in patience – Neville."

Holmes analyzed the paper and envelope closely. After a long day collecting information, he sat in front of the fire at Baker Street and retold the facts to Watson, hoping to use his friend as a conductor of light. Holmes felt that he had all of the information to find Neville St. Clair. If he could only discover why Mr. St. Clair had not returned to his wife, public scrutiny of one of his steadily earning buildings would disappear, and Holmes could deal with the wily lascar who had allowed issues to reach this point.

The next morning, Watson came back down to the sitting room to find Holmes perched cross-legged on a sort of eastern divan created from pillows and cushions from around the room. His pipe was between his lips, smoke curling upward, filling the sitting-room with a dense tobacco haze.

"Good morning, Watson."

"Holmes," Watson coughed through the dense smoke, "have you been up all night?"

"Yes. Pondering over the problem of the missing Mr. St. Clair. Dress quickly and we will have a morning drive," Holmes chuckled, seeming a different man than the somber thinker Watson had spent time with the night before. "I want to test a little theory of mine. I think I have the key of the affair now."

"Where is it?"

"In the bathroom. Oh, yes, I am not joking. I have just been there, and I have taken it out, and have got it in this Gladstone bag. Come on, my boy, and we shall see whether it will not fit the lock."

Holmes had, when he so willed it, the utter immobility of countenance of a red Indian, and Watson could not gather from his appearance whether he was satisfied with the case during their cab ride. While Watson yearned to know of the developments with the Bar of Gold problem, Holmes was only interested in discussing the Bertillon system of measurements, expressing his enthusiastic admiration of the French savant.

Their cab pulled up in front of the police courts on Bow Street, and Holmes handed Watson the Gladstone bag and a note. "Hand this to Inspector Bradstreet and come back out. He and I have had some correspondences in the past, but I am not willing to tempt fate and set foot inside that building."

Watson returned a few minutes later and Holmes ordered the cab to drive around the block and park up the street, where they could watch the door.

"What are we waiting for, Holmes?"

"I expect to soon see a man with damp hair and a beggar's outfit leaving the building," Holmes answered. "And when he does, we will give him a ride home."

As predicted, a man meeting Holmes' description stepped out and Holmes ordered the cab to pull up beside him.

"Mr. St. Clair," Holmes spoke out the window. "Or do you prefer that I call you Hugh Boone when you are dressed as so?"

Surprised, the man could only stare up at the man speaking to him.

"Get in the cab, Mr. St. Clair. We will take you back to your wife. She has been very worried about you."

Neville St. Clair climbed in suspiciously. "Are you the one who sent the officer in with the sponge?"

"You have caused enough problems, Mr. St. Clair. I will lead this conversation," Holmes said in his rigid and constrained demeanor. "Please correct me on any points of which I am in error."

Neville St. Clair nodded.

"For whatever reason, you have been passing yourself off as Hugh Boone, a professional beggar and you have been using the Bar of Gold as your dressing room at the beginning and end of

71

each day. At the end of the day on Saturday, you looked out the window of the second floor and saw your wife and she happened to look up and recognize your face. She tried to run upstairs, but was slowed by the door attendant, giving you time to change back into your beggarly clothes. When she finally made her way in, she only found Neville St. Clair's clothes and Hugh Boone. Is everything correct so far?"

"God help me, it's all true, sir," St. Clair moaned. "I don't know how you know all of this, but it's true. I would not have done all of this if it wasn't for my children. I wouldn't have them ashamed ..."

Holmes interrupted. "Your motives are not of interest to me. Clearing up this matter quickly is the only thing that concerns me at this time. I will continue. Your wife raised the alarm and the constable on duty came to her aid, but could not help her to find her husband. Seeing a small point of blood on the windowsill, which," Holmes nodded down at St. Clair's hand, "I can tell was not part of a murderous row, and also seeing your clothes on the floor, the beggar Boone was arrested for murder, prompting an investigation and you were put in jail. You were able to write your wife a letter, hoping that it would pacify her until the matter could be resolved. That was your plan until your ruse was discovered this morning when the officer washed your disguise away."

"Yes. I would have endured imprisonment, aye, even execution, rather than have left my miserable secret as a family blot to my children," St. Clair responded. "Did she send you after reading my letter? I never hoped to put her through such a trial."

Holmes held out St. Clair's signet ring. "The man you gave your letter to was unable to deliver it. Your wife knows nothing of this. Here we are," Holmes said as they pulled up to his house.

"You will reunite and tell your wife and the police any story that you choose, but it stops here. There will be no more of Hugh Boone and you will stay away from the Bar of Gold."

"I have sworn it by the most solemn oaths which a man can."

"In that case, I do not believe that any further steps need be taken. Now get out, Mr. St. Clair."

Dazed, Neville St. Clair stumbled from the cab.

As the cab pulled away, Watson looked at the man who was forever confounding him with some new phase of his astuteness. "Holmes, I am always amazed at your deductions!"

"I have found that at times, sitting and consuming an ounce of shag can help to focus one's thoughts. I think, Watson, that if we drive back to Baker Street, we shall just be in time for breakfast, and then I can deal with the wily lascar behind this whole problem."

Soon enough, the man who had been operating the Bar of Gold was dealt with. His departure sent a clear message across criminal London that rules were to be obeyed.

One day that September, Holmes had just returned from a meeting with members of the Paradol Chamber Society as a particularly violent gale began to lash the streets of London. Picking up his violin, he treated Watson to small performance.

"Bravo, Holmes! It is always a treat to hear you play, especially on a day when the weather is as sorry as this. Your talents gladly drown out the sound of the wind crying and sobbing in the chimney."

Holmes smiled. "You are quite descriptive doctor, perhaps if our criminal enterprises were to dry up, you should become a novelist."

Chuckling, Watson responded. "Oh, I hardly think I would be able to keep all of my facts and dates straight. Tell me, how did you come to become such a virtuoso on the violin?"

Lighting his clay pipe, Holmes settled into his chair. "Ah, that is an interesting story. While I was living in Montague Street, I had helped Scotland Yard in my own capacity and they allowed me to interview their prisoners. I told them that it was research for a monograph I was attempting on the criminal demeanor, but in truth, it was for my own personal knowledge. One of these opportunities allowed me to meet with the convicted murderer, Charles Peace, while he was waiting to be hanged. Our discussion on his methods and my youthful curiosity impressed the man so much that he treated me to a few pieces on his violin before my visitation was over.

Soon after that, I realized that my mind needed an outlet other than study. While walking down Tottenham Court Road one afternoon, I happened to see a beautiful violin in the window of a broker's shop. On a whim, I went inside and found it priced at only fifty-five shillings. My course of studies had led me to have a working knowledge of instruments and immediately recognized the violin in my hand as a Stradivarius, worth two hundred times what the broker was asking for it. I gladly bought the instrument and took to learning it every day, coming to rely on it as a form of introspection and enjoyment."

"Well, your talents are certainly remarkable, and enjoyable for me as well."

Suddenly, the bell rang. "Who would come tonight? Some friend of yours perhaps?" Watson asked.

"Except for yourself, I have none," Holmes answered. "I do not encourage visitors."

Holmes and Watson received a man named John Openshaw.

"I have heard of you, Mr. Holmes, from Major Prendergast. He told me how you saved him in the Tankerville Club Scandal."

Holmes smiled at the memory. "Ah, of course. He was wrongfully accused of cheating at cards."

"He said that you could fix anything and that you are never beaten."

"He said too much. I have been beaten four times – three times by men and once by a woman. I beg that you will draw your chair up to the fire, and favor me with some details as to your problem."

"It is no ordinary one."

"None of those which come to me are. I am the last court of appeal. Pray, give us the essential facts from the beginning, and

I can afterwards question you as to those details which seem to me to be most important."

The young man pulled up his chair and told Holmes his tale. Eighteen years ago, Openshaw's uncle returned to England after serving as a colonel in the Confederate Army and living as a successful farmer in Florida in the United States. He took a small estate in Sussex, and his quick temper and foul mouth made him disliked by most that met him. He allowed his nephew, Openshaw, to stay with him after taking a liking to the boy, but young Openshaw was forbidden from entering a certain room in the house and looking at his uncle's trunks from America.

In 1883, Openshaw's uncle received an envelope from Pondicherry, India that contained only five orange pips and the letters "KKK." The uncle immediately ran to the closed room and burnt stacks of papers from inside his locked trunk. A lawyer was also called that day and a will was drawn up, leaving the estate to young Openshaw's father. His uncle from then on would keep himself locked up in his room, or would become so drunk that he would tear about the garden with a pistol in hand. One night two months after the date of the strange mailing, his uncle was found dead: face down in the garden pond. The official cause of death was suicide, but Openshaw had an ominous feeling.

The estate was turned over to Openshaw's father, and two years later, he received an envelope postmarked Dundee, Scotland, containing five pips, three K's, and instructions to leave the papers on the sun dial in the garden. Young Openshaw pleaded with his father to take this message seriously and call the police, but his father did not pay attention to his warning. Three days later, Openshaw's father was found dead at the bottom of a nearby chalk pit.

Openshaw had inherited the cursed estate, and two days before his visit to Baker Street, he had received the same message that his father had two years earlier. The police believed that it was a practical joke, and Openshaw shared his despair with his friend, Major Prendergast.

"He pulled me aside, and told me confidentially of a man that fixes problems in London. The major has high words for you, Mr. Holmes, but to tell the truth, I feel helpless. I have felt like one of those poor rabbits when the snake is writhing towards it. I seem to be in the grasp of some resistless, inexorable evil, which no foresight and no precautions can guard against."

"Tut! Tut!" cried Holmes. "You must act, man, or you are lost. It is really two days since you had the letter. We should have acted before this. You have no further evidence, I suppose, than that which you have placed before us – no suggestive detail which might help us."

"There is one thing," said Openshaw, handing Holmes a piece of discolored, blue-tinted paper. "The day that my uncle burnt his papers, I found this single sheet upon the floor of his room, and I am inclined to think that it may be one of the papers which had fluttered out from among the others. The handwriting is undoubtedly my uncle's."

Holmes read the paper and handed it back to his visitor. "Now you must not lose another instant. We cannot spare time even to discuss what you have told me. You must get home instantly and put this piece of paper which you have shown us into the box which you've described. You must also put in a note to say that all the other papers were burned by your uncle, and that this is the only one which remains. You must assert in such words as will carry conviction. Having done this, at once put the box out upon the sundial. Do not think of revenge, or anything of the sort. I think that we may gain that by means of the law; but we have our web to weave, while theirs is already woven. Do you understand?"

"Entirely. Thank you," said Openshaw, rising and pulling on his coat. "You have given me fresh hope. I shall certainly do as you advise."

"Do not lose an instant. And, above all, take care of yourself in the meanwhile, for I do not think that there can be a doubt that you are threatened by a very real and imminent danger. The streets are still crowded, so I trust that you may be in safety. And yet you cannot guard yourself too closely."

"I am armed."

"That is well. Tomorrow I shall set to work upon your problem. Call upon me in two days with news," Holmes directed.

Openshaw shook hands with the men and left. Sherlock Holmes sat in silence with his head sunk forward for some time, eyes staring into the fire. After a while, he lit his pipe, leaned back in his chair, and watched the smoke drift upwards.

"I think, Watson, that of all our current irons in the fire, this is the most worrisome," Holmes remarked. "This John Openshaw seems to me to be walking amid peril."

"But have you formed any definite conception as to what these perils are?"

"There can be no question to their nature. But there is something larger than the imminent threat behind this. The ideal reasoner would, when he has once been shown a single fact in all its bearings, deduce from it not only all the chain of events which led up to it, but also all the results which would follow from it. We have not yet grasped the results which the reason alone can attain. It is not so impossible, however, that a man should possess all knowledge which is likely to be useful to him in his work, and this I have endeavored in my case to do.

"In the first place, we may start with a strong presumption that Colonel Openshaw had some very strong reason for leaving America. Men at his time of life do not change all their habits, and exchange willingly the charming climate of Florida for the lonely life of an English provincial town. His extreme love of solitude in England suggests the idea that he was in fear of someone or something, so we may assume as a working hypothesis that it was fear of someone or something which drove him from America. As to what it was he feared, we can only deduce that by considering the formidable letters which were received by himself and his successors. Did you remark the postmarks of those letters?"

"The first was from Pondicherry, India, the second from Dundee, Scotland, and the third from London."

"From East London. What do you deduce from that?"

"They are all seaports. That the writer was on board a ship."

"Excellent," Holmes replied. "We have a clue. There is the strong probability that the writer was aboard a ship. And now let us consider another point. In the case of Pondicherry seven weeks elapsed between the threat and its fulfillment; in Dundee it was only some three or four days. And the last one came from London. Now you see the deadly urgency of this new problem, and why I urged young Openshaw to caution. The blow has always come at the end of the time which it would take the senders to travel the distance. But this one comes from here in London, and therefore we cannot count upon delay.

"The papers which Openshaw carried are obviously vital to the person or persons in the sailing ship. I think that it is quite clear that there must be more than one of them. A single man could not have carried out two deaths in such a way as to deceive a coroner's jury. There is an organizing force with resource and knowledge behind all of this. The letters KKK is commonly known in America as the Ku Klux Klan, a terrible secret society formed by some ex-Confederate soldiers in the southern states after the Civil War. Its outrages were usually preceded by a warning sent to the marked man in some generally recognized way, a sprig of oak leaves, melon seeds or orange pips.

"They are a force in America, but how are they availing themselves upon the Openshaws here in London? That is the question which lies at the heart of this problem. But our first responsibility is to our paying customer. Once his matter is resolved, I will delve deeper into who is behind these murders."

The next morning, Watson arrived at the breakfast table to find Holmes already eating.

"You will excuse me for not waiting for you," said Holmes. "I foresee a very busy day before me in looking into this case of young Openshaw's."

"What steps will you take?"

"It will depend upon the results of my first inquiries. I may have to visit Openshaw today after all."

Watson lifted the unopened newspaper and glanced over the morning's headlines. A chill ran through him. "Holmes! You are too late."

"I feared as much. How was it done?" Holmes asked calmly, although Watson could see that he was deeply moved.

Watson read the report to him. "Tragedy near Waterloo Bridge. Between nine and ten last night Police Constable Cook of the H Division heard a cry for help and a splash in the water. The night was extremely dark and stormy, so that in spite of the help of several passersby, it was quite impossible to affect a rescue. The alarm was given, and by the aid of the water police, the body was eventually recovered. It proved to be that of a young gentleman whose name, as it appears from an envelope found in his pocket, was John Openshaw, and whose residence is near Horsham. It is conjectured …"

"That is enough," Holmes interrupted. After sitting in shaken silence for some minutes, he said, "That hurts my pride, Watson. It becomes a personal matter with me now, and, if God sends me health, I shall set my hand upon this American gang and expose their London agents. That he should come to me for protection, and that I should send him away to his death!"

Holmes sprang from his chair and paced the room. "They must be cunning devils. How could they have decoyed him down there? The embankment is not on the direct line to the train station. The bridge, no doubt, was too crowded, even on such a night, for their purpose. Well, Watson, we shall see who will win in the long run. I am going out now!"

Returning home that evening, Watson found that Holmes had not returned yet. Finally, after ten o'clock, he burst through the door. "I have them in the hollow my hand, Watson. Young Openshaw shall not remain long unavenged, and this client will not be a complete failure upon my name. I will first deal with the Americans. I will put their own devilish trademark upon them."

Holmes took an orange from the cupboard, tore it to pieces and squeezed the pips from it. Taking five of these, he thrust them into an envelope and wrote "S.H. for J.C." on the inside flap. He addressed the envelope to Captain James Calhoun, Barque *Lone Star*, Savannah, Georgia.

"Who is Captain Calhoun?" Watson asked.

"The American connection; I shall have the others but he is first. I have spent the whole day over Lloyd's registers and old papers, following the future career of every vessel which touched at Pondicherry in January and February in '83. There were thirty-six ships which were reported there during those months. Of these, the *Lone Star* instantly attracted my attention, since, although it was reported as having cleared from London, the name is that which is given to one of the States in the Union."

"Texas, I think."

Holmes nodded. "I searched the Dundee records, and when I found that the barque *Lone Star* was there in January, '85, my suspicion became a certainty. I then inquired as to vessels which lay at present in the port of London. The *Lone Star* arrived here last week. I went down to the Albert dock, and found that she had been taken down the river by the early tide this morning, homeward bound to Savannah. I wired to Gravesend, and learned she had passed some time ago. As the wind is easterly, I have no doubt that she is now past the Goodwins, and not very far from the Isle of Wight."

"What will you do, then?"

"Oh, I have my hand upon him. He is the only native-born American on the ship. The others are Finns and Germans. I also know that he was away from the ship to deliver payment before the ship left this morning. I had it from the stevedore, who has been loading their cargo. By the time their sailing ship reaches Savannah the mail boat will have carried this letter, and the cable will have informed the police of Savannah that the captain is badly wanted here upon a charge of murder."

But the man who ordered the murder of John Openshaw never received his orange pips. Holmes and Watson waited for news of the *Lone Star* in Savannah, but none ever reached them. At last, they heard that somewhere far out in the Atlantic a shattered sternpost of a boat was seen swinging in the trough of a wave, with the letters "L.S." carved upon it.

"Perhaps we will never know of the storm that sank the ship," Watson commented.

"Or perhaps the one hidden behind the whole affair did not wish me to have my vengeance and saw to it that the ship sank," Holmes mused. "There is a force at work here, Watson. Make no mistake we are about to tread into deep waters ourselves."

Chapter 6: Bold and Active

Over the next four months, Holmes busied himself with other endeavors while gathering information on the organizing force quietly working out of the Seven Dials and Whitechapel sections of London. Not allowing himself to become hyper-focused and exhausted as he had with Baron Maupertuis, Holmes slowly collected his information as to not arouse suspicion of his wily opponent. In the meantime, he wrote a monograph on the use of typewriters for detection, helped a Mr. Dundas disappear from his wife, and sent out a team to collect a back payment from Silas Etheredge, who had gone into hiding from him.

Then came a Saturday morning at the end of October. Watson was reading Holmes a news story about James Windibank, a petty thief who was headed to the gallows, when one of Holmes' street Arab messengers arrived with a note. After dispatching the boy, Holmes sprang up and clapped his hands.

"It is time for one of my greatest endeavors, Doctor!"

"You've found your rival finally?"

"No, but that will wait. Business must continue in the meantime, and tonight will certainly be business of note. A city branch bank has recently come into possession of 30,000 French gold napoleons, and I plan to have them. All of my wheels are in motion, and you will find today to be a glorious one."

Later that morning, a stout-built man with a splash of acid upon his forehead came to Baker Street.

"Watson, this is John Clay, the fourth smartest man in London. Not only is he a trusted thief, smasher and forger, but also a graduate of Oxford. I've sure you heard his name before."

"Of course," Watson nodded. "I believe I've sent you a note or two in the past at Mr. Holmes' request."

"Nice to meet you, Doctor Watson," Clay responded. "Everything is ready, Mr. Holmes. You seem to have done the thing very completely. I must compliment you."

"And I you," Holmes answered. "Your red-headed idea was very new and effective."

Turning to Watson, Holmes explained. When he first heard of the possible gold shipment to the bank, Holmes placed Clay as an assistant to a redheaded pawnbroker that had a shop next door to the bank. Discussing possible ploys, Clay suggested hiring the pawnbroker under the guise of a club for red-headed men. Liking the idea, Holmes organized everything. Clay and another employee lured the pawnbroker from his shop every day for a few hours to do what he thought was work for a red-headed league, allowing Clay to dig a tunnel from the cellar of the pawnbroker's shop to the basement vault of the bank. Clay informed Holmes that the tunnel would be completed tonight as planned.

Watson laughed at the genius of the plan. "The red-headed buffoon surely won't be seeing his payment this week!"

"On the contrary, my friend," Holmes said, "we cannot risk the pawnbroker arousing suspicion from the police or anyone else. He will surely be paid. He will have his alibi when the bank discovers the robbery on Monday morning, but he will be without his new employee."

Turning back to Clay, Holmes said, "Tonight's plans are laid out and I trust that you and Archie are equipped to deliver the gold. Once that is done, you will of course need to disappear for a time, as your pawnbroker will be able to describe you to the authorities."

"You may not be aware, Mr. Holmes, that I have royal blood in my veins. My family is known to be a charitable one, and I will be spending my time raising money for an orphanage in Cornwall. Once my alibi has been established, I plan to spend some time in Scotland."

"Very good then. I will see you tonight." After Clay left, Holmes turned to Watson, "Doctor, we've done our work, so it's time we had some play. A meal at Simpson's, and then off to violin land, where all is sweetness, delicacy, and harmony, and no more talk of red-headed pawnbrokers."

Holmes and Watson took to the streets and spent the afternoon enjoying a concert at St. James' Hall. After it ended, Holmes told Watson that he had to deal with the business for another client, Victor Savage, and that he would meet him back at Baker Street at ten.

When they met that night, Holmes said they had only to wait for Clay to show up, which would be sometime after midnight.

"Can you trust him to show up with the gold?" Watson asked.

"As I said earlier, Clay is one of the smartest men in London and his red-headed ploy was quite an inspired one. A criminal who is capable of such a thought is a man whom I should be proud to do business with." Chuckling, Holmes continued, "He is smart enough to show up. Otherwise a determined Inspector Jones from Scotland Yard will know how to find him in the morning."

Soon enough, there was a ring at the bell. Clay and his partner appeared loaded down with bags filled with gold bullion. Watson poured whiskey and water for everyone, the men described the night's activities, Holmes paid the men their share, and congratulations were passed around for what would surely be known as one of the biggest heists in London's history.

London was abuzz with the news of the bank robbery and suspicion was pointed in every corner for weeks. Holmes had planned in advance to keep a low profile during this time. His employees stayed dormant, he turned away a lucrative case from man named Bert Stevens who was later convicted of murder, and Holmes easily fended off a revenge plot from taking on Victor Savage as a client. But for the most part, the next two months were a quiet time for Holmes' empire.

But Sherlock Holmes had not planned on the boredom that would set in during this time. Watson often saw him lying about with his violin and books, hardly moving, save from the sofa to the table. The landlady, Mrs. Hudson, allowed for many of Holmes' eccentricities, from the throngs of singular and often undesirable characters to his incredible untidiness. She never dared to interfere with him, however outrageous his proceedings might seem. But this period of time proved to be too much for even her. Even though Holmes' criminal enterprises allowed him to pay princely sums for his rooms, enough to have purchased the rooms outright, Watson returned home to find her in a completely nervous state one afternoon.

"I am afraid for Mr. Holmes, Dr. Watson," she said imploringly.

"Why so, Mrs. Hudson?"

"After you was gone, he walked and he walked, up and down, and up and down, until I was weary of the sound of his footstep. Then I heard him talking to himself and muttering, and every time the bell rang out he came on the stairhead, with 'What is that, Mrs. Hudson?' And the gunfire!"

"Gunfire?" Watson responded.

"Yes. Every now and then I will hear shots fire from his rooms. I'm afraid to go in there, sir. You know how masterful he is. But this is too much of a strain, Dr. Watson. I don't complain about the music at strange hours or the scientific experiments, and his payments are enough for me to allow the atmosphere of violence and danger that hangs around him, but these past few weeks have been too much!"

"I don't think that you have any cause to be uneasy, Mrs. Hudson. I have seen him like this before. He is restless, but I will speak to him."

Watson entered 221B to find Holmes draped in his arm-chair with his hair-trigger pistol resting in his lap and a hundred Boxer cartridges at his feet.

"Ah, Watson, welcome home."

"Holmes! What have you done to the wall?"

Across the sitting room, Holmes had adorned the opposite wall with VR done in bullet pocks.

"It is my little way to celebrate Her Majesty's Golden Jubilee. It has done little to assuage my boredom, though."

"There is nothing of interest in the papers?"

"Bleat, Watson—unmitigated bleat!"

"Why not spend the next few hours making our rooms a little more habitable then? Mrs. Hudson is beside herself with the state of this room."

Holmes glanced around the sitting room in its disastrous state. Cigars sat in the coal scuttle, and tobacco in the toe end of a Persian slipper. Holmes' unanswered correspondence was attached by a jack-knife into the very center of the wooden mantelpiece. Chemicals and criminal relics cluttered numerous corners and tables around the room.

"These items are all placed for easy access, doctor. When I am of a mind to respond to the letters, they are accessible where they are. My chemical investigations are numerous, but in different states of completion and I would be remiss to upset them."

"But the papers, Holmes. Look around. Every corner is stacked with bundles. At the very least, they could be put away."

"I cannot deny the justice of your request, but first we must tend to Mrs. Hudson. I'm afraid that after the city bank robbery, I am still not at liberty to truly engage my energies, and I cannot promise that my behavior will not try her nerves again. Perhaps we should allow her to take a holiday. Have her set it up with Mrs. Turner to oversee the premises and send her off with my blessing and apologies."

"Splendid. You know, she does hold you in the highest regard."

"And I, her. She is a long-suffering woman," Holmes mused.

"And should I promise her that the rooms will be tidied up upon her return?"

"I suppose," Holmes sighed with a rueful face. Slowly, a mischievous look came to Holmes' eyes. "But first, perhaps you would care to hear of some of my early work?"

"Of course," Watson said, settling into his own chair. "You know that I often love to hear of them."

"As I've told you before, much of my work was premature and halting, but there were some pretty little problems among them. Perhaps I should tell you of Vamberry, the wine merchant?"

Completely forgetting about Mrs. Hudson, and the state of the sitting room now, Watson smiled. "That sounds delightful."

Holmes chuckled and wriggled into a comfortable position in his chair. "Arminius Vamberry was a Hungarian wine collector renowned for his vintage stock and was spoken of in the highest terms by Westhouse and Marbank, the great claret importers of Fenchurch Street. I had established a small agency by this time and was becoming known in certain circles and quite the stormy petrel of crime. Vamberry was in London and had made it his purpose to acquire bottles from British collectors that had survived the French blight of previous years. He had met with much resistance in France, as the wines from that era were treated as national treasures by their owners and hoped to find a more receptive audience abroad.

"You and I, Watson, may have our occasional glass of port after dinner, but the wines Vamberry was searching for would stagger you if you knew of their value. Let me say that the value was enough to interest the criminal element.

"The associates I had discussed the opportunity and we were of the opinion that we need only to follow Vamberry to where he would purchase the wines and then rob him of his money before he could spend it."

Watson chuckled at this. "I can hardly picture you doing so."

"Hardly. They say that genius is an infinite capacity for taking pains. It's a very bad definition, but it does apply to planning. I argued that crime should be treated as a fine art, and recommended my associates read an old article from Blackwood's Magazine that argued the same. This, of course, fell on deaf ears, but having done so well under my tutelage previously, they were willing to test out my method.

"We met with an unassuming grocer by the name of Cameron, and presented him with an opportunity. If he would allow us to place a forgery of the French wine in his attic and put him in touch with a connoisseur who would be willing to appraise it as a wine from the era Vamberry was looking for, we would allow him a portion of the sale. The man saw no harm in this, and we then met with a crooked wine connoisseur by the name of Mortimer Maberley who was more than willing to abet our plan, especially as he disliked Vamberry immensely.

"The grocer announced that he had found a dusty box in his attic that contained a few French items, apparently from a previous owner, and asked around what he should do with the bottles of wine that were also in the box. Our connoisseur stepped forward, appraised the wine for him, and announced that one of the bottles was one of the French wines that Vamberry was looking to buy. Vamberry swooped in and bullied the poor grocer for some time before he agreed to sell it to him at a price well below the wine's actual worth, but still more than Cameron would expect to make in half a year."

"But didn't Vamberry check the wine's authenticity before purchasing it?" Watson asked.

"I expect that he would have, but when his rival announced what Cameron had found and hinted that he would like to buy it from the grocer, Vamberry had to move quickly, and in doing so, acted rashly. I'm sure he soon found out the wine was a forgery, but I had made my profit and did not care to follow up on the matter at the time."

"While you seem to have always been creative in your methods, I'm glad to see you are more thorough now." Pacified by Holmes' story, Watson turned to pick up the latest textbook on pathology.

"Aren't you forgetting Mrs. Hudson's holiday?" Holmes asked innocently.

"Of course!" Watson laughed. "I will go down to see her right now. And seeing that it is almost supper time, I think I will step down to my club as not to worry her with preparing a meal. Unless you would care to eat?"

"No, my dear fellow. But when you pass Bradley's, would you ask him to send up a pound of the strongest shag tobacco? Thank you. I expect to be in a better mood in the morning. Good evening."

While Holmes' empire had built over the years, he continued his aversion to careless crimes and random street violence. His agents were encouraged to break up such matters when they saw them, creating the idea of a safer London. This philosophy led to an interesting event at the end of December that year.

Returning home from an extended Christmas visit to Murray, his old army orderly, Watson found Holmes lounging on the sofa in his purple dressing gown, studying a seedy and disreputable felt hat.

"You are engaged," Watson apologized. "I will not interrupt you."

"Not at all. I am glad to have a friend with whom I can discuss my results. The matter is a perfectly trivial one," Holmes said, jerking his thumb towards the old hat, "but there are points in connection with it which are not entirely devoid of interest, and even instruction."

Sitting in his arm-chair, Watson asked, "I suppose that, homely as it looks, this thing has some deadly story linked to it – or that it is the link in one of your upcoming plots?"

"No, no crime of mine. Only one of those whimsical little incidents which will happen when you have five million human beings all jostling each other within the space of a few square miles. The hat was found by my man, Redmond. Its owner is unknown. I beg that you will look upon it, not as a battered billycock, but as an intellectual problem. And, first as to how it came here. It arrived upon Christmas morning, in the company of a good fat goose, which is, I have no doubt, roasting at this moment in front of Redmond's fire. The facts are these. About four o'clock on Christmas morning, Redmond was returning from some small jollification, and was making his way homeward down Tottenham Court Road. In front of him he saw a tallish man carrying a white goose slung over his shoulder. As he reached the corner of Goodge Street a row broke out between this stranger and a little knot of roughs. One of the latter knocked off the man's hat, and he defended himself. Hoping to be commended for breaking up the assault, Redmond rushed forward and scared both parties. They took to their heels; the tall man leaving behind his hat and goose.

"Redmond brought round both hat and goose on Christmas morning, knowing my aversion to street toughs and my interest in small problems, especially these last two months when I have been lying quiet. Its finder carried off the goose to cook today on his wife's day off, while I continue to retain the hat of the unknown gentleman who lost his Christmas dinner."

"Did he not advertise?" Watson asked.

"No. The bird's leg had a small card with 'For Mrs. Henry Baker' printed upon it, and the initials H.B. are legible upon the lining of this hat. But, as there are some thousands of Bakers, and some hundreds of Henry Bakers in this city of ours, it would not be easy to restore the lost property to any one of them. I am left with only the hat to deduce his identity."

"But you are joking. What can you gather from this old battered felt?"

"You know my methods. There are a few inferences which are very distinct, and a few others which represent at least a strong balance of probability. The man was fairly well-to-do within the last three years, although he has now fallen upon evil days. These flat brims curled at the edge came in fashion three years ago and it is a hat of the very best quality. If this man could afford to buy so expensive a hat three years ago, and has had no hat since, then he has assuredly gone down in the world.

"He had foresight, but has less now, pointing to a moral retrogression, which, when taken with the decline of his fortunes, seems to indicate some evil influence, probably drink. He had the foresight to add a hat-securer. They are never sold upon hats. If this man ordered one, it is a sign of a certain amount of foresight, since he went out of his way to take this precaution against the wind. But since we see that he has broken the elastic, and has not troubled to replace it, it is obvious that he has less foresight now than formerly, which is a distinct proof a of a weakening nature. On the other hand, he has endeavored to conceal some of these stains upon the felt by daubing them with ink, which is a sign that he has not entirely lost his self-respect. It is also clear that his wife has ceased to love him,"

"My dear Holmes!" Watson exclaimed.

"This hat has not been brushed for weeks. When I see a married man with a week's accumulation of dust upon his hat, and when his wife allows him to go out in such a state, I fear that he has been unfortunate enough to lose his wife's affection. Other than

96

he is a man who leads a sedentary life, goes out little, is out of training entirely, is middle-aged, has grizzled hair which he has had cut within the last few days which he anoints with lime cream, and that it is extremely improbable that he has gas laid on his house, there is little that I can tell you about this man."

Watson had opened his mouth to reply, when a knock interrupted him. When Watson opened the door, Redmond rushed in with flushed cheeks and the face of a man who is dazed with astonishment.

"Sorry to interrupt, Mr. Holmes, but I knew you'd want to hear about this immediately. The goose, sir! See what my wife found in its crop!"

Holmes' employee held out his hand, and displayed a brilliant blue stone, smaller than a bean, but of such purity and radiance that it twinkled like an electric point.

Holmes sat up. "By Jove, Redmond. This is a treasure, indeed! I suppose you know what you have?"

"A gem sir, and a right pretty one!"

"It's more than that. It's the Countess of Morcar's blue carbuncle. Watson, being out of town these past few days, I doubt you've heard the news of it."

"I have missed most of the news as of late," Watson admitted.

"*The Times* has had advertisements about it every day lately. It is absolutely unique, and its value can only be conjectured, but the reward offered of a thousand pounds is certainly not within a twentieth part of the market price."

"A thousand pounds!" Redmond stared at the two men.

"You have done well to bring it here, Redmond. Putting such a jewel as this out in the market would surely bring us scrutiny that I hope to avoid. But let me make the good doctor aware of the facts before we discuss what to do with such a treasure."

Turning back to Watson, Holmes continued. "It was lost at the Hotel Cosmopolitan on the twenty-second of December, just five days ago. John Horner, a plumber, was accused of having taken it from the lady's jewel case. The evidence against him was so strong that the case has been referred to the Assizes. The hotel attendant testified that he had shown Horner up to the countess' dressing-room on the day of the robbery to fix a loose grate. The attendant was called away, leaving Horner in the room alone. When the attendant returned, he found Horner was gone and that the bureau had been forced open. Upon further inspection, the carbuncle was found to be missing."

Leaning back in his chair, Holmes mused, "The question now is to solve is the sequence of events leading from a rifled jewel case at one end to the crop of a goose in the other. You see, Watson, our little deductions upon this hat have suddenly assumed a much more important and less innocent aspect."

"But surely, it's of no consequence, how it got there. You have the carbuncle now, and surely it will net you a fortune," Watson offered.

"No, we will return this little stone. The officials are still crying for the culprit behind the city bank robbery. If this also goes unsolved, it will bring much more scrutiny upon the criminal class of London than I am comfortable with. Although it is tempting," Holmes sighed, looking at the glint of the jewel in the light. "No, it will be more valuable for us to turn this back over to its rightful owner."

Taking up a pencil and paper, Holmes wrote a note. "Now then, 'Found at the corner of Goodge Street, a goose and a black felt hat. Mr. Henry Baker can have the same by applying at 6:30 this evening at 221B Baker Street.' Redmond, please take this around to all the papers and have them run it. Also, I will ask you and your wife to not speak a word of your find to anyone. When I have connected to the two ends of our chain, you will return the carbuncle and keep a sizable portion of the reward. But until then, I would like to solve this puzzle. Also, have one of the Irregulars bring me a goose so that we may give it to this gentleman in place of the one which your family is now devouring."

Bright with the thought of his future reward, Redmond hurried out of the room to place Holmes' advertisement in the papers.

At 6:30 that evening, there was a knock on the door at Baker Street.

"Mr. Henry Baker, I believe," Holmes said, answering the door. "Is that your hat, Mr. Baker?"

Henry Baker was a large man with rounded shoulders, a massive head with a touch of red in his nose and cheeks. A slight tremor of his extended hand confirmed Holmes' surmise as to his drinking habit.

Baker answered in a slow, staccato fashion. "Yes, sir, that is undoubtedly my hat."

99

"We have retained these things for some days because we expected to see an advertisement from you giving your address. I am at a loss to know why you did not advertise."

"Shillings have not been so plentiful with me as they once were," the visitor remarked.

"Very naturally. By the way, about the bird – we were compelled to eat it."

"To eat it!"

"Yes, it would have been no use to anyone had we not done so. But I presume that this other fresh goose upon the sideboard will answer your purpose equally well?"

"Oh, certainly, certainly!" answered Baker with a sigh of relief. "That looks like quite an excellent bird."

Holmes glanced at Watson with a slight shrug of his shoulders before turning back to Baker. "There is your hat, then, and there your bird. By the way, would it bore you to tell me where you got the other one from? I am somewhat of a fowl fancier, and I have seldom seen a better grown goose."

"Certainly. There are a few of us who frequent the Alpha Inn near the Museum. This year our good host instituted a goose club, by which on consideration of some few pence a week, we were to receive a bird at Christmas. My pence were duly paid, and the rest is familiar to you. I am much indebted to you, sir." Baker bowed solemnly to Holmes and Watson and took his leave.

"So much for Mr. Henry Baker," said Holmes after he closed the door. "It is quite certain that he knows nothing whatever about the matter. I suggest we follow up this clue at the Alpha Inn while it is still hot."

Holmes and Watson followed the trail of the carbuncle, and found that the geese provided to the Alpha Inn goose club members came from a salesman in Covent Garden by the name of Breckinridge. Back out into the December cold they went, travelling onto the Covent Garden Market, where they found the stall bearing the name of Breckinridge just closing up for the day. Holmes questioned the salesman and found that the geese came from a breeder on Brixton Road. Holmes and Watson had barely moved away from Breckenridge when a little rat-faced fellow began pestering the salesman about his geese.

Watching the new man being shooed away by Breckenridge, Holmes whispered to Watson, "Ha, this may save us a trip to Brixton Road," and quickly caught up with the new arrival.

The man spun around, pale-faced and quivering. "Who are you? What do you want?"

"I could not help overhearing your discussion with the salesman. I think that I could be of assistance."

"You? Who are you? You couldn't possibly know anything of this matter."

"My name is Sherlock Holmes. It is my business to know what other people don't know."

At Holmes' name, the man turned even paler. "But you can know nothing of this?"

"I see that you recognize my name, so you understand that what you say is not true. You are endeavoring to trace some geese which were sold by Mrs. Oakshott, of Brixton Road, to a salesman named Breckinridge, by him in turn to Mr. Windigate of the Alpha Inn, and by him to his club, of which Mr. Henry Baker is a member." Holmes paused for a moment to let his grey eyes bore down on the man. "That goose had something very valuable to you in it, didn't it Mr. Ryder?"

Suddenly very worried, Ryder squeaked, "How do you know my name?"

"Mr. Ryder, you clearly know who I am so don't waste my time with such bleat. You are the head attendant at the Hotel Cosmopolitan, the same man who let a plumber into the Countess of Morcar's room the day that her carbuncle went missing. And now you've lost the gem. The game's up, Ryder."

As the cold air enveloped the men, Holmes moved in closer to Ryder and lowered his voice to a menacing tone. "If you recognize my name, then you know that a crime of such magnitude should have been run through my organization. It would have never fallen apart as it has, and you would be under my protection. But you weren't the force behind this theft, were you, Ryder?"

"Please, Mr. Holmes," Ryder stammered. "It wasn't my idea. I was only following orders, sir."

"Precisely. And from whom did the orders come? The orders to steal the carbuncle and place the blame on your plumber with a convenient criminal record so that there was no trail back to you or your superior in crime?"

"I never met with the man. I only got my orders through other people and notes. I swear, Mr. Holmes."

"A name, man. Give me a name!" Holmes growled.

Looking around fearfully, Ryder whispered, "Please, he can't know that I told you. He threatened my sister."

Holmes nodded curtly at the man's pleadings. Ryder took a deep breath and finally whispered, "His name is Moriarty."

Holmes placed his hand on the man's shoulder. "You are not cut out for this line of work, Mr. Ryder. I suggest that you return to the Hotel Cosmopolitan, and when John Horner returns to work in a few days, cleared of all charges, that you give him a significant raise."

"Of course, Mr. Holmes, anything you say. God help me!" Ryder burst into convulsive sobbing, with his face buried in his hands.

"Go!" said Holmes. "No more words. Go!"

As the man rushed off, Watson turned his surprised face to Holmes.

"After all, Watson," Holmes smiled, "it is the season of forgiveness. Chance has put in our way a most important brick in the case against our rival. My man will return the carbuncle, we will split the reward, John Horner will be released, and we may take up our case against a most singular foe."

Holmes paused for a moment, looking at the snow beginning to fall. "Yes, Watson, we have the man's name now. I feel that it is time that we got to know who this Moriarty really is."

Chapter 7: Dear Me, Mister Holmes

"I am inclined to think …" Watson started.

"I should do so," Holmes remarked impatiently.

"Really, Holmes, you are a little trying at times."

After learning the name of his new rival in December, Holmes had spent all of his energy learning everything that he could of his foe. His long hours of investigation had left him stand-offish, and this day in January was no different, as he was too absorbed with his own thoughts to answer Watson. Before tempers could flare from either man, there was a knock on the door and one of Holmes' messenger boys delivered him a note.

Holmes glanced at the envelope. "Thank you, Simpson. There will be no reply to this, but please see that these notes are delivered to Eckrich and Cochran."

Once the boy had left, Holmes turned his attention back to his correspondence. "It is Porlock's writing. I can hardly doubt that, though I have only seen it twice before. The Greek *e* with the peculiar top flourish is distinctive. But if it is from Porlock, then it must be something of the very first importance."

"Who is Porlock?"

"Porlock, Watson, is a *nom de plume*, a mere identification mark, but behind it lies a shifty and evasive personality. In a former letter he frankly informed me that the name was not his own, and defied me ever to trace him among the millions of this great city. Porlock is important, not for himself, but for the great man with whom he is in touch. Picture to yourself the pilot-fish with the shark, the jackal with the lion – anything that is insignificant in companionship with what is formidable. Not only formidable, Watson, but sinister – in the highest degree sinister. That is where he comes within my purview."

"The criminal Moriarty?" Watson asked.

"Yes. Professor James Moriarty. But you are uttering libel in the eyes of the law when you call him a criminal, and there lies the glory and the wonder of it. The masterful schemer, the organizer of every devilry that rivals my own organization, the man who wishes to be the new controlling brain of the underworld. That's the man. But so admirable in his management and self-effacement, that for those very words that you have uttered he could hale you to a court and emerge with your year's pension as a solarium for his wounded character. The man pervades London's underworld and yet no one save myself has heard of him. But our day will come."

"He is a professor, you say?"

"Yes. He is a man of good birth and excellent education, endowed by nature with a phenomenal mathematical faculty. He is a genius, a philosopher, an abstract thinker. At the age of twenty-one he wrote a treatise upon the Binomial Theorem. On the strength of it, he won the Mathematical Chair at one of our smaller universities, and had, to all appearances, a most brilliant career before him. The professor is the celebrated author of *The Dynamics of an Asteroid* – a book which ascends to such rarefied heights of pure mathematics that it is said that there was no man in the scientific press capable of criticizing it.

"And this professor is the man you have been hunting for all this time."

"He is. A criminal strain ran in his blood, which was increased and rendered infinitely more dangerous by his extraordinary mental powers. Dark rumors gathered round him in the university town, and eventually he was compelled to resign his chair and to come down to London, where he set up as an Army coach. So much is known to the world, but I have discovered more.

"I have been three times in his rooms, twice waiting for him under different pretexts and leaving before he came. Once – well, I will leave that to your imagination, Watson. It was on the last occasion that I took the liberty of running over his papers, with the most unexpected results – I found absolutely nothing. That amazed me. He is unmarried. His younger brother is a station-master in the West of England. His chair at the university was worth seven hundred a year. And yet, above his desk, hangs a Greuze painting, similar to one that fetched more than four thousand pounds at auction.

"You mean that he has a great income and that he must earn it in an illegal fashion?"

"Exactly. Of course I have other reasons for thinking so— dozens of exiguous threads which lead vaguely up towards the center of the web where the poisonous, motionless creature is lurking. I only mention the Greuze because it brings the matter within the range of your own observation. Moriarty is reminiscent of Jonathan Wild, a master criminal from the last century – 1750 or thereabouts. You see, Watson, everything comes in circles – even Professor Moriarty. Jonathan Wild was the hidden force of the London criminals, to whom he sold his brains and his organization of a fifteen percent commission. The old wheel turns, and the same spoke comes up. It's all been done before, and will be again."

"The same could be said for our company," Watson observed.

"Ah, but where I differ from Moriarty and Wild is that I take pains to perform my crimes in a gentlemanly fashion, devoid of violence, except for when totally necessary. I'll tell you one or two things about Moriarty which may prove this point. I also happen to know who is the first link in his chain – a chain with this Napoleon of crime at one end and a growing number of broken fighting men, pickpockets, blackmailers and cardsharpers at the other, with every sort of crime in between. His chief of staff is Colonel Sebastian Moran, as aloof and guarded and inaccessible to the law as himself. Moriarty supplies him liberally with money and uses him only in very high-class jobs which no ordinary criminal could undertake. You may have some recollection of the death of Mrs. Stewart, of Lauder, in 1887. No? Well, I am sure Moran was at the bottom of it; but nothing could be proven.

"I may also tell you that Moriarty rules with a rod of iron over his people. His discipline is tremendous. There is only one punishment in his code. It is death."

"How can London tolerate two organizations such as yours and Moriarty's? Surely, the force will begin to suspect a controlling force sooner or later," Watson pondered.

"I am aware of the conundrum. Again and again in case of the most varying sorts – forgery cases, robberies, murders, the perpetrators have operated under shield which forever stands in the way of the law, such as my own. But these were not crimes in which I have been consulted. This ex-professor of mathematical celebrity is the organizer of nearly all that is undetected outside of my range in this great city. But he is fenced round with safeguards so cunningly devised that, do what I will, it seems impossible to get to him. You know my powers, my dear Watson, and yet at the end of these months of work, I am forced to confess that I have at last met an antagonist who is my intellectual equal. But at last the time has come when I am able to seize my thread and follow it, until it led me, after a thousand cunning windings, to this man, Porlock."

"But what does this man Porlock tell you?" asked Watson.

"Ah, the so-called Porlock is a link in the chain some little way from its great attachment. Porlock is not quite a sound link, between ourselves. He is the only flaw in that chain so far as I have been able to test it. Hence his extreme importance. Encouraged by the stimulation of an occasional ten-pound note sent to him by devious methods, he has once or twice given me information which has been of value. I cannot doubt that if we had the cipher we should find that this communication is of the nature that I indicate."

Holmes flattened out the paper he was holding to reveal a numbered and lettered code, obviously an attempt to convey secret information. Holmes deduced quickly that the code referenced words in a page of some book. But which book?

In a very few minutes, there was another knock at the door and another message appeared.

"The same writing," Holmes remarked, as he opened the envelope. He read the message aloud to Watson. "'Dear Mr. Holmes, I will go no further in this matter. It is too dangerous. I can see that he suspects me. He came to me quite unexpectedly after I had actually addressed this envelope with the intention of sending you the key to the cipher. I was able to cover it up. If he had seen it, it would have gone hard with me. But I read suspicion in his eyes. Please burn the cipher message, which can now be of no use to you. Fred Porlock.'"

Holmes sat back for some time, staring into the fire.

"It's pretty maddening to think that an important secret may lie here on this slip of paper, and that it is beyond human power to penetrate it," Watson offered.

Puffing on his pipe, Holmes mused aloud. "I wonder! Let us consider the problem in the light of pure reason. This man's reference is to a book. That is our point of departure."

"A somewhat vague one."

"Let us see, then, if we can narrow it down. The cipher message begins with a large number, 534, does it not? We may take it as a working hypothesis that 534 is the particular page to which the cipher refers. So our book has already become a large book. The next sign is C2. What do you make of that, Watson?"

"Column!" Watson announced.

"Brilliant, Watson. You are scintillating this morning. Had the volume been an unusual one he would have sent it to me. Instead of that he had intended, before his plans were nipped, to send me the clue in this envelope. This would seem to indicate

110

that the book is one which he thought that I would have no difficulty in finding for myself. In short, Watson, it is a very common book."

"The Bible!" Watson cried triumphantly.

"Good, Watson, good! But not, if I may say so, quite good enough. The editions of the Holy Writ are so numerous that he could hardly suppose that two copies would have the same pagination. This is clearly a book which is standardized."

"The almanac."

"Excellent, Watson! But, today being the seventh of January, it is more than likely that Porlock took his message from last year's."

Holmes dashed to the cupboard and emerged with a yellow-covered volume. He sat down and began to work out the cipher.

"I have it Watson. 'There is danger may come very soon one Douglas. Rich. Country. Now at Birlstone House, Birlstone. Confidence is pressing.' There is our result, and a very workman-like bit of analysis it was. So, some devilry is intended against one Douglas, whoever he may be, residing as stated, a rich country gentleman. This may be a way to trail a crime back to Moriarty himself."

Holmes was still chuckling over his success when the door brought a knock again, and a Scotland Yard inspector sauntered into the room.

Watson was startled to see a member of the police force at 221B, but Holmes only smiled and welcomed his guest. "You are an early bird, Mr. Mac. I fear that a personal visit instead of a telegram means that there is some mischief afoot. Let me introduce my friend, Doctor Watson. Watson, Inspector MacDonald is an old acquaintance of mine back from my days on Montague Street."

"Yes," MacDonald acknowledged, "Mr. Holmes has helped me twice to attain success and a few other times on trifles. I know, Mr. Holmes, being the gentleman that you are, you don't care to mix with the more grisly crimes that come my way, but I am dearly in need of your services. A Mr. Douglas of Birlstone Manor House was horribly murdered this morning."

Holmes hid his surprise, but was startled by the news of so quick a development relating to Moriarty. "I am interested, Mr. Mac, and as I have no other pressing matters at the time, I would be happy to assist you. While we are on our way, Mr. Mac, I will ask you to be good enough to tell us all about it."

On their way to Sussex, MacDonald filled the two men in on what details he had. John Douglas had been found dead from a shotgun blast to the head. The alarm had been raised close to midnight, but so far, no arrest had been made.

When their train arrived, the three men were met by the chief Sussex Detective, White Mason, who took the men to the manor house, which lay encircled by a moat. White Mason filled in more details for the newcomers. He had found a sawed-off shotgun with an American inscription on the barrel. The bridge had been pulled up overnight and no signs of anyone exiting the moat were found on the far side.

Holmes moved into the study and inspected the body of the deceased. A shotgun blast had been administered at close range, leaving most of the victim's face unrecognizable. Holmes noticed a small piece of plaster on the angle of Douglas' jaw, apparently from shaving the day before. An old branded triangle was on Douglas' arm, and his wedding ring was missing. Beside the dead man lay a card with "V.V." and "341" printed on it. A large hammer lay on the ground, a smudge of blood like a boot mark was upon the windowsill, and a single dumbbell lay under the side table.

Mr. Cecil Barker was introduced to the men as an old friend of Mr. Douglas from California. Barker was a frequent visitor and friend who had been in the house the previous night. He heard the shot while in the guest room, rushed downstairs and saw the body of his friend and rang for the servants. When Douglas' wife appeared, Barker convinced her to return to her room upstairs. Mrs. Douglas corroborated Barker's story, but Holmes was surprised to hear that she had been talked into returning upstairs before seeing her husband's body.

After meeting with Mrs. Douglas and the servants, Holmes dispatched Watson to the village inn, while he remained at the murder scene. He returned at five that evening with a ravenous appetite.

"My dear Watson, when I have exterminated that fourth egg I will be ready to put you in touch with the whole situation. I don't say that we have fathomed it – far from it – but when we have traced the missing dumbbell-"

"The dumbbell!"

"Dear me, Watson, is it possible that you have not penetrated the fact that the case hangs upon the missing dumbbell? Well, well, you need not be downcast, for between ourselves, I don't think that Inspector Mac or the local practitioner has grasped the overwhelming importance of this incident."

Holmes lit his pipe and talked slowly, "A lie, Watson – a great big, thumping, uncompromising lie. The whole story told by Barker is a lie. But Barker's story is corroborated by Mrs. Douglas. Therefore she is lying also. What are they trying to conceal? And what is Moriarty's role in all of this? I think that an evening alone in that study would help me much. I shall sit in that room and see if its atmosphere brings me inspiration. By the way, you have that big umbrella of yours; I'll borrow that, if I may."

"Certainly – but what a wretched weapon! If there is danger ..."

"Nothing serious, Watson, or I should certainly ask for your assistance. But I'll take the umbrella."

The next morning after breakfast, Holmes asked MacDonald to send a note to Barker telling him that they planned to drain the moat the following day. The two officials objected to this maneuver, citing its impossibility, but Holmes admitted that it was only a ruse. After the note was delivered, Holmes, Watson, and the two detectives waited for the next step, which would come later that night.

After taking up a hiding spot on the far side of the moat that evening, Holmes, Watson, MacDonald and White Mason settled in for a long vigil. Finally, the window from the study was thrown open, and a man's shadow appeared. The man leaned out the window and stirred up the moat, attempting to fish something out of it. Running swiftly across the bridge, Holmes and his companions burst into the manor house and down to the study.

When they arrived in the study, Cecil Barker turned around, with a wet bundle at his feet. "What the devil is the meaning of all this? What are you after?"

Holmes replied, "This is what we are after, Mr. Barker. This bundle, weighted with a dumbbell, which you have just raised from the bottom of the moat."

Barker stared in amazement. "How in thunder do you know anything about this?"

"Simply that I put it there. Perhaps I should have said that I replaced it there. When water is near and a weight is missing it is not a very far-fetched supposition that something has been sunk in the water. Last night, with the crook of Dr. Watson's umbrella, I was able to fish up and inspect this bundle. It was of the first importance, however, that we should be able to prove who placed it there. This we accomplished by the very obvious device of announcing that the moat would be dried tomorrow. So, Mr. Barker, I think the word lies now with you."

White Mason picked up the sopping bundle, put it on the side table and undid the tie. He drew out a dumbbell, a pair of American made boots, a long knife and a bundle of commonplace American clothes. Turning back to Barker, he said, "We will keep you here until we have the warrant and can hold you."

Barker stared defiantly back at the policemen and they stared at their captive. The deadlock was broken by a woman's voice behind them.

"You have done enough for us, Cecil," Mrs. Douglas said, entering the room. "Whatever comes of it in the future, you have done enough."

"Mrs. Douglas," Holmes said, "I should strongly recommend that you ask *Mr. Douglas* to tell his own story."

Mrs. Douglas gave a cry of astonishment, but a man did appear, blinking as one who has just come into the light from the dark. "And you'll have it, gentlemen," Mr. John Douglas said. "Can I smoke as I talk? You'll guess what it is to be sitting for two days with tobacco in your pocket and afraid that the smell will give you away."

"Well, this beats me!" cried Inspector MacDonald. "If you are Mr. John Douglas, of Birlstone Manor, then whose death have we been investigating, and where in the world have you sprung from now?"

John Douglas leaned against the mantelpiece and told his story. He told the men that his real name was Birdy Edwards, a Pinkerton detective from Chicago. He had infiltrated a secret society in Pennsylvania and had to flee to England once he had been found out. Three days ago, Douglas spotted Ted Baldwin, an old American enemy, in a neighboring town. He knew to be on guard from then on out. The next night, Baldwin came for him after the house had been shut up and Douglas was making his nightly rounds. Douglas spotted Baldwin hiding behind the curtain of the study just in time to grab a hammer as Baldwin sprang at him with a knife. After an initial struggle, Baldwin pulled a shotgun from under his coat, and as they fought, the shotgun went off in Baldwin's face.

Cecil Barker was the only one to have heard the shotgun blast and hurried to the room. Seeing the same brand from the secret society on the dead man that was on his own arm, Douglas decided to trade identities with the would be assassin, and enlisted Barker's help. The dead man was quickly dressed in Douglas' clothes, and a piece of plaster was applied to what was left of his jaw and the murderer's clothes were lowered into the moat. The only thing Douglas didn't place on the dead man was his wedding ring, saying he couldn't bear to part with it. A fake boot mark was placed upon the windowsill to make it look like the murderer had escaped, and Douglas went into hiding. After letting Mrs. Douglas know what had happened, Barker raised the alarm, and the investigation began.

The room sat in silence after Douglas' tale until it was broken by Holmes. "I would ask you how did this man know that you lived here, how to get into your house, or where to hide to get you?"

"I know nothing of this," Douglas answered.

Holmes already knew, though, and very gravely responded, "The story is not over yet, I fear. You may find worse dangers than the English law, or even than your enemies from America. I see trouble before you, Mr. Douglas. You'll take my advice and still be on your guard."

Within a few days, John Douglas was quickly acquitted as having acted in self-defense and Holmes wrote to his wife, "Get him out of England at any cost. There are forces here which may be more dangerous than those he has escaped. There is no safety for your husband in England."

Two months went by, and Holmes continued his investigations into Moriarty's operation while keeping his own working smoothly, when, one morning, a note was slipped into Holmes' letter box that simply read, "Dear me, Mr. Holmes! Dear me!"

"Devilry, Watson!" Holmes remarked and sat quietly after that.

That night, a note from Cecil Barker appeared with disturbing news: John Douglas and his wife had been on a ship bound for South Africa when he was lost overboard. No one could say how the accident occurred.

"Ha! It came like that, did it?" Holmes said, thoughtfully. "Well, I've no doubt it was well stage-managed."

"You mean that you think there was no accident?" Watson asked.

"None in the world. There is a master hand here. It is no case of sawed-off shotguns."

"But for what motive?"

"Because it is done by a man who cannot afford to fail – one whose whole unique position depends upon the fact that all he does must succeed. A great brain and a growing organization have been turned to the extinction of one man. It is crushing the nut with the hammer – an absurd extravagance of energy – but the nut is very effectually crushed all the same.

"Having an English job to do and knowing that I would not deal in murder for hire, they took into partnership this new consultant in crime. From that moment their man was doomed. At first he would content himself by using his machinery in order to find their victim. Then he would indicate how the matter might be treated. Finally, when he read in the reports of the failure of this agent, he would step in himself with a master touch."

Stunned, Watson asked, "Do you tell me that we have to sit down under this? Do you say that no one can ever stop this king-devil?"

"No, I don't say that," Holmes said, his grey eyes looking to the future. "I don't say that he can't be beat. But you must give me time – you must give me time!"

Chapter 8: The Dominant Mind

The remainder of 1888 found Professor Moriarty increasing his efforts to wrest control of the criminal world from Sherlock Holmes. But the two intellectual adversaries knew that a war between their organizations would only end up hurting everyone involved, and even the winner could not come out of such a battle unscathed. Instead, these two criminal masterminds spent the next few months performing crimes that rang all across London and the continent, and caused London's criminals to pick a side in the battle.

Holmes was first to strike. After his defeat by allowing John Douglas to be murdered, Holmes dearly wished to reclaim his good name. Being a man who loved to dominate and surprise those who were around him, Holmes' next feat would be one that was the talk of two countries. Alexandre Lecomte had recently inherited his family's estate outside of Paris. But before the young man was able to move in, Holmes' associates slipped in under the cover of night and removed numerous paintings and jewels from the house. They were soon distributed to dealers in Riga, Latvia and St. Louis in the United States. One of France's most prominent detectives, Francois Le Villard investigated the theft. Holmes admired the man's quick intuition, for he was able to immediately deduce how the robbers gained access to the manor and how they were able to move the takings out so quickly. But Holmes knew that he could be beaten when it came to his exact knowledge of practical matters, and Le Villard was unable to trace the thieves' multiple routes out of the country. Therefore, he was able to catch up to the stolen goods only after rumors of their individual sales drifted back to France months later. Holmes' empire benefited greatly from the sales, and the authorities were left clueless by the crime.

Professor Moriarty was not a man who let the grass grow under his feet. His next crime was local but no less notorious. For weeks, the Nonparieil Club in London had been rumored to have an unbeatable whist player. Being a private club, the rumors stayed unfounded. The members of the club were hesitant to discuss the unbeatable man, Colonel Upwood, with outsiders. Not only was the man impossible to beat, but he had taken each of the members for grand sums of money. Colonel Upwood behaved so atrociously during his card games that the club feared public disgrace and for the honor of individual members for associating with such a man. Once the colonel had won all that he could from his club mates and some became suspicious of his methods, he quickly disappeared, citing an impending trip to Africa. Upwood was a known associate of Moriarty's lieutenant, Colonel Moran, so Holmes and most of the underworld knew that Moriarty had orchestrated, and most likely benefitted greatly, from the famous card scandal.

Holmes followed his lucrative Parisian heist by returning to one of his quieter, but steady forms of income: helping people to disappear from unpleasant situations. Amy Davenport was a beautiful young woman scheduled to have her coming out ceremony, when her stepmother woke one morning to find her gone without a trace on the day that she was to be presented at St. James' Palace. Miss Davenport's stepmother had done all of the necessary preparation for the presentation and had done all she could to make her stepdaughter a wildly coveted debutante that season. But unbeknownst to her, the young woman had employed Sherlock Holmes to escape the wicked woman. Miss

Davenport had learned that her stepmother planned to use her debutante season as a way to marry her off to the richest suitor, despite Miss Davenport's own preference for travelling abroad. Holmes listened to tales of the stepmother's behavior, and after pocketing his fee, arranged for the young lady's disappearance to New York. The stepmother was imprisoned for a time on a charge of murder, but when no proof could be produced, she was acquitted. The whole affair created such an uproar that her name never carried much weight in polite society again.

Moriarty's next work was blackmailing Dr. Robert Crammond, master of The Rugby School, and the most revered name in English education. Dr. Crammond was successfully blackmailed twice, but when Moriarty's men squeezed him a third time, he refused to pay, showing that Moriarty had gone back to his target one too many times. Moriarty abandoned the scheme, and he allowed pieces of the story to trickle out, letting others know that the professor's organization was happy to use blackmail as another tool in building his criminal empire.

During these months, Holmes showed an excitement that Watson had rarely seen. One evening, Watson sat, reading the British Medical Journal, when Holmes burst through the door in high spirits.

"A productive day out?" Watson asked as Holmes threw his hat into the basket chair and settled into his own.

"Nothing extraordinary, but this is a stimulating time nonetheless. This grand game Professor Moriarty and I are playing of one-upmanship is quite invigorating. Slips are common to all mortals and the greatest is he who can recognize and exploit them. This time we have got a foeman who is worthy of our steel, Watson!"

"I must say that I am surprised that all of this activity has not taken a toll on you."

"I have a curious constitution. I never remember feeling tired by work, though idleness exhausts me completely. And, there is nothing more stimulating than a competition where your rival is of this caliber. This work, the pleasure of finding such a field for my peculiar powers is such a reward that it would be unappreciative of me to not acknowledge it."

"Then you are willing to allow Moriarty to co-exist in London? This is a different strategy than I had expected of you."

"Hardly. There are times when a brutal front attack is the best policy, but not with a foe such as Moriarty. Not only must I contend with him, but the police also. I fully intend to dismantle his organization, but it must be done slowly. When a crime is coolly premeditated, then the means of covering it are coolly premeditated also. Moriarty must not see how I plan to move against him until it is too late."

"And surely, he has his motives against us," Watson said.

"Undoubtedly. Remember to keep your revolver near you night and day, and never relax your precautions, for this is a truly dangerous man and he seeks to have our agency as his own."

"But you must take pains to protect yourself as well, Holmes."

"Of course, doctor. I am well versed in single stick fighting, as well as Baritsu, the Japanese system of wrestling if it were to come to physical contact. But you surely know that I have other precautions in place. In fact, over the last year, I have made at least five small refuges in different parts of London in which I am able to change my personality. No, I hardly doubt that Moriarty's agents will detect me, and even so, they would not move against me yet. Moriarty is like a master chess player, and he has not yet meditated his crowning move in his scheming mind. But our time will come, Watson. Soon enough. Now, Watson, ring for Cartwright. I have a job for Mr. Lynch that I would like to have started very soon."

One evening in September, Holmes and Watson were discussing the finer points of Holmes' recent Bishopgate jewel heist, when Watson stated that Holmes' gift for plotting and execution must come from systematic training.

"To some extent," Holmes answered thoughtfully. "My ancestors were country squires, who appear to have led much the same life as is natural to their class. But, none the less, my turn that way is in my veins, and may have come with my grandmother, who was the sister of Vernet, the French artist. Art in the blood is liable to take the strangest forms."

Having never heard Holmes refer to his relations before, Watson was keenly interested. "But how do you know that it is hereditary?"

"Because my brother Mycroft possesses it in a larger degree than I do."

Watson was stunned by this news. Another Holmes? And one smarter than his friend? Over their years of friendship, Watson had come to regard Holmes as an orphan with no relatives living, due to Holmes' lack of reference to his own people.

"If there is another man like you in England, how is it that neither the police nor public has heard of him? And surely he cannot possess powers greater than yours!"

"My dear Watson," said Holmes, "how many of the public know my name? My name is known in certain circles only because I have allowed it to be for certain business reasons. And I cannot agree with those who rank modesty among the virtues. To the logician all things should be seen exactly as they are, and to underestimate oneself is as much a departure from truth as to exaggerate one's own powers. When I say, therefore, that Mycroft has better powers of observation than I, you may take it that I am speaking the exact and literal truth."

"Is he your junior?"

"Seven years my senior."

"How is it that he is unknown?"

"Oh, he is very well known in his own circle, the Diogenes Club, for example. It is the queerest club in London, and Mycroft one of the queerest men. He's always there from a quarter to five till twenty to eight. It's six now, so if you care for a stroll this beautiful evening, I shall be very happy to introduce you to two curiosities."

Five minutes later, Holmes and Watson were walking towards Regent Circus.

"You wonder," said Holmes, "why it is that Mycroft does not use his powers for public work. He is incapable of it."

"But I thought you said ..."

"I said that he was superior in observation and deduction. If the art of deduction began and ended in reasoning from an armchair, my brother would be the greatest public agent that ever lived. But he has no ambition and no energy. He would not even go out of his way to verify his own solutions, and would rather be considered wrong than take the trouble to prove himself right. Again and again I have taken a problem to him and have received an explanation which has afterwards proved to be the correct one. And yet he was absolutely incapable of working out the practical points which must be gone into before a case could be executed."

"Deduction is not his profession, then?"

"By no means. What is to me a means of livelihood is to him the merest hobby of a dilettante. He has an extraordinary faculty for figures, and audits the books in some of the government departments."

"The government! But Holmes, surely he knows of your profession!"

"He does. He does not approve, but tolerates it. We have an understanding that as long as my exploits do not infringe upon national issues and they stay away from more barbaric crimes, then he will allow me to have my reign. When I say that he will explain a problem to me, it is only in cases where the welfare of a client is involved. He is in no way interested in helping me defraud others for my own personal gain."

"But why would he tolerate behavior such as ours?"

"I have, from time to time, been able to do the leg work in matters for the government, which he is incapable of having the energy of doing himself."

Suddenly, it dawned on Watson. "The Secretary of State! Was he sent to you by your brother?"

"Yes, Mycroft knew that I could be trusted with such an issue as the potentate's letter. And because I do such favors for him, he is willing to look the other way when it comes to my chosen profession. I have no doubt that Mycroft could have found the missing letter, but he takes no exercise and is seen nowhere except his lodgings in Pall Mall, Whitehall, and the Diogenes Club, which is just opposite his rooms."

"I cannot recall the name of such a club."

"Very likely not. There are many men in London, you know, who, some from shyness, some from misanthropy have no wish for the company of their fellows. Yet they are not averse to the comfortable chairs and the latest periodicals. Being a club man yourself, Watson, you understand. It is for the convenience of these that the Diogenes Club was started, and it now contains the most unsociable and unclubbable men in town. No member is permitted to take the least notice of any other one. Save in the Stranger's Room, no talking is permitted. My brother was one of the founders, and I have myself found it a very soothing atmosphere."

"But I still fail to see how your brother could allow you to operate as you do."

"Mycroft intercedes from time to time. I understand that my position is a precarious one, and do not wish to upset those who could put a stop to it."

"What a mysterious man."

"It is a mistake to confuse strangeness with mystery."

The two men stopped at a door some little distance from the Carlton, and Holmes led the way in after cautioning Watson not to speak. Through the glass paneling, one could catch a glimpse of a large and luxurious room in which a considerable number of men were sitting about and reading papers, each in his own little nook. Holmes showed Watson into a small chamber which looked out on to Pall Mall, and then left for a minute, to return with a companion who could only be his brother.

Mycroft Holmes was a large and stout man, much more so than his brother. His body was absolutely corpulent, though his massive face preserved the same sharpness of expression as his brother. His watery grey eyes had a far-away introspective look when they met Watson's.

"I am glad to meet you, sir," Mycroft said, putting out a broad, flat hand, like the flipper of a seal. "You are a medical man, I see. A retired army surgeon.

"By the way, Sherlock," Mycroft continued, "I expected to see you round last week to consult me over that Manor House problem."

"No, I solved it," said the younger Holmes, smiling.

"Adams was the key, of course?"

"Yes, Adams held the answers."

"Very good. I was sure of it from the first. Your deductions are coming along nicely."

"Yes, detective work has always been an alternative profession had I cared to adopt it."

Mycroft grunted something close to a chuckle and the two brothers sat down in the bow-window of the club. "To anyone who wishes to study mankind this is the spot," said Mycroft. "Look at the magnificent types! Look at these two men who are coming towards us, for example."

"The billiard-marker and the other?"

"Precisely. What do you make of the other?"

"An old soldier, I perceive," said Sherlock.

"And very recently discharged."

"Served in India, I see."

"As a non-commissioned officer," Mycroft replied.

"Royal Artillery, I fancy."

"And a widower."

"But with a child," said Sherlock.

"Children, my dear boy, children."

Watson had seen Holmes perform such feats many times, but to see two such men at work, and one able to do better than his friend was astonishing. Mycroft saw the look on his face and smiled. He took snuff from a tortoiseshell box and brushed away the grains from his coat with a large silk handkerchief.

"By the way, Sherlock," Mycroft continued, "I have had something quite after your own heart – a most singular problem – submitted to my judgment. I really had not the energy to follow it up, save in a very incomplete fashion, but it gave me a basis for some very pleasing speculations. If you would care to hear the facts …"

"My dear Mycroft, I should be delighted."

Mycroft scribbled a note and rang the bell, handing it to the waiter when he appeared.

"I have asked Mr. Melas to step across," Mycroft said. "He lodges on the floor above me. He has come to me in his perplexity. Mr. Melas is Greek by extraction, and he is a remarkable linguist. He earns his living partly as interpreter in the law courts, partly by acting as guide to any wealthy Orientals who may visit. I think I will leave him to tell his own very remarkable experience in his own fashion."

As they waited, Mycroft congratulated Holmes on his latest writing on the influence of a trade upon the form of hands, and critiqued some minor points. Sherlock accepted the praise and criticism graciously. Watson was unsure if it were due to respect of his brother's intellect or to his position in the government. A few minutes later, a short, stout, olive-faced man came in and shook hands with the men, and his eyes sparkled with pleasure when he understood that Sherlock was anxious to hear his story.

"I do not believe that the police credit me – on my word I do not," said Melas in a wailing voice. "Just because they have never heard of it before, they think that such a thing cannot be. But I know that I shall never be easy in my mind until I know what has become of my poor man with the sticking-plaster upon his face."

"I am all attention," said the younger Holmes.

Melas told the men an extraordinary tale. Two nights ago, he was hired by a man named Harold Latimer to translate at an estate in Kensington. Melas was put into a carriage with its windows covered, and Latimer sat across from him. When Melas commented that they seemed to be taking a long route to Kensington, Latimer pulled out a bludgeon and told Melas that he was to ask no more questions. Latimer promised to pay him for his inconvenience, but said that if word ever got out about the night's business, Melas would be visited with violence. The two men sat in silence for the remainder of the two hour ride.

The carriage eventually arrived and Melas was hurried into a large and poorly lit house. Another man, nervous and giggling, was waiting in the room for them, and finally a deadly pale and terribly emaciated man was brought into the room, his face grotesquely crisscrossed with sticking-plaster. Melas was ordered to interrogate this poor man, and once he realized that the kidnappers did not know any Greek, Melas began to add his own questions to find out what he was involved in.

Through this process, Melas was able to find out that the man's name was Kratides, he was from Athens, he had only been in London for three weeks, the men were starving him, and he did not know where he was. From the questions he was being forced to ask, Melas could also figure out that then men were trying to force Kratides to sign over property, and that a woman was somehow involved.

Before Melas could find out any more information, a tall and graceful woman stepped into the room and was surprised to see Kratides there, calling out, "Oh my God, it is Paul! Brother!"

Kratides called out to his sister, Sophy, and rushed into her arms, only to have Latimer force her out of the room. Melas was paid five sovereigns and ushered back out into the carriage, but not before the giggling man could issue another warning to him not to speak of this to another human soul.

After Melas finished, the room sat silent for some time before Holmes asked his brother, "Any steps?"

Mycroft picked up the *Daily News* and read an advertisement. "'Anybody supplying any information as to the whereabouts of a Greek gentleman named Paul Kratides, from Athens, who is unable to speak English, will be rewarded. A similar reward paid to anyone giving information about a Greek lady whose first name is Sophy. X2473.' That was in all the dailies. No answer. They also know nothing at the Greek Legation."

"A wire to the head of the Athens police, then."

"Sherlock has all the energy of the family," Mycroft said to Watson. "Well, you take up the problem by all means, and let me know if you do any good."

"Certainly," said Holmes, rising from his chair. "I'll let you know, and Mr. Melas also. In the meantime, Mr. Melas, I should certainly be on my guard if I were you. For, of course, they must know through these advertisements that you have betrayed them."

Walking home, Watson asked Holmes, "There is no financial gain in this matter. Why are you taking an interest in it?"

"Mycroft does me a service by allowing my enterprises to continue by not raising an alarm, and when he presents a problem to me, it is my way of doing a service in return. And, as we have nothing else pressing at the moment, this problem allows me a modest protest against the monotony of existence when opportunities are scarce."

When the two men reached Baker Street, Holmes entered their rooms first and gave a start of surprise. Looking over his shoulder, Watson was also astonished to see Mycroft Holmes sitting and smoking in the armchair, absorbed in a collection of pictures of the modern Belgian masters.

Setting down the book, Mycroft said blandly, "Come in, Sherlock! Come in, sir. You don't expect such energy from me, do you, Sherlock? But somehow this problem attracts me."

"How did you get here?"

"I passed you in a hansom."

"There has been some new development?"

"I had an answer to my advertisement. It came within a few minutes of your leaving."

"And to what effect?"

Mycroft produced a sheet of paper. "Here it is. Written with a J pen on royal cream paper by a middle-aged man with a weak constitution. 'Sir,' he says, 'in answer to you advertisement of today's date, I beg to inform you that I know the young lady in question very well. If you should care to call upon me, I could give you some particulars as to her painful history. She is living at present at The Myrtles, Beckenham. Yours faithfully, J. Davenport.' He writes from Lower Brixton. Do you not think that we might drive to him now, Sherlock, and learn these particulars?"

"My dear Mycroft, the brother's life is more valuable than the sister's story. I think we should call at Scotland Yard for Inspector Gregson and go straight out to Kensington."

"Better pick up Mr. Melas upon our way. We may need an interpreter," Watson suggested.

"Excellent, Watson!" said Holmes.

"A splendid idea. I can see his importance to your organization," smiled Mycroft.

"Watson, send the boy for a four-wheeler, and we shall be off at once." Holmes opened the table drawer and slipped his revolver into his pocket. Noticing Watson's glance, he said, "Yes, I should say from what we have heard that we are dealing with a particularly dangerous gang."

"Can I be of assistance?" Watson asked.

"Your presence might be invaluable," Holmes smiled.

When the men reached Pall Mall, Melas was gone. The landlady told them that a nervous, laughing gentleman had called for him and that they drove away in a carriage. Watson and the Holmes brothers rushed to Scotland Yard, only to be delayed by more than an hour for Gregson to comply with formalities that would allow them to legally enter the house. Holmes' decision to work outside of the law was only reinforced by such a delay.

When they finally reached the house described by Melas, it was empty, and wheel tracks showed Holmes that a heavily loaded carriage had left an hour prior. Gregson hammered loudly at the door and pulled the bell, without any success while Holmes slipped away. Returning after a few minutes, Holmes stated, "I have a window open."

The inspector, noting the clever way in which Holmes had forced back the catch of the window, noted, "Well, I think that, under the circumstances, we may enter. It is a mercy that you are a law-abiding citizen, Mr. Holmes."

One after the other, the men made their way into the house and heard a low moaning above their heads. They dashed up the stairs, Holmes and the inspector leading with Watson at their heels, while Mycroft followed as quickly as his bulk would permit.

Holmes burst through the door from which the moans emanated, only to burst back out with his hand at his throat. "It's charcoal! Give it time. It will clear."

Peering in, they could see that two men were crouched against the wall. Rushing in, they got to the poisoned men and dragged them out onto the landing. Both men were blue lipped and swollen. Mr. Melas survived the ordeal, but Watson could quickly see that they had arrived too late to help the emaciated man.

Once he was able to talk, Melas told the rescue party his story. He was threatened at his own apartment by the giggling man and brought back here for another interview. Kratides was being threatened even harder this time, but did not give in. Finally, the captors hurled him into the poisonous room and turned on Melas, shaking the newspaper advertisement in his face. He was struck from behind and remembered nothing else until he was pulled out of the room by Gregson and Watson.

Melas had also learned during the interview that Sophy was from a wealthy Grecian family, and while on a visit to England met Harold Latimer. He had convinced her to fly away, and her friends alerted her brother, Paul, who came to England after her. When he found Latimer and his foul associate, they realized that Paul was ignorant of their language and made him prisoner in the house, without the girl's knowledge until he would sign away their property.

That was the end of the adventure of the Greek interpreter until months later, when a curious newspaper cutting was forwarded to Baker Street. It told how two Englishmen had met with a tragic end in Budapest. They had each been stabbed and the

Hungarian police were of the opinion that they had quarreled and had inflicted moral injuries upon each other.

After reading this, Holmes looked to Watson, "If one could find the Grecian girl, one might learn how the wrongs of herself and her brother came to be avenged."

"Was the newspaper story sent from your brother?" Watson asked.

"No. If Mycroft had sent it, it would have been marked from Pall Mall. This is clear of any identifying marks."

"There were did the cutting come from?"

"I propose that Professor Moriarty has been keeping an eye on our activities, just as we have been observing his."

Chapter 9: Possession of a Considerable Treasure

"Which is it today," asked Watson, "morphine or cocaine?"

"It is cocaine," Holmes answered languidly. "A seven percent solution. Would you care to try it?"

"No, indeed. And consider the cost!" Watson said earnestly, his hand stealing towards his old war wound. "Why should you, for a mere passing pleasure, risk the loss of those great powers with which you have been endowed? Remember that I speak not only as a comrade, but as the medical man on staff, and therefore I am answerable to your constitution."

Putting his fingertips together, Holmes leaned his elbows on the arms of his chair. "Of course, my dear doctor. Even though we found ourselves in such an exciting chain of events with brother Mycroft just last week, here we sit with nothing on the horizon. My mind rebels at stagnation. Give me problems, give me work, give me the most abstruse cryptogram or the most intricate analysis, and I am in my own proper atmosphere. I can dispense then with artificial stimulants. But I abhor the dull routine of existence. I crave mental exaltation."

"But how can you say that there is nothing on the horizon when you create your own activities? As the head of our agency, surely you are truly the master of your own destiny."

"You may not be aware, but our rival, Professor Moriarty, and his minions were involved in a situation in Mitcham just recently, and our current game of one-upmanship has stirred up the official forces. We must lay low. And other than our continuing counterfeit operation in Berkshire, we find ourselves in a quiet and uneventful time in London."

"Your writings then? Couldn't they fill this time for you?"

"My technical monographs are of interest, but do nothing for me at this time. I cannot summon up the interest in something as intricate as distinctions between ashes of various tobaccos or the use of plaster of Paris as a preserver of footprints."

"You do have an extraordinary genius for minutiae," Watson marveled. Hoping to keep Holmes distracted from his drug use. "Your talent is of the greatest interest to me. Would you think me impertinent if I were to put your theories to a test?"

"On the contrary, I should be delighted to look into any problem which you might submit to me."

"I have a here a watch which has recently come into my possession. Would you have the kindness to let me have an opinion upon the character or habits of the late owner?"

Holmes balanced the watch in his hand, gazed hard at the dial, opened the back, and examined the works and then handed it back to Watson. "There are hardly any data. The watch has been recently cleaned, which robs me of my most suggestive facts," he remarked.

"Though unsatisfactory," he continued, "my research has not been entirely barren. Subject to your correction, I should judge that the watch belonged to your elder brother, who inherited it from your father."

"That you gather, no doubt, from the H. W. upon the back?"

"Quite so. The W. suggests your own name. The date of the watch is nearly fifty years back, and the initials are as old as the watch: so it was made for the last generation. Jewelry usually descends to the eldest son, and he is most likely to have the same name as the father. Your father has, if I remember right, been dead many years. It has therefore, been in the hands of your eldest brother."

"Right so far," Watson replied. "Anything else?"

"He was a man of untidy habits - very untidy and careless. He was left with good prospects, but he threw away his chances, lived for some time in poverty with occasional short intervals of prosperity, and finally, taking to drink, he died. That is all I can gather."

Bitterly, Watson spat, "This is unworthy of you, Holmes. If you wished to know of my family, you should have asked me, not sent out agents to make inquiries into the history of my unhappy brother, and then pretend to deduce this knowledge in some fanciful way. You cannot expect me to believe that you have read all this from his old watch!"

"Watson, pray accept my apologies. Viewing the matter as an abstract problem, I had forgotten how personal and painful a thing it might be to you. I assure you, however, that I never even knew that you had a brother until you handed me the watch. True, I have looked into your background before you came to work for me, but that was only an inquiry into your military and employment history."

"Then how in the name of all that is wonderful did you get these facts? They are absolutely correct in every particular. Surely it could not have been mere guesswork!"

"No, no: I never guess. It is a shocking habit – destructive to the logical faculty. What seems strange to you is only so because you do not follow my train of thought or observe small facts upon which large inferences may depend. For example, I began by stating that your brother was careless. If you observe the lower part of that watchcase you notice that it is not only dented in two places, but it is cut and marked all over from the habit of keeping other hard objects, such as coins or keys, in the same pocket. Surely it is no great feat to assume that a man who inherits a watch of such value is well provided for in other aspects

"It is very customary for pawnbrokers in England," Holmes continued, "when they take a watch, to scratch the numbers of the ticket with a pin-point upon the inside of the case. There are no less than four such numbers visible to my lens on the inside of this case. Inference – that your brother was often at low water. Secondary inference – that he had occasional bursts of prosperity, or he could not have redeemed the pledge. Finally, I ask you to look at the inner plate, which contains the keyhole. Look at the thousands of scratches all 'round the hole marks where the key has slipped. You will never see a drunkard's watch without them. He winds it at night, and he leaves these traces of his unsteady hand."

Just as Watson was opening his mouth to reply, the crisp knock of Mrs. Hudson was at the door. She entered, presenting a card. "A young lady for you, sir."

Holmes read the card aloud. "'Miss Mary Morstan.' Hum! I have no recollection of the name. Ask the young lady to step up." Turning to Watson, he smiled. "We may have something to occupy us yet!"

Miss Morstan entered the room with an outward composure, a young blonde lady, small, dainty, well-gloved, and dressed in the most perfect taste. Her large blue eyes accentuated her sweet and amiable expression. Even though Watson had an experience of women extending over many nations and three continents, he was smitten with the refined and sensitive face he looked upon that day.

"I have come to you, Mr. Holmes," Miss Morstan said, "because you once enabled my employer, Mrs. Cecil Forrester, to unravel a little domestic complication. She was much impressed by your skill."

"Mrs. Cecil Forrester," Holmes repeated thoughtfully. "Yes, I believe that I was of some slight service to her. The problem, however, as I remember it, was a very simple one. State your case," he said in a brisk, businesslike tone.

Miss Morstan laid her tale for the two men. In 1878, her father, an officer in the Bombay Infantry, telegraphed her to meet him at the Langham Hotel. When she arrived, she found that her father had gone out the previous night and never come back. Although she asked an old comrade of his, Major Sholto, and had tried everything else she could think of, no trace was ever found of her father.

Four years later, an advertisement appeared in the *Times* asking for her address. After she provided it, she received a large pearl in the mail, and continued to do so every year for six years from an unknown source. She showed the two men her collection of pearls. But that morning, Miss Morstan received a letter stating that she was a wronged woman and if she would meet her unknown benefactor at the Lyceum Theater that night, she would have justice. She was allowed to bring two friends, but no police.

After the mention of pearls, Holmes became more interested in the young lady's story. "You trust this person?" he asked her.

"I'm not sure, Mr. Holmes. But the writer's hesitance at police involvement made Mrs. Forrester think that you would be an appropriate chaperone for tonight."

"Ah, then you understand that my methods may not always follow the letter of the law?"

"I understand and upon Mrs. Forrester's recommendation, I place my trust in your judgement."

"Very well then, Miss Morstan. Judging from the pearls you have shown us, treasure of some sort awaits you at the other end of this mystery."

"I care not for the treasure, Mr. Holmes. I will gladly give you a significant portion of it if you are able to find out what happened to my father ten years ago! Will you go tonight?"

"I believe your offer would suit me. We shall most certainly go – you and I and – yes, why Dr. Watson is the very man."

"You are both very kind," she replied.

"We shall look out for you, then, at six," Holmes said, "*Au revoir*, then."

With a bright, kindly glance at the two men, Miss Morstan hurried away.

Watching her walk briskly down the street, Watson exclaimed, "What a very attractive woman!"

"Is she?" Holmes responded, leaning back in his chair with his pipe. "I did not observe."

"You really are an automaton - a calculating machine! There is something positively inhuman in you at times."

Holmes smiled. "It is of the first importance not to allow your judgement to be biased by personal qualities. A client is to me a mere unit, a factor in a problem. The emotional qualities are antagonistic to clear reasoning."

"In this case, however-"

Holmes held up his hand to stop his friend. "I never make exceptions. An exception disproves the rule. I am going out now. I have some few references to make."

Returning to Baker Street that evening, Holmes stated, "There is no great mystery in this matter. The facts appear to admit of only one explanation. Major Sholto died upon the 28th of April, 1882."

"I may be obtuse, Holmes, but I fail to see what this suggests."

"You surprise me. Look at it in this way, then. Captain Morstan disappears. The only person in London whom he could have visited is Major Sholto. Major Sholto denies having heard that he was in London. Four years later Sholto dies. *Within a week of his death* Morstan's daughter receives a valuable present, which is repeated each year and now culminates in a letter which describes her as a wronged woman. What wrong can it refer to except this deprivation of her father? And why should the presents begin immediately after Sholto's death, unless Sholto's heir knows something of the mystery and desires to make compensation?"

"Why should he write a letter now, rather than six years ago? What justice can she have? It is too much to suppose that her father is still alive."

"There are certainly difficulties, but our expedition of tonight will solve them all."

Miss Morstan arrived in a four wheeler and answered all of the questions about her father and Major Sholto that Holmes asked her.

"By the way, a curious paper was found in Papa's desk which no one could understand," she said. "I don't suppose that it is of the slightest importance, but I thought you might care to see it."

Holmes took the paper. "It is of native Indian manufacture. It has at some time been pinned to a board. The diagram upon it appears to be a plan of part of a large building with numerous halls, corridors, and passages. At one point is a small cross done in red ink, and above it is '3.37 from left' in faded pencil writing. In the left hand corner is a curious hieroglyphic like four crosses in a line with their arms touching. Beside it is written, in very rough and coarse characters, 'The sign of the four – Jonathan Small, Mahomet Singh, Abdullah Khan, Dost Akbar.' It is evidently a document of importance. Preserve it carefully, Miss Morstan, for it may prove to be of use to us. I begin to suspect that this matter may turn out to be much deeper and more subtle than I at first supposed, I must reconsider my ideas."

The party of three was hardly at the meeting spot at the Lyceum Theater when a small, dark man came up to them. After assuring the man that they were not police officers, he ushered them into a cab and mounted the front of it himself. As they drove, Holmes muttered the names of the streets that they passed, making their way out of fashionable districts of London.

When they arrived at the only inhabited house on a questionable and foreboding street, the door was thrown open by an Indian servant, and the three guests were led down a poorly lit hall to a door on the right, where a small man with a very high forehead stood.

The balding man wrung his hands together. "Your servant, Miss Morstan. Your servant, gentlemen," his thin high voice said. "Pray step into my little sanctum. Mr. Thaddeus Sholto, that is my name. You are Miss Morstan, of course. And these gentlemen…"

"This is Mr. Sherlock Holmes, and this is Dr. Watson," she answered.

"A doctor, eh!" Sholto cried. "Have you your stethoscope? Might I ask you – would you have the kindness? I have grave doubts as to my mitral valve, if you would be so very good. The aortic I may rely upon, but I should value your opinion upon the mitral."

Watson glanced at Holmes, who shrugged his shoulders. He listened to the man's heart and replied, "It appears to be normal. You have no cause for uneasiness."

"You will excuse my anxiety, Miss Morstan," Sholto remarked airily, "I am a great sufferer. Had you father refrained from throwing a strain upon his heart, he might have been alive now."

Enraged at the man's callous and offhand reference to so delicate a matter, Watson took a step forward to strike Sholto across the face, but he was stopped by Miss Morstan's words.

"Please, no, Doctor. I knew in my heart that he was dead."

"I can give you every information," Sholto said. "What is more, I can do you justice; and I will, whatever Brother Bartholomew may say. We can show a bold front to Brother Bartholomew in Norwood. But let us have no outsiders – no police or officials. We can settle everything satisfactorily among ourselves."

Everyone agreed. Sholto began to fidget with a hookah and prattle on about French paintings.

"Excuse me, Mr. Sholto," Miss Morstan cut in, "but I am here at your request to learn something which you desire to tell me. It is very late, and I should desire the interview to be as short as possible."

"Yes," Watson added. "If we are to go to Norwood, it would perhaps be as well to start at once."

"That would hardly do!" Sholto cried. "No, I must prepare you by showing you how we all stand to each other."

Sholto explained to his visitors that his father was Major Sholto, a friend to Miss Morstan's father. In 1882, Major Sholto received a letter and, as his health declined, he hoped to reveal all to his sons. On his deathbed, Major Sholto told his two sons that Captain Morstan had visited him the night of his disappearance, as they had arranged to divide a considerable treasure that they brought back from their time in India. The men argued, and in a fit of anger, Morstan suffered a heart attack and died. The treasure was a secret between the two men, so Major Sholto and his servant disposed of the body. He showed his sons a chaplet of pearls, saying that he wished them to go to Morstan's orphan.

As he was about to tell the location of the remaining treasure to his sons, Major Sholto began to scream at something in the window. The sons turned around to see a bearded face with wild, cruel eyes pressed against the window. When they turned back to their father, he was dead. The two sons searched outside for evidence of the intruder, but only found a single footprint. The next morning, the window to Major Sholto's room was opened, the room had been ravaged, and a piece of paper lay on the dead man's chest with 'The sign of the four' scrawled across it.

Since that day, the brothers had searched the family home, Pondicherry Lodge, for the Indian treasure. Just the day before, Bartholomew had found it. Thaddeus quickly communicated with Miss Morstan. And now that the story had been told, the four of them headed to Pondicherry Lodge.

When the party arrived, Sholto knocked on the door and it was opened by a short, deep-chested man. "That you, Mr. Thaddeus? But who are they? I had no orders about them from the master. He hain't been out o' his room today and I have no orders to let anyone else in. I can let you in, but your friends they must just stop where they are. I don't know none o' your friends."

"Oh, yes, you do, McMurdo," cried Holmes genially, stepping into the light. "I don't think you can have forgotten me."

"Not Mr. Sherlock Holmes! God's truth! How could I have mistook you? If instead o' standin' there so quiet you had just stepped up and given me that cross-hit of yours under the jaw, I'd ha' known you without a question. In you come, sir, in you come – you and your friends. Very sorry, Mr. Thaddeus, but orders are very strict. Had to be certain of your friends before I let them in."

As McMurdo closed the door behind them, they heard the shrill whimpering of a frightened woman.

"It is Mrs. Bernstone," said Sholto. "She is the only woman in the house. Wait here. I shall be back in a moment."

As Thaddeus disappeared to talk to the housekeeper, Holmes picked up a lantern to peer at the house. In the past few hours, Mary Morstan's questions had been answered, but the treasure was still to be split. In her time of distress, Miss Morstan reached out and grasped Watson's hand with her own, needing the feeling of comfort and protection.

"There is something amiss with Bartholomew!" Sholto cried as he rushed back towards them.

Leaving Miss Morstan to sit with the housekeeper, the three men made their way to Bartholomew's room, only to find it locked from the inside. Holmes looked through the keyhole and with a sharp intake of breath rose and asked Watson's opinion. Watson peered in and saw a face that mirrored Thaddeus Sholto's fixed in a horrid, unnatural grin as the body lay prostrate in a chair.

"The door must come down," Holmes stated. He and Watson threw all their weight against it and the door gave way with a sudden snap.

Inside, Bartholomew Sholto sat dead. Watson examined the body and stated that death had come hours before. His body was hard as a board, possibly death from some powerful alkaloid. On the table next to the body lay a brown stick with a stone head like a hammer, rudely lashed on with coarse twine. Next to that was a torn sheet of notepaper with "The sign of the four" scrawled upon it.

"This means murder," Holmes stated, pointing to a long, dark thorn sticking in the skin just above Bartholomew's ear. "This is certainly not an English thorn."

"The treasure is gone!" Thaddeus cried from behind them. "They have murdered my brother and robbed him! There is the hole through which we lowered it. I was the last person who saw him! I left him here, and I heard him lock the door as I came downstairs. The police will suspect that I had a hand in this. But you don't think so? Is it likely that I would have brought you here if it were I? Oh, dear!"

Holmes grasped Sholto's shoulder and stared into his face. "I know that you wished to resolve this matter without interference of the police, but that time has passed. Take my advice and drive down to the station to report the matter. Offer to assist them in every way. We shall wait here until your return."

The little man stumbled out of the room and Watson asked, "Should we leave before the police arrive?"

"No. Too many people know that we are here and our absence would only turn the detectives on to our trail instead of the murderer's. Now, Watson, we have half an hour to ourselves. Let us make good use of it, for I plan to find this treasure before the official force. My case is almost complete; but we must not err on the side of overconfidence. Just sit in the corner there, that your footprints may not complicate matters. In the first place, how did these folk come and how did they go? The door has not been opened since last night. Window is snubbed on the inner side. Frame work is solid. No hinges at the side. Let us open it. No water pipe near. Roof quite out of reach. Yet a man has mounted by the window. It rained a little last night. Here is the print of a foot in mold upon the sill. And here is a circular muddy mark, and here again upon the floor, and here again by the table. See here, Watson!"

"That is not a footmark," Watson said.

"It is something much more valuable to us. It is the impression of a wooden stump. But there has been someone else – a very able and efficient ally. Could you scale that wall, Doctor?"

"It is absolutely impossible."

"Suppose you had a friend up here who lowered you this stout rope which I see in the corner. Then you might swarm up, wooden leg and all. You would depart in the same fashion, and your ally would draw up the rope, shut the window, snib it on the inside, and get away in the way that he originally came."

"This is all very well, but how about this mysterious ally? How came he into the room?" Watson asked.

"The grate is much too small. You must apply my precept. When you have eliminated the impossible, whatever remains, however improbable, must be the truth. We know that he did not come through the door, the window or the chimney. We also know that there is no concealment possible in the room."

"He came through the hole in the roof! Holmes, I cannot but think what a detective you would have made had you turned your energy and sagacity in defense of the law!"

"Of course he came through the roof. If you will have the kindness to hold the lamp for me, we shall now extend our researches to the room above – the secret room in which the treasure was found."

Climbing into the room above, Holmes and Watson spied a trap door leading to the roof outside. Holmes held the lamp to the floor of the secret room, looking for footprints and found prints of a clear, well defined naked foot, but one that was hardly half the size of an ordinary man's.

"Holmes," Watson whispered, "a child has done this!"

"There is nothing else of importance here," Holmes said, as he lowered himself back into Bartholomew Sholto's room. "We are certainly in luck!" he crowed suddenly. "We ought to have very little trouble now. Number one has had the misfortune to tread in the creosote in the room. I know a dog that would follow that scent to the world's end. The answer should give us the – but hallo! Here are the accredited representatives of the law."

A burly man with a pair of very small keen eyes came into the room, followed by a uniformed inspector and Thaddeus Sholto. "Here's a pretty business!" the man cried in a husky voice. "Who are all these? Why, the house seems to be as full as a rabbit warren!"

"My name is Sherlock Holmes, Mr. Athelney Jones. I don't know if you recollect me, but I'm sure if you ask Gregson or Lestrade, they may vouch for my good name."

"Of course I do!" he wheezed. "It's Mr. Sherlock Holmes, the theorist. I'll never forget how you lectured us on causes and inferences. But here we are, bad business! Stern facts here – no room for theories. How lucky that I happened to be out at Norwood on another case! What d'you think the man died of?"

"Oh, this is hardly a case for me to theorize over," Holmes replied dryly.

"No, no. Dear me! Door locked. Jewels worth half a million missing. How was the window?"

"Fastened, but there are steps on the sill."

"Well, well, if it was fastened the steps could have nothing to do with the matter. That's common sense. Man might have died in a fit; but then the jewels are missing. Ha! I have a theory. These flashes come upon me at times. Just step outside, Inspector, and you, Mr. Sholto. What do you think of this,

153

Holmes? Sholto was, on his own confession, with his brother last night. The brother died in a fit, on which Sholto walked off with the treasure. How's that?"

"On which the dead man very considerately got up and locked the door on the inside. You are not quite in possession of the facts yet. This splinter of wood, which I have every reason to believe to be poisoned, was in the man's scalp where you still see the mark; this card was on the table, and beside it lay this rather curious stone instrument. How does all that fit into your theory?"

"Confirms it in every respect. You see that I am weaving my web round Thaddeus. House is full of Indian curiosities. Thaddeus brought this up, and if the splinter be poisonous, Thaddeus may as well have made murderous use of it as any other man. The card is some hocus pocus. The only question is, how did he depart? Ah, of course, here is the hole in the roof."

Holmes and Watson watched the man spring into the garret and heard him proclaim that he had found the trap door to the roof.

"He can find something, at least," Holmes murmured to Watson.

Jones reappeared from the hole in the roof. "You see! Facts are better than theories, after all. My view of the case is confirmed. It shows how our gentleman got away. Inspector!" he called out. "Bring Mr. Sholto this way! Mr. Sholto, I arrest you in the Queen's name as being concerned in the death of your brother."

"There now! Didn't I tell you!" cried Sholto, looking at Holmes and Watson. "I brought you here on business, and now I am implicated in my own brother's murder!"

"Don't trouble yourself, Mr. Sholto," Holmes said. "I think that I can engage to clear you of the charge."

"Don't promise too much, Mr. Theorist!" Jones snapped. "By the way, why is it that you are here tonight, Mr. Holmes?"

"Mr. Sholto wished to show the treasure to Miss Morstan, the young lady downstairs, and having never met either of the Sholtos before, she retained Doctor Watson and I to accompany her."

Jones accepted this response with a nod and then turned back to the scene.

Holmes ushered Watson out to the head of the stairs. "The police involvement has caused us to lose sight of the original purpose of our journey."

"I have just been thinking so. It is not right that Miss Morstan should remain in this stricken house."

"No. You must escort her home. I will remain here and attempt to contain the tenacious imbecile that is complicating matters. We shall work the problem out independently and leave this fellow Jones to exult over any mare's nest which he may choose to construct. When you have dropped Miss Morstan, I wish you to go on to No. 3 Pinchin Lan, down near the water's edge at Lambeth. The third house on the right hand side is an old friend of mine, Sherman the bird-stuffer. Knock old Sherman up and tell him, with my compliments, that I want Toby at once. A queer mongrel, with a most amazing power of scent. I would rather have Toby's help than that of the whole detective force of London."

Two hours later, as the clock passed three in the morning, Watson returned to Pondicherry Lodge. Holmes was standing on the doorstep, smoking his pipe.

"Ah, Watson! You have him there! Good dog, then! Athelney Jones has gone. He has arrested not only Thaddeus, but our old friend McMurdo, the housekeeper, and the Indian servant. After you left, I inspected number one's escape route and found these."

Holmes held out a small pouch woven of colored grasses with a few beads strung around it. Inside were six spines of the dark wood, like that which had struck Bartholomew Sholto. "I'm delighted to have them," Holmes said, "for the chances are that they are all he has. Are you game for a trudge, Watson?"

"Certainly."

"Then here you are, doggy! Smell it, Toby, smell it!" Holmes pushed a creosote stained handkerchief under the dog's nose and then fastened a stout cord to the dog's collar, and led him to the foot of the water barrel that he had found to be the escape route.

Toby followed the scent from the property to the half-rural roads which led back into London, passing street laborers and dockmen.

"Does the rush of the chase outweigh the reward for you, Holmes?" Watson pondered as they moved down side streets of London.

"Hardly. Crime is, or ought to be, an exact science and should be treated in the same cold and unemotional manner. I will enjoy our spoils when this adventure is over, but I cannot allow emotion to interfere now."

As the sun began to rise, the two men followed Toby down towards the riverside, and right down to the water's edge, where there was a small wooden wharf.

"We are out of luck. They have taken to a boat here," said Holmes.

"Then the treasure is lost?" Watson asked.

"I don't believe they have flown just yet," Holmes smiled, looking at the small brick house next to the wharf. Above the door hung a sign that read 'Mordecai Smith, Boats to hire by the hour or day.'

Within a few moments, Holmes had learned that a wooden-legged man had hired the steam launch, the *Aurora*, one of the fastest boats on the Thames.

Walking away from the wharf, Holmes commented to Watson, "This is just the time where the Baker Street Irregulars might be invaluable. I will wire their dirty little lieutenant, Wiggins, and I expect that he and his gang will be with us before we have finished our breakfast."

That morning's paper carried a short notice titled 'Mysterious Business at Upper Norwood' outlining the previous night's activity and detailing all of Athelney Jones' arrests.

"I think that we have had a close shave ourselves of being arrested for the crime!" Watson stated.

"So do I," Holmes responded. "I wouldn't answer for our safety now, if he should happen to have another attack of energy. We must wrap this matter up quickly."As Holmes spoke, Wiggins appeared to receive his orders.

"Ah, Wiggins. I want to find the whereabouts of a steam launch called the *Aurora*, owner Mordecai Smith, black with two red streaks. She is down the river somewhere. I want one boy to be at Mordecai Smith's landing stage opposite Millbank to say if the boat comes back. You must divide it out among the boys and do both banks thoroughly. Let me know the moment you have news. Now off you go!"

"If the boat is above water they will find it," Holmes said, handing the scraps of his meal down to Toby. "Look here, Watson; you look done in. Lie down there on the sofa, and see if I can put you to sleep."

Taking up his violin, Holmes began to play some low, dreamy, melodious air of his own improvisation as Watson drifted peacefully to sleep, thinking of the sweet face of Miss Mary Morstan.

It was late in the afternoon when Watson woke, finding Holmes sitting in his chair, deep in a book. "Have you had news?" he asked.

"Unfortunately, no," Holmes confessed. "I am surprised and disappointed. Wiggins has just been up to report. He says that no trace can be found of the launch."

"Then I shall call upon Mrs. Cecil Forrester. She asked me to when I escorted Miss Morstan home."

"Call on Mrs. Forrester?" Holmes asked with a twinkle in his eye.

"Well, of course, on Miss Morstan, too. They were anxious to hear what happened."

"I would not tell them too much. Women are never to be entirely trusted – not the best of them."

Watson shook his head at Holmes' sentiment, took up Toby's leash to return him and left Holmes with his pipe and book.

Holmes waited for word of the launch all that night and the next day, pacing the floors and making himself worn and haggard. He directed Watson to stay in their rooms the third day while he donned the disguise of a sailor to investigate down the river. As Watson read the morning paper, he saw two items of interest to their current problem: Athenley Jones had had to release his prisoners for lack of evidence and an advertisement asking for information on the *Aurora* to be called upon at Baker Street. The long day of waiting for word continued until Holmes returned in his disguise around three that afternoon.

"I have been working in that get-up all day," Holmes said as he tossed a white wig onto a chair and lit a cigar. "A good many of the criminal classes begin to know me, whether they work for us or not. I can only go on the warpath under some disguise, especially if I don't want Professor Moriarty to catch a whiff of what we are on to!"

"Then you have news?"

"A break in the chain, to be sure. We will have a fast steam launch waiting for us at the Westminster Stairs at seven o'clock. But no more of this problem until then. Dinner will be ready in half an hour."

Their meal that night was a merry one. Holmes talked brilliantly on a quick succession of subjects: miracle plays, medieval pottery, Stradivarius violins, Buddhism of Ceylon and warships of the future, handling each as though he had made a special study of it. When the dinner had ended, Holmes poured two glasses of port and handed one to Watson.

"One bumper to the success of our little expedition. And now it is high time we were off. Grab your pistol, Watson. It is well to be prepared."

As they mounted the launch, Holmes turned to Watson and laid out his day's activities for him. In his seaman's garb, he inquired at all the repair yards down the river until he came upon one where the *Aurora* was being hidden. It was set to leave at eight o'clock that night and Holmes had stationed one of the Irregulars close by to signal them when it began to leave.

The lookout signaled to them, and the *Aurora* took off like the devil! Holmes commanded his engineer to take off at full speed and to catch the boat at all costs. The *Aurora* had slipped unseen behind two or three small craft and had fairly got her speed up before Holmes' craft took after her, and she was flying down the stream, near the shore going at a tremendous rate. Holmes' boat's own furnaces roared, and the powerful engines whizzed and clanked like a great metallic heart, quivering like a living thing. They followed behind the *Aurora*'s wake, flashing past barges, steamers and merchant vessels, in and out, behind one and round another, following close upon her track.

"Pile it on, men, pile it on!" Holmes cried, looking down into the engine-room, while the fierce glow from below beat upon his eager, aquiline face. "Get every pound of steam you can."

Suddenly, a tug with three barges in tow plowed in front of them. Only by putting the helm down did they avoid a collision, and after they rounded it, the *Aurora* had gained two hundred yards on them. The boilers strained and the frail shell vibrated and creaked as the engineers piled on the coal, and still the *Aurora* chugged on. Holmes could see the figures upon her deck. One man sat on the stern, stooped over something black between his knees.

The flying manhunt down the Thames continued as Holmes' boat steadily drew in on its prey yard by yard. The man on the stern of the *Aurora* continued to crouch with his arms moving as though he was busy, glancing up every now and again as his pursuers came nearer and nearer. Next to him appeared a little man with a great misshapen head and a shock of tangled hair. When the pursuers closed to only four boat lengths away, the man in the stern of the *Aurora* sprang up on his wooden leg and cursed in a cracked voice.

"Fire if that little man raises his hand," Holmes told Watson.

As the chase closed to only one boat length between them, the little man plucked a short, round piece of wood and clapped it to his lips. Holmes and Watson fired automatically, and the little man whirled around as the bullets hit him. He fell into the river with a choking cough as Holmes' boat sped by his dying body.

The wooden legged man pulled hard on the rudder and the *Aurora* made straight for the bank. Holmes' boat shot by them, but quickly pulled back around only to find that the wooden-legged man had run off the boat and had become trapped in the marshy soil. Holmes ordered a rope to be tossed around the fleeing man and he was hauled aboard like some evil fish.

Once the captive and treasure were loaded onto Holmes' launch, he dispatched Mordecai Smith and the *Aurora* back to his wife. Striding into the cabin of his own boat, Holmes lit a cigar and faced his prisoner.

"Well, sir, I am sorry that it has come to this."

"And so am I. I don't believe that I can swing over the job. I give you my word on the Book that I never raised a hand against Mr. Sholto. It was the little hell-hound Tonga who shot one of his cursed darts into him. But it seems you've given him his punishment. I had no part in it, sir."

"I am hardly worried about that. My interest is in reclaiming Miss Morstan's treasure."

"It's a bad job for you, then!" the man crowed. "I have put it away where you shall never lay hand on it. It is my treasure, and if I, Jonathan Small, can't have the loot, I'll take darned good care that no one else does! I tell you that no living man or woman has any right to it, unless it is three men who are in the Andaman convict barracks and myself. I know now that I cannot have the use of it, and I know that they cannot. Well, I know that they would have had me do just what I have done, and throw the treasure into the Thames rather than let it go to kith or kin of Sholto or Morstan!"

Enraged by this, Watson struck the man in his mouth. Equally perturbed but still curious, Holmes placed a hand on his shoulder.

"Let him continue, Watson."

Small leaned back and laughed aloud. "It was not to make them rich that we did it. You'll find the treasure where little Tonga is. When I saw that your launch must catch us, I put the loot away in a safe place. There are no rupees for you this journey! Oh, it went to my heart to do it, though. I was half mad when you came up with us. However, there's no good grieving over it. I've had ups in my life, and I've had downs, but I've learned not to cry over spilled milk."

Holmes sighed. "This is a serious matter for you, Small. If you had helped me procure the treasure, you could have walked away from this." He turned and walked out of the cabin. "Engineer, take us back up to the Isle of Dogs. I remember seeing a police launch. We will unload our man there."

The next morning, Watson returned to Camberwell to tell the disappointing end of the treasure hunt to Miss Morstan and Mrs. Forrester. When he returned to Baker Street that afternoon, he found Holmes smoking in silence.

"Watson, make a call upon that McMurdo chap from the Sholto manner, will you? I believe he would be a welcome addition to

163

our organization. And find me someone at the port who would be willing to let us know when the Thames will be dredged next. I would like to have some men on that crew."

"Gladly, Holmes. Until the river is dredged, I think that should be the end of our little drama," Watson mused. "And I fear that it may be the last one in which I shall have the chance of studying your methods. Miss Morstan has done me the honor to accept me as a husband."

Holmes groaned. "I feared as much. I really cannot congratulate you. She is one of the most charming young ladies I ever met, but love is an emotional thing, and whatever is emotional is opposed to that true, cold reason which I place above all things."

"I trust that my judgment may survive the ordeal," Watson laughed. "But the division seems rather unfair. You have done all the work in this business. I get a wife out of it, Jones gets his man and public credit, and if nothing comes from the dredging of the river, pray what remains for you?"

"For me, there still remains the cocaine bottle."

Chapter 10: Signs of Renewed Activity

Watson found marriage to be a happy position. Although his wife was vaguely aware of Holmes' shadowy enterprises, having been a client herself, she urged her husband to begin his own practice, one not tied to Holmes' shadier dealings. After weeks of pressure from his wife, Watson finally conceded and visited Baker Street to deliver the news to Holmes.

Holmes set aside the commonplace book into which he was placing a newspaper cutting and welcomed his friend warmly. "Wedlock suits you, Watson. You have put on seven and a half pounds since I saw you."

"Seven!" Watson answered.

"Indeed, I should have thought a little more. Just a trifle more, I fancy, Watson, and you have hired a most clumsy servant girl at your practice."

"My dear Holmes, this is too much. I fail to see how you work such things out."

"I deduce it," Holmes answered, lighting a cigarette. "You see, but you do not observe. The distinction is clear. For example, you have frequently seen the steps which lead up from the hall to this room."

"Frequently."

"Then how many are there?"

"How many! I don't know."

"Quite so! You have not observed. And yet you have seen. That is just my point. Now, I know that there are seventeen steps, because I have both seen and observed," Holmes chuckled to himself and rubbed his long nervous hands together.

"I fear that I have news to bring you," Watson started.

"Mrs. Watson would prefer you to spend more time as a doctor and less time assisting in my enterprises?"

Smiling and shaking his head, Watson continued, "I would of course be happy to assist you when I can, but Mary does deserve a respectable life," Watson offered.

"I cannot begrudge you this one selfish action," Holmes sighed. "You have been a most stalwart companion in our association. I would, however, like to retain your services on an as-needed basis. Surely, Mrs. Watson cannot deny me that request?"

Laughing, Watson replied, "Surely not, my good man! Perhaps I can even persuade you to forgo your Bohemian habits and visit us every now and again."

"Don't expect too much of me, Watson."

Relieved to have gotten Holmes' blessing, Watson sold the pearls his wife had inherited and bought a connection in the Paddington district from an old Mr. Farquhar. Farquhar had once been an excellent general practitioner, but his affliction of St. Vitus' dance and his increased age had thinned his clientele. Watson directed all his energy into revitalizing the practice, and within a year from its purchase, business was steadily rising and the practice was well on its way to be as flourishing as ever.

During this time, Holmes continued his own work, and took care of a most lucrative problem for the Vatican during May of that year. When the two men would meet, Holmes would regale Watson with stories from his latest exploits. One day would find Holmes retelling how he helped Lestrade solve a murder in Boscombe Valley or accepting a commission to help an escaped Princetown convict to relocate to South America, while the next meeting would have Holmes giving the details of how he used a bogus laundry operation to remove countless jewels from families all throughout Piccadilly. Watson never seemed to tire of the charm of variety Holmes' exploits contained.

But many of their conversations revolved around the Ripper murders.

During this time, London was in an uproar of the outrageous murders of young women in the Whitechapel neighborhood and the taunting letters from the alleged murderer that were being sent to the Central News Agency. Watson pored over the daily news reports and speculations just like every other Londoner, and was anxious to hear Holmes' thoughts on the matter.

"You know that I abhor violence in my city, Watson," Holmes stated. "Of course something like this could not be tolerated. But this Ripper is on a completely different plane of existence from the pickpockets and smashers that my employees have been told to squash unless they worked for me. This man is a shadow, and a possible lunatic. He has my people, especially the female ones, that live in Whitechapel terrified. I have not taken an active role in pursuing the fiend, but have instructed my employees to always travel in twos and threes, and to offer any ladies safe passage at night. These murders do not have a logical progression or pattern, so I fear that my skills would not be useful in such matters."

"But Holmes," Watson protested, "surely you are doing more in this matter! Mycroft has not contacted you in this matter?"

"Brother Mycroft deals on the world stage. While he views this matter as an unfortunate and horrendous one, it is not one in his purview."

"And you are comfortable sitting by your fire while this madman terrorizes London?"

Holmes drew his clay pipe from the top of a line of reference books beside the mantelpiece. "I am not retained by the police to supply their deficiencies. The 'Ripper Murders,' as the press has sensationalized them, is not an area that directly affects my livelihood. My time is better spent gathering any morsel of information I can on Professor Moriarty's organization."

"I cannot accept that you will sit in your rooms doing nothing while this monster is on the loose! You once told me that you strove to elevate crime to a gentlemanly manner and that you abhorred the circle of misery and fear that senseless violence created. These words are an exact description of Jack the Ripper. This attitude of compliance is beneath you, Holmes."

Holmes absorbed his friend's words and puffed on his pipe for a few moments. "Your words ring true, Watson. I have become calloused in your absence. I saw no monetary gain from this matter, and pushed it out of my mind. But your moral compass has always been truer than mine, even for a man involved in as many crimes as you have. I am ashamed to say that I turned Inspector Gregson down when he asked for my thoughts on the matter. If you would, please send word to the inspector that I plan to give the matter serious thought tonight and will have a possible profile of the Ripper for him tomorrow if he would be so good to call upon me."

"Don't be so hard on yourself, Holmes," Watson smiled. "I'm sure Gregson and London will be glad for your help, no matter how tardy it may be."

Holmes waved his hand dismissively. "Thank you for your words Watson. Now, if you will leave me to smoke. This will be quite a three-pipe problem, and I intend to give it my full attention for the time being."

As Watson left, he looked over his shoulder at Holmes curled up in his chair with his thin knees drawn upon his hawk-like nose, with his eyes closed and his black clay pipe thrusting out like the bill of some strange bird.

As promised, Holmes presented Inspector Gregson with his detailed opinion about the Ripper the next morning. Soon after, the murders came to a close. If the man had been caught, killed, or escaped, Holmes never knew, for he had contributed what he could, and the matter had been tucked away into a corner of his brain-attic.

One July morning, Holmes appeared at Watson's Paddington office.

"It is good to see you Watson," Holmes greeted. "Your neighbor is a doctor I see by the brass plate."

Smiling from under his mustache, Watson responded, "Yes. He bought a practice as I did. Both have been ever since the houses were built."

"Ah, then you got hold of the better of the two."

"I think I did. But how do you know?"

"By the steps, my boy. Yours are worn three inches deeper than his. I am sorry to see that you've had the British workman in the house. He's a token of evil. Not the drains, I hope?"

"No, the gas."

"Ah! He has left two nail-marks from his boot upon your linoleum just where the light strikes it. Since I see no patients in your waiting room or paper work on the desk, and that you still smoke the Arcadia mixture of your bachelor days, can I entice you to smoke a pipe with me? "

Watson handed Holmes a tobacco pouch, and they seated themselves opposite one another and smoked for some time in silence. After some time had passed, Watson asked for news of Holmes' exploits.

"I fear that the days of great capers may be past."

"That surely cannot be true!" Watson cried.

"You know me too well to think that I am exaggerating. It appears that Professor Moriarty and I may have finally come to a stalemate. I have just recently thwarted one of his employees, a Colonel Carruthers, but he has also able to put an end to one of my schemes with the tired captain we have employed from time to time. We seem to be at a point where we are sniping at each other and our battles continue to draw the attention of the official force," Holmes sighed. "I have recently submitted a monograph to the *Anthropological Journal* on the formation of the human ear, but other than reading a slim volume by Petrarch, my time is filled with too much leisure. You know how these periods of inaction can seize me, Watson. I dread the days ahead where I can only lie upon the sitting-room sofa, hardly moving a muscle from morning to night."

Holmes' nostrils dilated with the purely animal lust for crime, but his hands were tied. Crimes worthy of his abilities were not able to be carried out while he and Moriarty were at a loggerhead.

"Perhaps I could convince you to step round to my club some evening?" Watson ventured.

Smiling at his friend's attempt, Holmes replied, "Thank you Watson, but you know how I loathe every form of society. No, I shall remain in my lodgings buried among my old books."

The two men continued their visit until they were interrupted by a patient looking for Doctor Watson. Holmes took his leave and made his way back to Baker Street.

But the next day brought adventure for Sherlock Holmes.

Watson's old schoolmate, Percy Phelps, sent for Watson to make a house call in Woking. Phelps had just recovered from a case of brain fever and needed his friend's advice on regaining his strength. During the doctor's interview with his patient, he learned that Phelps had risen to a responsible position in the Foreign Office but a horrible misfortune nine weeks prior had caused his illness. Although Phelps was looking for medical advice, Watson was more intrigued with the incident that was the catalyst.

Phelps had been in possession of a secret treaty between England and Italy of the utmost importance. So much so that he was only able to work on copying it at night once the rest of his office staff had left. While working on it, he had called for a cup of coffee to help him stay alert. When the coffee did not arrive, Phelps left the treaty on his desk, went down the hall to the commissionaire's desk and found the coffee boiling over as he slept.

Suddenly, Phelps heard the bell from his office ring and he raced back, only to find that the treaty was gone. Knowing that there was only one other way out from his office besides the hallway that he had been standing in with the sleeping commissionaire, Phelps rushed out the door but found nothing. The police were called but they could find no clues to help. Driven to despair, Phelps returned home. When his mother and fiancée saw him, a sick room was made up for him in the room where his fiancée's brother had been staying. Nine weeks later, he was coherent enough to ask for a doctor, and he remembered his old schoolmate, Watson.

Watson gave his friend orders and promised to visit again in two days. Leaving Woking, he headed straight to Baker Street, instead of his office. When Watson arrived, he found Holmes seated at his side-table, clad in his mouse-colored dressing gown

172

and working over a chemical investigation. He hardly glanced up as Watson entered, and Watson seated himself in an armchair and waited. Holmes dipped into different bottles, drawing out a few drops of each with his glass pipette, and finally brought a test tube containing a solution over to the table where he dropped some of the solution onto a piece of litmus paper. Holmes observed the results and scribbled off several telegrams, handed them to the page boy that had let Watson into the room, and threw himself down in the chair opposite Watson, drawing up his knees until his fingers clasped round his long, thin legs.

"A very commonplace little murder," Holmes said. "Since I have only seen you just yesterday, I fancy you have something better for me, Watson. What is it?"

Watson retold Phelps' story to Holmes, noting that although it didn't have any payoff for him, it did present a problem like the letters he retrieved in 1886, with which he was happy to help.

"True, your friend's problem is of interest. And, more importantly, it will occupy me for some time."

"I wondered if you had heard anything of this from your brother."

"No, brother Mycroft prefers to use me when the problem is unknown to the public. Because the police were called in, this would not be something Mycroft would engage me for. However, if I brought it to him of my own accord, he would not begrudge me the details to help my own investigation. Let me change out of my dressing gown and we may head to the Diogenes Club for a visit."

Holmes and Watson waited for Mycroft to join them in the Stranger's Room at his club where Watson again marveled at the odd atmosphere of a social club where men were not allowed to be sociable to one another. When Mycroft's bulk came through the door, he shook Watson's hand and turned to his younger brother, "Your monograph on the dating of manuscripts had two errors in it. Sloppy work, Sherlock."

"One. The other was an error by the printer. But I'm not here to quibble over my research. I have recently been made aware of a missing treaty with Italy."

Mycroft pursed his lips. "And how did you learn of that?"

Watson spoke up. "Percy Phelps is a patient of mine and described the incident to me today. I brought the issue to your brother thinking that he may be able to help such as he did with the letters for the Secretary of State three years ago."

"That is very good of you, Doctor," Mycroft said, "But we are all aware of my brother's line of work and if he were ever to be found out ..."

Holmes let out a sharp laugh at that.

Mycroft glared at the younger Holmes, and then turned back to Watson, "If he were ever to be found out, the government could not be seen as retaining someone with such an *illustrious* work history." Turning to his brother, he continued. "But, since you have found this out on your own accord, I cannot stop you from investigating out of patriotic duty."

"It is beneficial for you that I have been spiritless as of late. Clearly the Foreign Office's investigations have uncovered little."

"Spiritless or hampered by a mathematics professor?" Mycroft shot back. "No matter. You've come to me for information. Proceed."

Ignoring Mycroft's comment, Holmes continued. "Could the Foreign Minister have been overheard giving instructions to Phelps?"

"Out of the question."

"Then if the Foreign Minister and Phelps were the only people with knowledge that Phelps was to copy the treaty that night, the thief's presence in the room was purely accidental. He saw his chance and he took it."

"Precisely," Mycroft nodded.

"What are the results if the details of the treaty become known?"

"Very grave results."

"And have they occurred?"

"Not yet. If the treaty had reached another country's Foreign Office, I would have known."

"The thief has not been fielding bids for the highest price?"

"No. And if he waits much longer, he will get no price at all. It will not be a secret in a few months."

"Very instructive...," Holmes muttered.

175

"About Mr. Phelps," Watson cut in, "how will he fare in all of this?"

"This incident will have a very prejudicial effect upon his career," Mycroft answered, shaking his head. "It is a shame, for what his uncle has said of him, Mr. Phelps was a most trustworthy and tactful employee."

"His uncle?" Holmes asked.

"Why Sherlock!" Mycroft laughed. "The Foreign Minister is Percy Phelps' uncle. You are lacking in many facts of this case, brother. Perhaps I should also tell you about the commissionaire's wife that was visiting him at the office that night or Mr. Phelps' coworker, Charles Gorot, who was the last person in the office before Phelps took out the treaty?"

"No, this information will be enough. Thank you, Mycroft," Holmes said. As they parted ways for the day, Holmes said to Watson, "Doctor, I believe tomorrow we should go check on your patient."

When Holmes and Watson arrived in Woking the next day, they found Percy Phelps very agitated. There had been an attempted break-in the night before, in the very room that Phelps was recuperating. Watson introduced Holmes as someone who might be able to help recover his missing treaty.

"Mr. Phelps, I believe I can present the treaty to you tomorrow morning if you would allow me one thing," Holmes offered.

"Anything!" Phelps replied.

"You must return to London today with Watson. Tell your fiancée that it is under his orders as your physician and that the house should be closed up until you return."

Confused, Phelps looked at Watson.

Shrugging, Watson replied, "I have known Mr. Holmes for years and he produces results."

Once Phelps assented, he had his fiancée pack him items for two days of travel and ordered the house to be closed up. Holmes, Watson and Phelps headed to the train station, where Holmes ordered two tickets to London.

"Two?" Watson inquired.

"Please set up Mr. Phelps in your old room at Baker Street, and I will meet you there tomorrow for breakfast."

"But my patients, Holmes!"

"We've discussed your neighbor's lack of patients. He clearly has time to watch your practice for a few hours while you save England from war." Holmes handed Watson the tickets and strode away.

The next morning, Watson was in the Baker Street rooms as ordered, waiting beside Percy Phelps when the door burst open and Holmes strode in.

"You've found it?" Phelps asked eagerly.

"You will do me the liberty of enjoying breakfast, Mr. Phelps. Remember that I have breathed thirty miles of Surrey air this morning." Turning the door, he shouted, "Mrs. Hudson!"

The landlady brought in three covered dishes as the men sat at the table, Holmes buoyant, Watson curious, and Phelps beside himself with anticipation.

"Mrs. Hudson has risen to the occasion. Her cuisine is a little limited, but she has as good an idea of breakfast as a Scotchwoman. Mr. Phelps, please help yourself to some sustenance."

"Thank you, I can eat nothing," Phelps said.

"Oh, come! Try the dish before you!"

"Thank you, I would rather not."

"Well then," Holmes urged, "I suppose that you have no objection to helping me? Please lift the lid, Mr. Phelps."

Phelps did so and uttered a scream as he stared down at the missing treaty on his breakfast plate.

"Watson here will tell you that I never can resist a touch of the dramatic," Holmes smiled.

"God bless you, Mr. Holmes! You have saved my honor!"

"So I have," Holmes said as he swallowed a cup of coffee and turned his attention to his ham and eggs. "I wouldn't expect to see your fiancée's brother anytime soon. He is the thief. I caught him as he retrieved the papers from a floorboard of your sick room – his old bedroom. When I approached him, he struck at me with a knife, but he found himself on the ground, able to see out of only one eye."

"He is a villain and a thief!" Phelps cried.

"Hum! I was asked to retain the treaty, not arrest ruffians, so I could not tell you what has happened to him. But he is a gentleman to whose mercy I should be extremely unwilling to trust."

"How did you know where the papers were?" Phelps asked.

"My analysis was that he came to visit you that night in your office, rang the bell when you were not in, saw the treaty lying out, took it and fled in hopes of selling it to another country's representative. When you took ill and were being tended to 'round the clock, he had no way of retrieving the papers. But when you were beginning to regain your strength, you were no longer in need of a nurse to sit by you through the night. He saw his chance to retrieve the papers, hoping you were asleep. After that attempt failed, I knew that he would jump at the chance to enter the room while you were away and in London. And now the Queen's realm can rest easy."

"And to think that during these long weeks of agony, the stolen papers were within the very room with me all the time!"

"So it was, Mr. Phelps," Holmes responded, nodding to Watson.

"Percy, if you don't plan on eating breakfast..." Watson began.

"Not at all, Watson," Phelps chirped. "I must return these to the Foreign Office immediately. Thank you, thank you, Mr. Holmes!"

Holmes saluted Phelps with his fork as the man rushed out the door. Turning to Watson, he said, "Now, Watson, does your practice require you back so soon, or can you read to me the story from the *Times* I see about the Garcia murder case?

Inspector Baynes is doing fine work these days, and he is one for me to keep my eye on…"

Chapter 11: Fly for Your Life

Watson's practice continued to flourish. While he treated cases of apoplexy, dyspnoea and rheumatism, Holmes continued to steer his agency while also chipping away at his rival's. As 1889 rolled into 1890, Holmes' organization faced a major setback when his counterfeiting operation was discovered.

The counterfeiting operation was set up in an old country house in Berkshire. It was a steady and quiet source of income, until the hydraulic press used in the counterfeiting of coins stopped working. Holmes always expected to know when routine processes were upset and would approve of the routes to correct them. But the man overseeing the counterfeiting, a retired army colonel, named Lysander Stark, chafed at what he felt were the overly restrictive practices of Holmes' empire, and scoffed at his assistant's reminder that he should wire to London to let them know of the issue.

Stark decided to take care of the matter himself, and tracked down an apprentice hydraulic engineer to get the machine back in gear to resume the process. When the engineer became inquisitive of the operation, Stark attempted to murder the man, but only managed to sever his thumb with a cleaver. Worried that Stark's attempt to repair the press would lead to the authorities being alerted and his comfortable position in Holmes' empire being endangered, his assistant, Mr. Ferguson, rushed out to telegraph Holmes.

Holmes received the news bitterly, and thought back to the debacle of the opium den years earlier. He ordered Ferguson to torch the building before it could be found out, dealing a heavy blow to the finances of his own organization. Holmes sent word to Stark that his services were no longer needed and suggested that he spend time on the Continent. Knowing a veiled threat when he saw one, Colonel Stark immediately embarked on a trip to India, and was never seen in England again.

Just a few months after this fiasco, murmurs of a lost train began to circulate around London. Intrigued, Holmes began to look into the issue. After an uneventful day investigating pawnbrokers' shops in areas of interest, Holmes discussed the matter with Watson back at his practice that evening.

"There is a powerful force behind this, Watson. You can tell an old master by the sweep of his brush. I can tell a Moriarty when I see one."

"But what is the profit in making a train disappear? Moriarty is not in this business for showmanship."

"That is what I intend to find out. Moriarty is not a showman, but perhaps he appreciates a touch of the dramatic, as do I. The chain of events is certainly one of extraordinary interest. My instinct now is to work form the other end. Instead of investigating the missing train, perhaps I should investigate the missing passengers that had engaged it."

After a day of furious correspondence, Holmes met Watson at Baker Street the next evening to update his old friend on his progress. "We have our man, Watson! Although official circles are reluctant to discuss the matter, I have found that the two men who engaged the lost special were Louis Caratal, a well-known financier and political agent in Central America, and his violent but loyal ally, Eduardo Gomez. The two men were on their way to Paris with all due speed to deliver incriminating information on some of the greatest men in France. Certainly, this evidence he held would mean ruin to all of them."

"Then Caratal was targeted by these men and they made sure that he did not arrive?" Watson asked.

"And who would be engaged to carry out such a task? My supposition that Professor Moriarty is behind this mystery is strengthened."

Holmes spread out his big map of London and leaned eagerly over it. "It is certain that the train left Kenyon Junction. It is certain that it did not reach Barton Moss. It may have taken one of the seven available side lines, but we may reduce our improbables to the three open lines, which I exhausted yesterday."

Holmes lit it pipe and stared hard at the map while Watson watched in rapt attention. "It is highly unlikely, but still possible that it may have departed the listed railways," Holmes continued. "Where would an engine and passenger car be disposed of branching off from this line?"

After tracing numerous paths with his forefinger and muttering about each of their likelihoods, Holmes finally stood back up after almost an hour hunched over the map. "You have a grand gift of silence, Watson," said he. "It makes you quite invaluable as a companion. 'Pon my word, it is a great thing for me to have someone to talk to, for my own thoughts are not over-pleasant."

"You have it then?" Watson asked.

"I believe I do. Hearthstone mine is some miles away from this path, but it used to be connected. An ingenious schemer could see that it would only require replacing a few rails to connect it once more. Once done so, the lost special could be smoothly thrown full speed into the abandoned mine and Monsieur Caratal would no longer be a threat to anyone. Moriarty has done it beautifully if I am correct. I would look over the site of the mine, but already know that no clues have been left. And if anyone were to be investigating the area, placing myself in proximity to the mine would only lead suspicion back to our doorstep."

"Then your interest in this mystery is over so quickly?"

"I may pen an anonymous letter to direct inquiry, but there is nothing for me to gain in following this line of reasoning. No, we may score one for Professor Moriarty, Watson.

Looking for a new line of revenue after the counterfeiting catastrophe, Holmes turned to gambling circles, particularly horse races. A fan of betting on the horses now and again himself, Holmes hired George Burnwell and Fitzroy Simmons to build up a bookmaking operation while he infiltrated the local syndicates that unofficially oversaw the local horse races. Holmes maneuvered around London and its surrounding area, making inroads with the notables in each ring. Through promises of profits, and some threats of exposure, Holmes was allowed to have a say in many horse racing matters.

When Silver Blaze, the favorite to win the Wessex Cup, disappeared, it threatened to upend his entire gambling organization. Hesitant to travel to Dartmoor after the area's nonsensical reaction to the ghost hound events in the news two years prior, Holmes' curiosity finally won out and he found himself scouring the moor in search of the missing horse. There Holmes eventually found Silver Blaze at a competitor's stable. The stable happened to be owned by Lord Backwater, the same man that Holmes had turned down when he offered to hire him for a job on the night of McMurdo's benefit fight years ago.

Backwater knew that he stood to lose money on yet another race, but was keen to keep up appearances by entering his horse nonetheless. When the consulting criminal showed up at his gate, Backwater agreed to keep the horse hidden from the public until race time and make a small profit on the side with gambling. Using this information to his advantage, Holmes' bookmakers raked in bet after bet that resulted in one of the greatest windfalls in horse racing history.

Holmes used some of this windfall to finance an extended trip to France on New Year's Day 1891. While the day-to-day operations were left to his trusted lieutenants, Holmes continued to order attacks on Moriarty's crime syndicate. Providence allowed him to cross paths with a small Moriarty operation within days of his arrival in Narbonne, which he happily derailed with little effort.

Merridew, an abominable man that Holmes held in such low regard, had orchestrated a quick but profitable robbery of the Franco-Midland Hardware Company. Included in the man's haul was a sizeable payment from the French government for a contract they had just placed with the company. Although Holmes would not benefit financially from this, he quietly tipped off police agents, and Merridew and his spoils were hastily picked up, dealing a large monetary blow to Moriarty.

But Moriarty's organization was a busy one, and the following month, Holmes' international agents informed him of a plot Moriarty was hatching against the royal family of Scandinavia. Through well-placed intermediaries, Holmes toppled the plan and word reached the royals through back channels that a Mr. Sherlock Holmes of London was to thank. A quiet but sizable thank you was made to one of Holmes' discreet bank accounts soon after.

After this endeavor, Holmes returned home. He had been back in London only a few days when Moriarty finally made just a little trip. It was small, but it was more than he could afford after years of Holmes being so close upon him. Holmes took his chance and wove a net round Moriarty until it was ready to close. He had the locations and evidence on all of the key players in Moriarty's organization and had coordinated with Inspector Patterson of the Yard to collect the head and lieutenants of his rival's organization. The plan only needed a few more days for every lieutenant to be back in London and available for the coordinated capture.

On the morning of April 24th, Holmes was sitting in his room, reading the latest publication by Sven Hedin, when the door opened and Professor Moriarty stood before him.

Surprised, Holmes looked upon the man who had plagued his organization for the past four years. This was their first face-to-face interaction, but Holmes was quite familiar with how his nemesis looked. In the doorway stood an extremely tall and thin man, with a forehead that domed out into a white curve that sat over two deeply sunken eyes. His shoulders rounded, Moriarty's face protruded forward in an ever slowly oscillating motion from side to side in a reptilian fashion.

"You have less frontal development than I should have expected," Moriarty greeted Holmes as he peered from the doorway with great curiosity through his puckered eyes. "It is a dangerous habit to finger loaded firearms in the pocket of one's dressing gown."

Holmes drew the revolver out of his pocket and laid it cocked upon the table beside him.

Moriarty smiled and his puckered eyes blinked at Holmes. "You evidently don't know me."

"On the contrary," Holmes answered, "I think it is fairly evident that I do. Pray take a chair. I can spare you five minutes if you have anything to say."

"All that I have to say has already crossed your mind."

"Then my answer has crossed yours."

Moriarty's head continued to move from side to side. "You stand fast?"

Not moving a muscle, Holmes replied, "Absolutely."

Moriarty clapped his hand to his pocket. Holmes' hand darted forward and raised the pistol at the professor. But Moriarty only produced a memorandum book and began to read from it.

"You crossed my path in France on the 4th of January. On the 23rd you incommoded me here in London. By the middle of February my activity with the royal family of Scandinavia was seriously inconvenienced by you. At the end of March I was absolutely hampered in my plans by your organization's existence. And now, at the close of April, I find myself placed in such a position through your continual persecution that I am in positive danger of losing my liberty. The situation is becoming an impossible one."

"Have you any suggestion to make?" Holmes asked, hand still on the revolver.

"I do. Imagine what the two of our organizations could accomplish under the same banner. Nothing would be beyond our reach if we worked in conjunction instead of opposing each other."

"I suppose the banner that flew over the union would bear the Moriarty name."

"It is the only way. My men will not succumb. Their hatred of you knows no bounds."

"I am quite aware of it. I believe three of them have already vowed to murder me the first chance they have. I would rather cease all business today than be associated with such men. My organization strives to elevate crime to a gentlemanly manner."

"Don't fool yourself, Mr. Holmes," Moriarty hissed. "We are both common criminals, no matter how intelligent and well-hidden we are."

Holmes stared hard at his opponent, his eyes contracting until they were like two menacing points of steel.

"Very well. You must drop it, Mr. Holmes," Moriarty said, his face swaying about. "You really must, you know."

"After Monday."

"Dear me, Mr. Holmes, dear me! I am quite sure that a man of your intelligence will see that there can be but one outcome to this affair. It is necessary that you should withdraw. London is mine. Take your talents to Paris or Berlin. I will grant you that out of respect. You have worked things in such a fashion that we have only one recourse left in London. It has been an intellectual treat to me to see the way in which you have grappled with this affair, and I say, unaffectedly, that it would be a grief to me to be forced to take any extreme measure. You smile sir, but I assure you that I would."

"Danger is part of my trade. Surely no man would take up our profession if it were not the danger that attracts him."

"This is not danger," Moriarty said. "It is inevitable destruction. You stand in the way not merely of an individual, but of a mighty organization, the full extent of which you, with all your cleverness, have been unable to realize. You must stand clear, Mr. Holmes, or be trodden underfoot."

Holmes rose, his eyes never leaving his nemesis. "I am afraid that in the pleasure of this conversation, I am neglecting business of importance which awaits me elsewhere."

The professor shook his head sadly. "Well, well. It seems a pity, but I have done what I could. I know every move of your

189

game. You can do nothing before Monday. It has been a duel between you and me, Mr. Holmes. You hope to place me in the dock. I tell you that I will never stand in the dock. If you are clever enough to bring destruction upon me, rest assured that I shall do as much to you. Your organization will not survive this gambit."

"You have paid me several compliments, Mr. Moriarty. Let me pay you one in return when I say that if I were assured of the former eventuality I would, in the interests of the public, cheerfully accept the latter. Although, I hardly think you are up to the task."

Finally showing a crack in his cool demeanor, Moriarty snarled at Holmes, "I can promise you the one but not the other!" Turning his rounded back on Holmes, he left the room.

Slightly shaken by the professor's soft, precise fashion, Holmes mulled over the singular interview. After deciding that there was nothing to do in the matter, Holmes went out that afternoon to follow up on business on Oxford Street. As he passed the corner of Bentinck Street, a two-horse van furiously whizzed round the corner headed straight for him. He jumped back up to the footpath and missed being trampled by only a fraction of a second.

As Holmes continued down Vere Street, a brick came falling down from the roof of one of the houses, shattering to fragments at his feet. He hailed a constable to have the place examined, and the officer reported that it must have been that the wind toppled over a loose brick that was part of a pile for repairs. Knowing better, Holmes hailed a cab and spent the rest of the day in Mycroft's rooms in Pall Mall.

That night, as Watson sat reading by a single lamp, Holmes entered.

"Have you any objection to my closing your shutters?" Holmes asked as he edged his way around the wall.

"You are afraid of something?" Watson asked.

"I am. Air guns."

"My dear Holmes, what do you mean?"

Holmes drew in the smoke from a cigarette."I must apologize for calling so late and I must further beg you to be so unconventional as to allow me to leave your house presently by scrambling over your back garden wall. Is Mrs. Watson in?"

"She is away upon a visit. I am quite alone."

"Then it makes it easier for me to propose that you should come away with me for a week on the Continent."

"But Holmes, you've just returned from France," Watson protested. "Your pale face tells me that your nerves are at their highest tension. There is more to this than a trip."

"Moriarty. The time has come for me to strike. In three days, that is to say on Monday next, matters will be ripe, and the professor, with all the principal members of his gang, will be in the hands of the police, leaving the rest of his employees to absorb into my syndicate. I'm sure you remember Porlock, my confederate in Moriarty's organization."

Watson nodded.

"After Moriarty began to suspect him, I helped Porlock to disappear until I needed him. Now, I have acquired enough information, that with his testimony against the professor, I can topple his organization and reclaim the entirety of the London criminal element. If I could beat that man, if I could free society of him, I should feel that my own career had reached its summit. Never have I risen to such a height, and never have I been so hard-pressed by an opponent. He can cut deep, and yet I just undercut him."

Holmes quickly told Watson of his plan, the meeting with Moriarty, and the attempts on his life already today.

"You will spend the night here," Watson offered.

"No, my friend. You might find me a dangerous guest. I have my plans laid, and all will be well. Matters have gone so far now that they can move without my help as far as the arrest goes. It is obvious that I cannot do better than get away for the few days which remain before the police are at liberty to act. It would be a great pleasure if you could come on to the Continent with me. It would make a considerable difference to me, having someone with me on whom I can thoroughly rely."

"You know that I have an accommodating neighbor. I would be glad to come."

"And to start tomorrow morning?"

"If necessary."

"Most necessary. Obey these instructions to the letter. You are now playing a double-handed game with me against the cleverest rogue and a most powerful syndicate of criminals in

Europe. Now listen!" Holmes gave Watson explicit instructions on what to do with his luggage and how to approach Victoria Station.

"Where shall I meet you?" Watson asked.

"At the station. The second first-class carriage from the front will be reserved for us."

Holmes bid Watson goodbye and disappeared out to the garden and over the back wall.

The next morning, Watson followed Holmes' instructions and arrived at the only carriage marked "Engaged" but did not find his friend there, only an old Italian priest, who spoke very broken English. As the train started to leave the station, Watson felt a chill of fear, worried that Holmes had fallen to Moriarty over the night.

"My dear Watson," said a familiar voice, "you have not even condescended to say good morning."

The aged priest turned his face towards Watson and for an instant, the wrinkles disappeared, the eyes shone bright, and the lower lip ceased to protrude, transforming into Sherlock Holmes. A moment later, it all collapsed back into the visage of an old priest.

"Every precaution is still necessary," Holmes as the priest whispered. They are hot upon our trail. Ah, there is Moriarty himself."

Glancing back, Watson saw a tall man pushing furiously through the crowd and waving to stop the train, but it was too late.

"Even with all our precautions, you see that we have cut it rather fine," Holmes laughed. "Have you seen the morning paper?"

"No."

"Then you haven't seen about Baker Street. They set fire to our rooms last night. No great harm was done."

"This is intolerable, Holmes!"

"They must have lost my track completely. Otherwise they could not have imagined that I had returned to my rooms. They have evidently taken the precaution of watching you, however, and that is what has brought Moriarty to Victoria. Did you recognize your coachman?"

"No."

"It was my brother Mycroft. It is an advantage to get about in such a problem with help from a brother such as Mycroft. But we must plan what we are to do about Moriarty now."

"This is an express train. I should think we have shaken him off very effectively."

"My dear Watson, you do not imagine that if I were the pursuer I should allow myself to be baffled by so slight an obstacle. Why then should you think so meanly of him?"

"What will he do then?"

"What I should do. Engage a special. This train stops at Canterbury; and there is always at least a quarter of an hour's delay at the boat. He will catch us there."

"What then?"

Holmes paused for a moment's thought. "We shall get out at Canterbury and then we must make a cross country journey to Newhaven, and so over to Dieppe. Moriarty will then get on to Paris, mark down our luggage, and wait at the depot for two days. In the meantime, we shall treat ourselves to a couple of carpet bags and make our way into Switzerland, via Luxembourg and Basle."

As they disembarked at Cantebury, Holmes pointed up the line. "Already, you see."

Sure enough, coming from the Kentish woods rose a thin spray of smoke and a minute later a carriage and engine flew along the open curve which led to the station. Holmes and Watson ducked behind a pile of luggage as the train rattled and roared past them.

Holmes and Watson made their way to Brussels and spent two days there, moving onto Strasburg on the third day. From there, Holmes telegraphed London, and received a reply that evening.

"I might have known it," Holmes groaned. "He has escaped!"

"Moriarty?"

"Yes. The police secured the whole gang with the exception of him and his chief lieutenant. I think that you will find me a dangerous companion now. This man's occupation is gone. He is lost if he returns to London. If I read his character right he will devote his whole energies to revenging himself upon me. I should certainly recommend you return to your practice in London."

"I will do no such thing," Watson responded resolutely. "Don't bother to debate with me, Holmes. As an old campaigner as well as an old friend, my decision will not be swayed."

Holmes knew better than to argue. For hadn't he hired Watson for his reliable nature? They spent the week moving up the Valley of the Rhone and through Alpine villages. But Holmes' quick glancing eyes and sharp scrutiny of every face that passed did not rest, constantly aware of the danger which dogged his every step.

On May 3rd, the duo reached the village of Meiringen and put up at the Englischer Hof. At the advice of the landlord, Holmes and Watson set off with the intention of crossing the hills and spending the night at the Hamlet of Rosenlaui, after stopping to visit the Reichenbach falls.

Standing upon the falls, Holmes and Watson gazed upon the fearful place. The swollen torrent plunged into a tremendous abyss, creating spray that rose up like smoke from a burning house. The river hurled itself into an immense chasm lined by glistening coal black rock. The two stood near the edge peering down at the gleam of the breaking water far below against the black rocks and listening to the half-human shout that came booming up with the spray out of the abyss.

When they moved to return to the path, a Swiss boy came running along with a letter addressed to Dr. Watson from the landlord. It said that within a few minutes of their departing the inn, an English lady had arrived in the late stages of consumption. She was overtaken by a sudden hemorrhage and was thought to have only a few hours left to live. It would be a consolation to her to see an English doctor, a summons which Watson could not ignore.

Holmes and Watson parted there, agreeing to meet that evening at Rosenlaui. When Watson looked back over his shoulder, he saw his friend leaning against a rock wall with his arms folded as he gazed down at the rush of the water. The sight pained Watson and caused the doctor to worry the entire trip back.

After passing another man walking towards the falls very rapidly, Watson finally reached Meiringen an hour later, only to find out that there was no English woman dying of consumption. He had been tricked! Before the landlord could offer any possible explanations, Watson hurried back up the mountain to the falls, where his worst fears were coming true.

After Watson's departure, Holmes waited patiently for what he knew was to come. When the sinister figure of Professor Moriarty appeared on the narrow pathway, Holmes read an inexorable purpose in his cold, grey eyes.

"I regret that it has come to this, Mr. Holmes," Moriarty shouted over the roar of the falls.

"I do not," Holmes said flatly.

"You may have struck me a heavy blow in London. But my reach is far beyond the metropolis. My company will rise again and spread throughout the Continent. You did not believe me when I said you do not realize the extent of my organization."

"I realize it. And I intend to have what is left of it, professor. It is a shame that you did not stay in London. I would have arranged for you to have comfortable lodgings in Newgate."

Moriarty chuckled. "Oh, I was quite aware of what you had in store for me, Mr. Holmes. You are not the only one with friends on the force and in the government. It was not so easy to trace you to Victoria Station, but following your friend, Dr. Watson, told us what we needed to know."

Moriarty took a step toward Holmes. "I hope you know that our little tete-a-tete has been a most stimulating exercise for me."

"Then you will grant me one courtesy – to write a short note to my friend."

"Of course," Moriarty replied with a wave of his hand. "Let it not be said that I am not a gentleman."

Tearing three pages from his notebook, Holmes addressed a final note to Watson.

"My dear Watson, I write these few lines through the courtesy of Mr. Moriarty, who awaits my convenience for the final discussion of those questions which lie between us. He has been giving me a sketch of the methods by which he avoided the English police and kept himself informed of our movements. They certainly confirm the very high opinion which I had formed of his abilities. I am pleased to think that I shall be able to free society from any further effects of his vile presence, though I fear that it is at a cost which will give pain to my friends and employees, and especially, my dear Watson, to you. I have already explained to you, however, that my career had in any case reached its crisis, and that no possible conclusion to it could be more congenial to me than this. Indeed, if I make a full confession to you, I was quite convinced that the letter from Meiringen was a hoax, and I allowed you to depart on that errand under the persuasion that some development of this sort would follow. Tell Inspector Patterson that the papers which he needs to convict the gang are in pigeon-hole M., done up in a blue envelope and inscribed 'Moriarty.' I made every disposition of my property before leaving England, and handed it to my brother Mycroft. Pray give my greetings to Mrs. Watson, and believe me to be, my dear fellow, very sincerely yours, Sherlock Holmes."

Holmes set the note on top of a rock jutting on to the path and weighted it down with his silver cigarette case. Leaning his alpenstock walking stick against the rock as well, he turned to walk the rest of the way up to the falls, with the professor right behind him.

When Holmes reached the end of the path, he turned and Moriarty sprang at him with a snarl. Knowing that Holmes had ended his game, the professor threw his long arms around

Holmes, and was only anxious to have his revenge, future plans be damned.

As the mist of the falls soaked their clothes and skin, the two men tottered on the brink of the cliff, the endless chasm of rock and crashing water awaiting them. Holmes slipped through Moriarty's grip with a Baritsu move, and Moriarty kicked madly for a few seconds and clawed the air with both hands. But for all of his efforts, the professor could not regain his balance. Over he went, falling into the darkening void with a terrible scream, eventually striking and bounding off of a rock and splashing into the water far below.

Holmes stood at the precipice and regained his breath, astonished at how close to death he had just come. Knowing that the arrest of Moriarty's gang would lead to a bloody crime war in London, he weighed his options. Fate had presented Sherlock Holmes with a chance to disappear, leaving the world to think that he was dead. At least three other prominent criminals had vowed to kill Holmes, all working for Moriarty, and their vengeance would only be incensed by the death of their leader.

Turning away from the falls, Holmes had made up his mind. A few small footholds presented themselves on the rock face behind him, and Holmes started to make his way up to the rock ledge above. The falls roared beneath him, and one mistake would lead him to the same fate as Moriarty. As he climbed, tufts of grass came out in his hand and his foot slipped in the wet notches of the rock from time to time. Holmes struggled upward, and at last, reached the ledge above him just in time to roll out of sight as Watson returned to the scene of the final confrontation.

Watson stood for a minute or two, collecting himself. Looking around, the damp soil told him the story all too well: Holmes and Moriarty met, grappled at the cliff face, and went over together. No footsteps returned from the cliff. Watson laid down on the soil with his face over the abyss and called Holmes' name in vain.

No sound came back.

Only the cry of the water plunging down.

Standing, Watson turned around and spotted Holmes' alpenstock and cigarette case. He took up the letter and read the words of goodbye that his friend had left for him. Numb with shock, Watson could barely register the fact that Sherlock Holmes was gone. He turned and stared at the Reichenbach Falls once more before slowly starting back down the path, utterly alone, and leaving behind the best and wisest man that he had ever known.

Chapter 12: Back in Baker Street

After Watson departed from the ledge above the Reichenbach Falls, Holmes took a deep breath and meant to spend a few minutes contemplating the end of his adventure, only to have a huge rock come falling from above and boom past him. The stone struck the path and bounded into the chasm below. He looked up and saw a man's head against the darkening sky right before another large stone smashed into the ledge he was laying on, only inches from his head.

Holmes knew immediately that Moriarty was not the only villain on that cliff. A dangerous man still remained, and he had waited for the right moment to strike. The man's face peered over the edge again and Holmes knew that another stone would soon be speeding towards him.

As he scrambled down the wet and dangerous path, another stone sang by Holmes, yet again just missing him. Slipping, torn and bleeding, Holmes eventually escaped the hunter and did ten miles over the mountains in the darkness, finally escaping to Florence. But he knew that there was still a member of Moriarty's organization out there who knew that he was alive, and this was a dangerous man that Holmes would eventually have to contend with.

Once he had arrived safely in Florence, Holmes telegraphed Mycroft to alert him to the situation. After a brief and coded conversation, the brothers Holmes agreed that it was all-important that no one else should know that Sherlock Holmes was still alive. Although Holmes deeply regretted the pain he knew this would cause Watson, Mycroft agreed with Sherlock's assessment that news of his survival would only ignite the criminal underworld like a powder keg. Mycroft sent Sherlock money and said that he would be in touch soon. Once his brother was settled and safe, Mycroft sent for Watson to visit him at the Diogenes Club.

When Watson arrived, he was in a state of mourning, with which Mycroft played along. The two men consoled each other on their losses, and Mycroft turned to look out the window.

"Doctor, I am aware of what my brother's line of work was. As a rule, I did not interfere. This will be my one and only exception to that rule."

Taken aback at Mycroft's bluntness, Watson began to speak, but Mycroft Holmes held up his broad, flat hand.

"Pardon me doctor, but I must continue. The Moriarty organization is done, but at least two dangerous players escaped capture. I know that one of them is here in London, while the other is abroad. The man in London is not a man to be trifled with, and although I do not know your plans, I would wager that you entertain thoughts of carrying on in my brother's stead. I can tell you that doing so would put you out of your depth and you could not count on the accommodations I afforded Sherlock."

"I had considered it as a tribute to your brother. But to be honest, I cannot say that I am up to such a task at this point," Watson confessed.

Softening slightly, Mycroft nodded. "Of course not. You are still reeling from a tragic loss. We both are. And you will excuse my saying so, but you could not carry out the organization's dealings to meet my brother's standards. My advice to you, Doctor, is to send word to your former workers that they are in danger from Moriarty's man and that they should leave London for a time. I believe that your medical practice should sustain you and that if you do not attempt to re-enter the criminal underworld, you shall be safe from the man until he can be brought to justice."

Nodding solemnly, Watson replied, "Yes, I agree that will be best. To think that this has all been brought upon by a man I have only seen once in passing! But if only there were a way that I could finish Holmes' work by eradicating Moriarty's men…"

"Doctor Watson, you were my brother's a trusted friend, but you must not attempt to have vengeance on his behalf. It could only end in disaster for you. You have your wife and medical practice. Other than the succinct reports that appeared in the Journal de Geneve and the Reuter's dispatch, there has not been, nor will there be any mention of the incident at the Reichenach Falls in the press. Be content with that and your memories and adventures with Sherlock."

The two men shook hands and parted, Mycroft returning to his governmental duties and routines, and Watson to a world without Sherlock Holmes.

While Holmes rested for a few days in Florence, Mycroft arranged a money transfer to him as well as a destination to keep him occupied: Tibet.

Holmes joined up with Captain Hamilton Bower's expedition, under the guise of Sigerson, a Norwegian explorer. For the next two years, he helped map the area with Captain Bower, and later with another explorer, William Rockhill, until they reached the boundary around Lhasa, where no Englishman was allowed to pass. That night at camp, Holmes slipped out unnoticed. Through a combination of disguises and diplomatic entreaties, he worked his way into Lhasa, where he studied Buddhism for some time. By happenstance, he was even allowed to spend some time with the head lama, and departed again before overstaying his welcome.

When his time in Tibet was over, Holmes took on an assignment for the Foreign Office that led him through Persia during its political unrest, and allowed him to look in at Mecca. His time there was brief. The region was in the midst of a civil war, and all outsiders were met with extreme suspicion. After collecting his needed information on the Russian threat there, Holmes escaped the area safely and travelled across the Red Sea to deliver a message to the Khalifa at Khartoum. Not one to take orders, and especially ones that put him in the middle of political conflict, Holmes informed Mycroft that his tenure as an international agent was terminated and he moved onto France.

Once in France, Holmes settled in Montpellier and found a medical school where he was allowed the use of a small laboratory. Here he spent some months conducting research into coal-tar derivatives. Sherlock Holmes, the criminal mastermind, had died in Switzerland, and Sigerson, the adventurer, had disappeared from public knowledge, but the student of chemistry deep inside Holmes was still alive, and he spent days upon days rekindling the inquisitive spirit that Watson first saw in the lab at St. Bart's hospital so many years ago. Once he had settled in the southern French city, Holmes reconnected with Mycroft, and it was then he learned that Mary Watson had died. Holmes was saddened by his friend's loss and took up his pen to write Watson. But fearing Watson's affectionate regard for him might tempt him to some indiscretion which would betray his secret, Holmes knew that it would be impossible to reach out to his old comrade.

Although Holmes was enjoying his studies and experiments, he never forgot about the face from the cliff above the Reichenbach Falls. When he learned from his brother that two of Moriarty's men had escaped capture, Holmes knew that now two men knew that Sherlock Holmes was alive, and he must always be alert.

Holmes enjoyed the French cafes and spent many days reading the papers with some attention there. On one such afternoon in early spring of 1894, Holmes was reading the day's story of the boulevard assassin, when a man sat down across from him and struck up a conversation, much to Holmes' annoyance.

"It's been a long time since anyone's seen you, Mister Sherlock Holmes," the small, bespectacled man sneered.

Holmes lowered his newspaper and stared coldly at the man. "I believe you are mistaken, sir."

The man tittered. "Hardly so. We've been watching you for a few days going in and out o' that lab a few streets over. No, I'd say we know who we're dealing with, all right."

Cocking an eyebrow, Holmes said, "We? I only see one of you."

The waiter set down two cups of coffee in front of the men and disappeared.

"Colonel Moran would stick out quite a bit here in France, so he's stayed home in London. I've been in charge of catching up with you here while the colonel sets up shop back in London."

Holmes sipped his coffee and smirked at the man. "I can't imagine your colonel would appreciate you sharing that information, Mr. Morgan."

The little man ran his hand through his thinning hair before he took a large drink of his own coffee. "So you're aware of me, Mister Holmes? I've not seen anyone following me."

"That is what you may expect to see when I follow you."

"No matter now," Morgan continued. "You've been found and dealt with. I don't expect you'll make it back to London. Hell, you won't even make it back to you rooms today."

"And why do you believe that? Is it because of the cyanide you had delivered to me in this coffee? My, what a blind beetle I have been to fall for such a ruse." Holmes held up his cup and took another sip.

Shocked, Morgan leaned forward. "What's your game, Holmes?"

Holmes nodded and the waiter returned with a baguette. "My friend here is happy to help me look after my health. I'm afraid our coffee cups may have been switched upon delivery."

Realization slowly spread over Morgan's face. "You devil…"

Holmes drained his cup and handed it to the waiter, who left the two men alone. Leaning in, Holmes' eyes contracted into two menacing points. "As the career poisoner you are, it's a shame that you did not notice its almond-like scent. I can only deduce that is because you were too confident of your own work, or that you are not able to smell such scent. You will know that is the case with many victims. You will also know, that at this point, your body is slowing down, and the tired feeling you are fighting valiantly against will soon overtake you."

Morton's mouth moved groggily, but no sound came out.

Holmes' gaze bore down on the little man. "I will leave you now to your own ends, but don't worry, Mr. Morton. I will meet with Colonel Moran soon. You don't mind paying the bill, do you?" Patting his pockets dramatically, he continued, "I seem to have left my wallet at the laboratory. And after all, the coffee was your idea." Rising from the table, Holmes took his bread, nodded to the waiter and slipped out the back door.

Now that only one enemy remained and was attempting to resurrect Moriarty's empire in London, Holmes knew that it was time to plan his return. The next day, he opened the newspaper in his rooms to read of an unidentified English man who had quietly died of heart failure in a local street café. That day's newspaper also told of the death of the Honorable Ronald Adair, second son of the Earl of Maynooth, who had been murdered on March 30, under the most unusual and inexplicable circumstances. Adair had been found dead from a gunshot wound to his head after returning home from a night of playing whist at his club with Mr. Court Murray, Sir John Hardy, and Colonel Sebastian Moran.

London was immensely interested in the murder of Ronald Adair. Doctor Watson was no exception. On April 5, Watson found himself at on Park Lane, where Adair had lived. He found a group of loafers standing around on the pavement and staring up at the window to the room where Adair's body had been found. After overhearing some ill-advised man give his theory, Watson drew away from the crowd in disgust, and bumped into an elderly deformed man behind him, knocking down several of his books. Endeavoring to apologize for the accident, Watson was given a snarl of contempt from the old man before he turned and his curved back and side-whiskers disappeared among the crowd.

Watson returned to his study and had not been there five minutes when the maid entered and announced a person to see him. Astonishingly, it was the strange, old book-collector from Park Lane.

"You're surprised to see me, sir," the collector said in a strange, croaking voice. "Well, I've a conscience, sir, and when I chanced to see you go into this house, as I came hobbling after you, I thought to myself, I'll just step in and see that kind gentleman, and tell him that I was a bit gruff in my manner.

There was not any harm meant, and that I am much obliged to him for picking up my books."

"You make too much of a trifle," Watson answered. "May I ask how you knew who I was?"

"Well, sir, if it isn't too great a liberty, I am a neighbor of yours, for you'll find my little bookshop at the corner of Church Street. Maybe you collect yourself, sir; here's *British Birds*, and *Catullus*, and *The Holy War* – a bargain every one of them. With five volumes you could just fill that gap on that second shelf. It looks untidy, does it not?"

Watson moved to look at the cabinet behind him. When he turned again, Sherlock Holmes was standing smiling at him across the study table.

For the first and last time in Watson's life, he fainted.

"My dear Watson, I owe you a thousand apologies. I had no idea that you would be so affected," the well-remembered voice said after undoing Watson's collar and putting brandy to his lips.

Watson gripped Holmes by the arm. "Holmes! Is it really you? Can it indeed be that you are alive? Is it possible that you succeeded in climbing out of that awful abyss? Tell me how you came alive out of that dreadful chasm."

Lighting a cigarette in a nonchalant manner, Holmes answered, "I had no serious difficulty in getting out of it, for the very simple reason that I never was in it. My note to you was absolutely genuine. I had little doubt that I had come to the end of my career when I perceived the somewhat sinister figure of the late Professor Moriarty standing upon the narrow pathway which led to safety. I read inexorable purpose in his grey eyes. I exchanged some remarks with him and obtained his courteous permission to write the short note which you afterwards received. I left it with my cigarette-box and my stick and I walked along the pathway, Moriarty still at my heels. When I reached the end I stood at bay. He drew no weapon, but he rushed at me and threw his long arms around me. It was only the knowledge of the Japanese system of wrestling, Baritsu, which saved me."

"Amazing," Watson whispered.

"Hardly," Holmes dismissed with a wave of his hand. "I spent the next three years traveling through Asia and Europe. I was about to return when my movements were hastened by the news of this very remarkable Park Lane Mystery, which appealed to me by its connection with the remaining member of Moriarty's organization and his attempt to revive it. I came over at once to London, called in my own person at Baker Street, threw Mrs. Hudson into violent hysterics, and found that Mycroft had preserved my rooms and my papers exactly as they had always been. So it was, my dear Watson, that at two o'clock today I found myself in my old armchair in my own old room, and only wishing that I could have seen my old friend Watson in the other chair which he has so often adorned."

Softening his features, Holmes continued. "I have heard the sad news of Mrs. Watson. Work is the best antidote to sorrow, my dear Watson. And I have a piece of work for us both tonight which, if we can bring it to a successful conclusion, will in itself justify a man's life on this planet. If I may ask for your cooperation, we have a hard and dangerous night's work ahead of us. You'll come with me?"

"When and where you like, Holmes. But what is the task?"

"You will hear and see enough before the morning," Holmes answered. "We have three years of the past to discuss. Let that suffice until half-past nine, when we start upon the notable adventure of the empty house."

The old friends spend the remainder of the evening catching up on each other's recent histories. Watson shared the sad story of Mary Watson's death earlier that year, and Holmes entertained Watson with stories of his travels.

Soon enough, though, it was like old times for Holmes and Watson, as they traveled across London in a hansom. Holmes was stern and silent, while Watson's heart beat with the thrill of adventure and his service revolver rested in his pocket. The cab stopped at the corner of Cavendish Square, and Holmes led the way on foot from there, taking the utmost pains to make sure that they were not followed. After many twists and turns, the two men arrived at the back of a deserted house. Holmes opened the door with a key, and they stepped in and shut the door behind them. Holmes and Watson moved through the dark house until they were in a large, square empty room, heavily shadowed in the corners, but faintly lit in the center from the lights of the street.

Leaning close, Holmes whispered, "Do you know where we are?"

"Surely that is Baker Street," Watson answered, staring through the dim window.

"Exactly. We are in Camden House, which stands opposite to our own old quarters. It also commands so excellent a view of our rooms. Might I trouble you to draw a little nearer to the window, taking every precaution not to show yourself, and then to look up at our old rooms – the starting point of so many of our little adventures? We will see if three years of absence have taken away my power to surprise you."

Watson crept forward and, as his eye fell upon the window, he gave a gasp of amazement. The blind was down and a strong light was burning in the room. The shadow of a man seated in a chair threw a hard, black outline upon the screen of the window.

"Good heavens, Holmes!" Watson ejaculated. "It is marvelous. It looks just like you!"

"The credit of the execution is due to Monsieur Oscar Meunier, of Grenoble, who spent some days in molding the bust in wax. The rest I arranged myself during my visit to Baker Street this afternoon."

"But why?" Watson asked.

"Because I had the strongest reason for wishing certain people to think that I was there when I was really elsewhere. I knew the rooms were watched by my old enemies, Watson. They knew that I was still alive. Sooner or later they believed that I should come back to my rooms. They have watched the rooms continuously and this morning, I recognized their sentinel when I glanced out of my window. He is a harmless enough fellow,

Parker, a garrotter by trade. I cared nothing for him, though. I care a great deal for the much more formidable person who was behind him, the man who is attempting to resurrect Moriarty's empire. He is the second most cunning and dangerous criminal in London. That is the man who is after me tonight, Watson, and that is the man who is quite unaware that we are after *him*."

Watson moved back to the darkness of the corner and the two men continued their vigil until midnight. Watson clutched Holmes' arm suddenly. "The shadow has moved!"

"Of course it moved. Am I such a farcical bungler, Watson, that I should erect an obvious dummy and expect that some of the sharpest men in Europe would be deceived by it? We have been in this room two hours, and Mrs. Hudson has made some change in that figure eight times. She works it from the front so that her shadow may never be seen. Ah!"

Holmes drew in his breath with a shrill, excited intake. In the dim light, he pulled Watson back even further into the shadows. A low, stealthy sound came from the back of the very house they waited in. Watson's hand closed upon his army revolver. A large man entered the room and crept forward, crouching, menacing into the room. The sinister figure was within three yards of them, yet he had no idea that Holmes and Watson were in the same room. The man stole over to the window, and noiselessly raised it six inches.

The light of the street fell upon the man's face. His face shone with excitement, and his features working convulsively. A huge grizzled mustache covered a large portion of his gaunt face. The rest of his face was scored with deep, savage lines. He carried what appeared to be a walking stick, but the man set about to

214

pulling objects out of his overcoat which turned the stick into a sort of gun. He crouched down, rested the end of the barrel upon the ledge of the open window, and peered through the sights. With a sigh of satisfaction, he sighted the target, and tightened his finger on the trigger.

There was a strange, loud whiz and a long, silvery tinkle of broken glass.

At that moment, Holmes sprang like a tiger onto the marksman's back and hurled him flat upon his face. The man was up again in a moment, and seized Holmes by the throat with convulsive strength. Watson landed a blow to the villain's head with his revolver, and the man dropped to the floor. Watson fell upon him, and held the stranger to the floor while a clatter of feet ran into the room.

"That you, Allard?" asked Holmes into the darkness.

"Oui, Monsieur Holmes," came the reply in a heavy French accent.

Two large men entered the room with lanterns and fell upon the would-be assassin, tying him up. A few loiterers had begun to collect in the street, and Holmes closed the window and the blinds.

"Ah, Colonel!" said Holmes, arranging the man's rumpled collar. "This is what it is like to face your prey. Not hiding in a dark room or behind tumbling rocks. At least Morgan was brave enough to sit across a table from me."

"You fiend," the colonel muttered, staring at Holmes as if in a trance.

Holmes turned to Watson. "I have not introduced you yet. This, gentlemen, is Colonel Sebastian Moran, once of Her Majesty's Indian Army, and the best heavy game shot that our Eastern empire has ever produced. I believe I am correct, Colonel, in saying that your bag of tigers still remains unrivalled?"

The fierce old man said nothing, only glaring at Holmes.

"I wonder that my very simple stratagem could deceive so old a shikari. It must be very familiar to you. Have you not tethered a young kid under a tree, lain above it with your rifle, and waited for the bait to bring up your tiger? You have possibly had other guns in reserve in case there should be several tigers, or your own aim failing you. These," Holmes pointed at Watson and the two large men, "are my other guns."

Holmes picked up the powerful air-gun. "An admirable and unique weapon. Noiseless and of tremendous power. I knew Von Herder, the blind German mechanic, who constructed it to the order of the late Professor Moriarty. For years I have been aware of its existence, though I have never before had the opportunity of handling it."

Holmes quickly broke the gun over his knee and leaned in close to Moran.

"You are nowhere near the caliber of your former employer. It was foolish for you to think that you could perform a feat that the so-called 'Napoleon of Crime' could not do."

Holmes turned to the two men. "Gentlemen, Inspector Lestrade will be awaiting Colonel Moran and would like to talk to him about the murder of Ronald Adair."

Holmes' men nodded and unceremoniously dragged Moran out of the room.

On their way back to the Baker Street rooms, Watson turned to Holmes. "You said that Moran was the second most dangerous man in London. Who is the first?"

Smiling, Holmes responded, "That honor, my dear Watson, belongs to me." Holmes took a deep breath of the night air. "It is good to be back in London again!"

Chapter 13: A Curious Collection

At Holmes' request, Watson sold his practice and moved back in to 221B Baker Street. A young doctor named Verner purchased the practice with little argument to the high price that Watson asked. When he moved back in, Watson was glad to find that the old chambers had been left unchanged through the supervision of Mycroft and the care of Mrs. Hudson. The old landmarks were still all in their place. There were the chemical corner and the acid-stained table. Upon a shelf was the row of formidable scrapbooks of reference. The diagrams, the violin case, and the pipe rack – even the Persian slipper which contained Holmes' tobacco – all met Watson's eyes as he glanced around.

After disassembling Holmes' organization, Doctor Watson kept track of most of the employees, a fact that delighted Holmes, leading him to tell Watson that he would never get his friend's limits. Watson's actions allowed Holmes to restart his empire quicker than he had anticipated after his hiatus and the Colonel Moran incident. Forgers and fences were quickly re-established. Robberies were scouted and competitors discouraged. Word spread quickly through the London underworld of the return of Sherlock Holmes.

Society hardly noticed, and the few police officers that asked were simply told that Holmes had been on an extended holiday abroad. His eccentricities were so well by known by his acquaintances at this point, that follow-up questions were never asked. To keep up the charade as an eccentric gentleman writer, Holmes threw himself into a writing on early English charters, while alternating between cocaine injections and planning his next criminal endeavors.

Over the next year, Holmes' employees pilfered an ancient British barrow of its singular contents, helped a banker named Crosby launder money from his employer, inserted themselves into the Smith-Mortimer succession for financial gain, and took care of an embarrassing matter for a well-known tobacco millionaire for a sizable sum.

As the days passed one into another, Holmes and Watson would often find themselves sitting after pleasant little meals. During these respites, Holmes would allow himself to expound upon his topic of the day. One day after Holmes had spent the day reading of Paganini in the British museum, he told anecdote after anecdote of the virtuoso when he arrived back in Baker Street that evening.

Watson poured them both another glass of claret and said off-handedly, "His imagination must have known no bounds. Improvising on the violin as you do, do you ever find yourself envious of such a man's imagination?"

"Oh, I value imagination and dare say I employ it every day in my own line of work! When planning crimes, I must imagine and balance probabilities and choose the more likely. It is the scientific use of imagination, but we have always some material basis on which to start. And to avoid capture, I must imagine myself as one of the Yarders. Having lowered my intelligence to their level, I try to imagine how I should myself have followed the clues under the same circumstances."

"You can hardly state that every Yarder is of sub-par intelligence!"

"Hardly. There a quite a few workman-like officials of the force, and some, such as Inspector Gregory, are extremely competent officers. But they are not gifted with imagination, and that is how I continue to score over them. The Yard does not value imagination. We imagine what might happen when the Yarders investigate, preempt the supposition, and find ourselves justified."

Before the conversation could continue, their new page-boy Billy arrived with a note.

"Our dinner conversation has been a delightful one, Watson, but a Mr. Slaney of Chicago promises a nice payment to meet him in Hyde Park. I would be remiss to pass up an opportunity to discuss business with one of our American cousins. Good night!"

One day in April of 1895, Holmes was studying a palimpsest with a powerful lens while Watson read a recent treatise on surgery, when there was a knock at the door, and Cartwirght, one of the Irregulars, delivered a message to Holmes.

"It is a message from Archie Stamford in Farnham, Watson. It seems that he has found Woodley and Carruthers."

"But I thought there were six more months until their return from South Africa."

"Yes, that was the original plan. According to Stamford, they have been back for some weeks now."

"And they haven't called upon you? You were the one who advanced them the money for their trip!" Watson snorted.

"Precisely. Perhaps you will go down to Farnham and collect our payment from the two gadabouts. I trust you to act as your own judgment advises. Then, having collected what you will, come back to me and report how the two men fared on their South African prospecting."

The next day, Watson left Waterloo station on the 9:13 to Surrey. Once he reached the village of Farnham, Watson headed straight for the pub, the center of public gossip. He made inquiries of the garrulous landlord, only to be told that one of the men he had described was in the next room. Watson moved into the tap room, and greeted Woodley seated at a table.

"I ain't got no money now, Doctor Watson, but I swear in just a few days' time, we'll be payin' Mister Holmes back. Carruthers and me got a nice angle here in this town."

"You will not speak my employer's name in public, Mr. Woodley," Watson said flatly. "I'm not interested in what you plan to do. I'm here to collect payment on what you owe from past services."

Woodley changed to a sneer. "Listen here, Doctor. I said we ain't got the money. Now, you can either let me have my time to hang up the ladle with a nice little flower for her money, or you can shove off!"

Watson took a deep breath. "Woodley, you agreed to the terms with our agent. Whether you found gold or not in South Africa, you knew what you would be expected to pay when you returned. And my employer is not pleased that we had to hear about your return to England from someone other than you and your partner. I will return on Saturday, and you will have a payment for us."

Woodley gulped down the last of his beer and slammed the empty mug on the table. "We'll just see about that, Doctor," and strode out of the bar.

Watson returned to Baker Street that night and relayed the story to Holmes, who was not surprised.

"I had to believe that my absence from London would lead some to acts such as this. I will accompany you to Farnham on Saturday. We will have to make an example out of Mr. Woodley," Holmes sighed.

That Saturday, Holmes and Watson took the train to Surrey, and once again, Woodley could be found in the tap room of the local pub.

"Well, well, it's the doctor," he sneered. "And it looks like you brought another pimp with you to run off at the sauce-box and do your boss's dirty work, eh?"

Watson began to correct him, but Holmes held up his hand. "Mister Woodley, we are here to collect payment for an advance you received for your trip to South Africa. We understand that you were not successful, so we will allow you to begin a payment plan."

"Oh, you'll allow me will ya? What if I tell you I ain't got the money, and there's not a damn thing you can do about it unless you want to get batter-fanged?"

Holmes grimaced. "That is unfortunate. I believe we should also speak to Mister Carruthers and see what he has to say."

"That capon will do what I tell him to or else I'll cop 'is mouse. And so will you!"

Woodley's backhand struck out so quickly, that Holmes was caught off guard and took a wicked blow to his forehead. Holmes staggered back and then moved back in with his hands in a boxer's position.

Woodley grinned at the prospect and charged, only to have his face met with straight left, dropping him to the floor. Holmes stepped back and allowed him to stand. Woodley raced back in and delivered one flailing hit to Holmes' face, splitting his lip. Holmes quickly returned a series of three punches that put the man down so hard that when he staggered to his feet, he immediately slunk out of the pub without another word.

Holmes turned to the landlord, and described Carruthers.

"He's got a place out by Charlington. Got servants and everything. There's a pretty gal out there, too."

Holmes started to walk towards Charlington, when Watson offered to call a cart.

"No. We will walk. I get so little active exercise that it is always a treat to be outdoors," Holmes said, and the two men began their trek to the manor where Carruthers was hiding.

After some time, an empty dog-cart came cantering down the road, its reins trailing behind it.

"Stop the horse, Watson!" Holmes cried. "This can hardly be a coincidence."

Holmes and Watson climbed into the dog-cart and Holmes snapped the reins to take off down the road. A bearded man pedaling furiously on a bicycle soon appeared and hollered for Holmes and Watson to stop, blocking the road with his bicycle.

"Where is Miss Violet Smith?" the man demanded.

Holmes looked at the man. "I don't know who that is. And why are you wearing a fake beard?"

Ignoring Holmes' question, the man responded, "You're in her dog-cart. You ought to know where she is."

"We met this dog-cart on the road with no one in it. We are driving it back," Holmes answered.

"Good Lord!" he cried. "What shall I do? They've got her, that hellhound Woodley and the blackguard parson. Come, man, if you can help. Stand by me and we'll save her, if I have to leave my carcass here."

The man took out a pistol and ran towards a gap in the hedge along the side of the road. Holmes and Watson looked at each other and then followed, only to come upon a young man about seventeen lying unconscious in the grass.

"That's Peter, the groom," the man cried. "He drove her. The beasts have pulled him off and clubbed him. We can't do him any good, but we may save her from the worst fate that can befall a woman."

Suddenly, a woman's shrill scream pierced the air from the thick green clump of bushes in front of them. Breaking through the bushes into a lovely glade, they saw a group of three people. One of them was a woman, drooping and faint with a handkerchief around her mouth. One of the men present was a gray-bearded man, wearing a short surplice over a light tweed suit. The other man present, holding the woman, was Woodley.

"By Jove, Holmes," Watson panted, "this is the marriage he was speaking of! He must have made his way out here while we spoke with the landlord!"

"Yes. We are mixed up in more than a simple collection," Holmes stated.

Woodley advanced towards the newcomers. "You can take that damn beard off, Bob. So these two found you, eh? Well, you and your pals have just come in time for me to be able to introduce you to Mrs. Woodley. You'll have your money soon enough, gents."

The man snatched off the dark beard and threw it to the ground, raising his gun as he did so. "Yes. I am Bob Carruthers, and I'll see this woman righted if I have to swing for it. I told you what I'd do if you molested her, and by the Lord, I'll be as good as my word."

"You're too late!" Woodley laughed. "She's my wife!"

"No. She's your widow."

The revolver cracked, and blood spurted from Woodley's waistcoat. He screamed and fell to his back.

The preacher cursed and pulled out his own pistol, but found himself looking at Holmes' weapon before he could use his own.

"Enough of this," said Holmes coldly. "Drop that pistol. Watson, pick it up. Hold it to his head! You, Carruthers, give me that revolver. We'll have no more violence. Hand it over!"

Carruthers looked at Holmes with confusion. "Who are you?"

"My name is Sherlock Holmes."

"Good Lord! Mister Holmes, I didn't know it was you! Woodley told me that your man came to collect, and I swear we were in the process of getting your money, but that brute muddled everything up."

"Enough!" Holmes barked. His masterful presence dominated the scene as everyone stood frozen. The preacher and Carruthers carried Woodley to the house while Watson escorted the frightened girl.

Once inside, Watson examined Woodley and pronounced that he would live.

"What!" cried Carruthers. "I will go upstairs and finish him off now!"

"You will do no such thing, Mister Carruthers," Holmes said flatly. "Sit down."

Once the man had followed orders, Holmes continued. "What we witnessed today was a sham marriage. I don't know why, nor do I care, but it was certainly not legal." Holmes glared at the preacher, who withered under his gaze.

"Now," he continued, "as for my reason to be here. Mister Carruthers, you and Jack Woodley owe me a nice sum of money for your expedition to South Africa. It is lucky for you that Mister Woodley will live, otherwise you would be responsible for his portion."

"Mister Holmes," Carruthers said meekly, "we didn't score anything like we had hoped to in South Africa, but we met a man over there, this young lady's father. He found plenty of gold, but died on the way home, leaving his fortune to her."

For the first time that day, the young woman spoke, "My father is dead?"

Carruthers nodded. "I'm sorry, Miss Smith. I had hoped to gain your trust before telling you."

Watson laughed. "That's a lie! Woodley said the plan was to marry her for money to pay your debt!"

"That was the original plan," Carruthers admitted, "but I began to have feelings for Miss Smith, and I had hoped to protect her from Woodley."

Holmes sighed. "I am not interested in your emotional status, Carruthers. We are here to settle an outstanding account."

"I will pay it," the young woman stated flatly.

All eyes turned to her, unsure of what to say next.

"If what you say is true," she continued, "That my father had found gold and is now dead, I am not interested in anything associated with his death or the horrible events that have followed. Mister Carruthers, you have tried to help me and I thank you for that, but I can never look upon you without knowing that you concealed my father's death from me and that you were once in partnership with that brute. No, my father's gold was never mine and it can only remind me these horrid events."

Holmes took the opportunity presented. "Miss Smith, this is a very noble gesture, and it will certainly absolve Mister Carruthers of his debt to me. I would also like to volunteer my services in helping you to find a profession and lodgings in London or anywhere you choose."

"Thank you, Mister Holmes. I appreciate your kindness. May I ask one other favor, as well?"

"Of course," Holmes answered graciously.

"Would you be able to find a place for me where Jack Woodley will never find me?"

Holmes nodded. "Miss Smith, I promise you that Jack Woodley will never bother you again."

Holmes turned to the sham preacher. "You will transport him to London on tomorrow's train. Woodley will be left at the Bar of Gold and you will leave England. Do I make myself clear?"

The terrified preacher nodded.

"Mister Holmes," Carruthers began.

Holmes waved his hand dismissively. "Go away, Carruthers. My business with you is finished."

Carruthers and the preacher slunk from the room and Holmes turned back to Miss Smith. "I will arrange everything with your father's estate. I will leave a train ticket for you. Here is my card. If you would call on me in three days' time, I will have everything ready for you to begin a new life away from this place."

Watson and Holmes escorted the young woman to her lodgings and took the day's train back to London.

"Holmes, surely that gold is worth much more than Woodley and Carruthers owe," Watson ventured.

"Quite so. The young lady did not want it, so I will graciously take it off of her hands. Some of it will be used for her arrangements. And the rest, Doctor Watson, the rest will find a nice home in our coffers."

"And Woodley? What are your plans for him?"

Holmes touched the spot on his forehead. "Mister Woodley owes me quite a bit. And he will be working off his debt to me for quite a long time. In fact, I may put him to work with the notorious canary trainer that my other employees detest so much." Holmes chuckled, "That should teach him to find out who he is talking to before he throws a punch."

Chapter 14: Brother Mycroft is Coming Round

"Ignorance can be dangerous, Watson," Holmes mused one morning, flipping down the newspaper.

"How so, Holmes?"

"You are obviously unaware of the attempt on our lives last night."

Watson slammed down his cup and wiped coffee from his mustache. "Nonsense. Surely, you realize it is too early for such a joke."

"You prove my point. You are ignorant of the danger that you were in just hours ago. Last night, an agent of ex-President Murillo made an attempt on our lives. We were only saved by the alarm being raised by the sentry I had placed opposite our door."

"How could I know nothing of this?"

"It could be that no sound reached your room upstairs. Or it could be that the effects of your drink during billiards last night had a stronger effect than you imagined," Holmes smiled.

"Nonetheless. What are we to do about this, Holmes? How can you sit so idly knowing that a powerful man wishes you – us – dead?"

Holmes waved his hand. "Murillo is no longer a powerful man. His attempt last night was quite possibly his last attempt at relevance. Since he has been deposed by his former subjects, he commands no power. And the final card he had to play was the lone agent that was so quickly dispatched by my own men. However, I suppose we should take some precautions for future safety."

Holmes wrote out two notes while Watson wrestled with the fact that after all these years, Holmes was still able to surprise him.

"These two moves should ensure future safety for us, Watson. Dispatch Allard to San Pedro to ensure that Mister Murillo is no longer a threat to us. And I would like to hire a discreet builder to construct a secret room for us in Baker Street just to make sure that we have a last line of defense. I believe Mister Oldacre in Norwood would be acceptable."

Watson read the notes and rang for the maid. "But why didn't you tell me of the danger from Murillo? I don't remember ever hearing his name from you before."

"Do you recall the theft we orchestrated from the Dutch steamship *Friesland*?"

"Or course. It was a beautiful case."

"Our heist from that ship was bound for San Pedro to fortify then-President Murillo's war chest from his usurpers. And when the payment never arrived, Murillo was ungraciously removed from office. I'm sure he blames me for his departure from power, but I can hardly be at fault for his poor management, now can I?" Holmes smiled.

"Hardly," Watson chuckled. "but I would ask you to keep me aware of future threats."

"Of course. It was callous of me to not do so. In fact, you are in danger at this very moment."

Watson started. "From whom?"

Holmes chuckled and took up a pipe from the Moroccan table next to his chair. Stuffing it with the plugs and dottles left from his smokes of the day before, he replied, "From everyone, my dear Watson. You should always remember that our line of work creates enemies and competitors that wish us ill. It would do you well to always keep that in mind. Think of the danger that thugs such as Brooks or Woodhouse pose whenever you start to feel comfortable with your position in this city."

Watson nodded in agreement and returned to his coffee. "Well, Holmes, since we were not murdered last night, what is on the docket for today?"

"I am expecting a payment of four thousand pounds from to arrive from Threadneedle Street before noon. And I had originally meant to spend today planning a robbery of one of richest men in London, Lord Mount James, but after a review of his person yesterday, I realize that the man is such a miser that his house would hardly have anything worth our time. I suppose I can turn my attention to Sir Eustance Brackenstall in Kent."

"I believe I've heard that name before. Isn't he a confirmed drunkard?"

"That he is. His household is considerable, but also a tumultuous one. That should allow our men cover one evening. He is a perfect fiend when he is drunk. There was a scandal about his drenching a dog with petroleum and setting it on fire that was only hushed up with some difficulty. Between you and I, he is the type of man that I thoroughly enjoy taking from."

"Capital," Watson replied. "What are your intentions for Sir Eustance?"

"He has recently had many modern changes and an entirely new wing added to his house. All of the servants sleep in this modern wing. The central block is made up of the dwelling-rooms, with the kitchen and Brackenstall's bedroom above, with his wife's maid sleeping above their room. There is no one else, and no sound could alarm those who are in the farther wing.

"We will endeavor to lure Mrs. Brackenstall and her maid away from her home for an evening. That same night, one of our men will engage Sir Eustance in town and invite him for a drink to discuss leasing his land for a hunt. Our man will ply Sir Eustance with enough drink and a little additive to make sure that he sleeps through the night. Our expert force will then have a fairly free reign."

Watson smiled at his friend's plan as the maid entered. She took the two notes from Watson and handed Holmes a telegram.

"Well, well!" said Holmes. "Brother Mycroft is coming round."

"And why not?" Watson asked. "It would do well for your brother to visit you once in a while instead of constantly ordering you to his club."

"Why not? It is as if you met a tram-car coming down a country lane. Mycroft has his rails and he runs on them. His Pall Mall lodgings, the Diogenes Club, Whitehall – that is his cycle. Once, and only once, he has been here for that business with the

Greek interpreter. What upheaval can possibly have derailed him? The Brackenstall business must wait, I'm afraid."

"Does he not explain?"

Holmes handed Watson the telegram and paced in front of the fireplace. It read, "Must see you over Cadogen West. Coming at once.–Mycroft."

"The name recalls nothing to my mind. But that Mycroft should break out in this erratic fashion! A planet might as well leave its orbit." Holmes stopped suddenly and faced Watson. "By the way, do you know what Mycroft is?"

"You told me that he had some small office under the British government. But he strikes me as someone with more influence than a typical worker bee. Your family seems to be one full of secrets…"

Holmes smiled. "I did not know you quite so well in those days. One has to be discreet when talking of high matters of state. You are right in thinking that he has a more substantial role under the British government. You would also be right in a sense if you said that occasionally he *is* the British government."

"My dear Holmes!"

"I thought that might surprise you. Mycroft draws four hundred and fifty pounds a year, remains a subordinate, has no ambitions of any kind, will receive neither honor nor title, but remains the most indispensable man in the country."

"But how?" Watson asked.

"Well, his position is unique. He has made it for himself. There has never been anything like it before, nor will be again. You could say that is a family trait. He has the tidiest and most orderly brain, with the greatest capacity for storing facts, of any man living. The same great powers which I have turned to crime he has used for this particular business. The conclusions of every department are passed to him, and he is the central exchange, the clearinghouse, which makes out the balance. All other men are specialists, but his specialism is omniscience. We will suppose that a minister needs information to a point which involves the Navy, India, Canada and the bimetallic question; he could get his separate advices from various departments upon each, but only Mycroft can focus them all, and say offhand how each factor would affect the other. They began by using him as a shortcut, a convenience; now he has made himself an essential. In that great brain of his everything is pigeon-holed and can be handed out in an instant. Again and again, his word has decided the national and international policy."

"The unseating of President Murillo…" Watson interjected.

Holmes nodded. "It was beneficial to us both. Mycroft thinks of nothing else other than governmental policy save when, as an intellectual exercise, he unbends if I call upon him and ask him to advise me on one of my little problems. You can now see why I defer to him in so many matters?"

"Of course, having such a powerful ally, and he having you to carry out certain deeds, must be a great boon for both of you."

"Yes, but Jupiter is descending today. What on earth can it mean? Who is Cadogen West and what is he to Mycroft?" Holmes mused.

"I have it!" Watson cried, and plunged among the litter of papers on the sofa. "Yes, here he is! Cadogen West was the young man who was found dead on the Underground on Tuesday morning."

Holmes sat up at attention, his pipe halfway to his lips. "This must be serious, Watson. A death which has caused my brother to alter his habits can be no ordinary one. What in the world can he have to do with it? Please, Doctor, enlighten me upon this case."

"Well, the young man had apparently fallen out of the train and killed himself. He had not been robbed, and there was no particular reason to suspect violence. There has been an inquest and a good many fresh facts have come out. Looked at more closely, I should certainly say that it was a curious case."

"Judging by its effect upon my brother, I should think it must be a most extraordinary one." Snuggling down in his armchair, Holmes continued. "Let us have the facts."

"The man's name was Arthur Cadogen West. He was twenty-seven years of age, unmarried, and a clerk at Woolwich Arsenal."

"Government employ. Behold the link with Brother Mycroft!"

"He left Woolwich suddenly on Monday night. Was last seen by his fiancée, Miss Violet Westbury, whom he left abruptly in the fog about 7:30 that evening. There was no quarrel between them, and she can give no motive for his action. The next thing heard of him was when his dead body was discovered by a plate-layer, just outside Aldgate Station on the Underground system in London at six on Tuesday morning. It was lying wide of the metals upon the left hand of the track at a bend. The head was badly crushed – an injury which might well have been caused by a fall from the train. The body could only have come on the line in that way. Had it been carried down from any neighboring street, it must have passed the station barriers, where a collector is always standing. This point seems absolutely certain."

"Very good. The case is definite enough. The man, dead or alive, either fell or was precipitated from a train. So much is clear to me. Continue."

"It can be stated for certain that this young man, when he met his death, was travelling in this direction at some late hour of the night, but at what point he entered the train it is impossible to state."

"His ticket, of course, would show that."

"There was no ticket in his pockets."

"No ticket! Dear me, Watson, this is really very singular. According to my experience, it is not possible to reach the platform of a Metropolitan train without exhibiting one's ticket. Was it taken from him in order to conceal the station from which he came? It is possible. Or did he drop it in the carriage? That is also possible. But the point is of curious interest. I understand that there was no sign of robbery?"

"Apparently not. His purse contained two pounds fifteen. He had also a checkbook on the Woolwich branch of the Capital and Counties Bank. There were also two dresscircle tickets for the Woolwich Theater, dated for that very evening. Also a small packet of technical papers."

Holmes gave an exclamation of satisfaction. "There we have it at last, Watson! British government – Woolwich. Arsenal – technical papers – Brother Mycroft, the chain is complete. But here he comes, if I am not mistaken, to speak for himself."

A moment later the tall and portly form of Mycroft Holmes was ushered into the room. At his heels came Inspector Lestrade. Watson bristled at having an official of the Yard in their rooms, but knew certain formalities must be adhered to if he and Holmes were to stay undetected by the force.

Mycroft struggled out of his overcoat and settled into an armchair. "A most annoying business, Sherlock. I extremely dislike altering my habits, but the powers that be would take no denial. Given the present state of Siam, it is most awkward that I should be away from the office. But it is a real crisis. I have never seen the Prime Minister so upset. As to the Admiralty – it is buzzing like an overturned beehive. Have you read up the case?"

"We have just done so," replied the younger Holmes. "What were the technical papers?"

"There's the point! Fortunately, it has not come out. The press would be furious if it did. The papers which this youth had in his pocket were the plans for the Bruce-Partington submarine. Its importance can hardly be exaggerated. It has been the most jealously guarded of all government secrets. You may take it from me that naval warfare becomes impossible within the radius of a Bruce-Partington's operation. Every effort has been made to keep the secret. The plans, which are exceedingly intricate, comprising some thirty separate patents, each essential to the whole, are kept in an elaborate safe in a confidential office adjoining the arsenal, with burglar-proof doors and windows. Under no conceivable circumstances were the plans to be taken from the office. If the chief constructor of the Navy desired to consult them, even he was forced to go to Woolwich. And yet here we find them in the pocket of a dead junior clerk in the heart of London. From an official point of view it's simply awful."

"But you have recovered them?"

"That's the pinch. We have not. Ten papers were taken from Woolwich. There were seven in the pocket of Cadogen West. The three most essential are gone – vanished. You must drop everything, Sherlock. It's a vital international problem that you have to solve. Solve this problem, and you will have done a good service for your country."

"It seems to me perfectly clear," said Lestrade, who had been listening impatiently. "He took the papers to sell them. He saw the agent. They couldn't agree to the price. He started home again, but the agent went with him. In the train, the agent murdered him, took the more essential papers, and threw him from the carriage. I don't see the need to include a civilian in such a matter of national importance."

Mycroft looked at Lestrade as a professor would look at a young child explaining the laws of physics. "My brother has been specifically requested by the Prime Minister after a previous dealing, of which the police force was not aware. While the government appreciates the work that your force does, there are some times when a private citizen can be more useful than a battalion of officers."

Trying to keep Lestrade's ego from derailing the conversation, Holmes interjected. "Of course I would be happy to assist the government and the official force in any way possible. At the moment, I am only working on a monograph of the Polyphonic Motets of Lassus, which can certainly wait until this more pressing matter has been resolved. Lestrade, I am at your disposal."

After investigating where the body was found with Watson and Lestrade, Holmes wrote a telegram to Mycroft. "See some light in the darkness, but it may possibly flicker out. Meanwhile, please send by messenger, to await return at Baker Street, a complete list of all foreign spies or international agents known to be in England, with full address. –Sherlock"

Once on the train and away from Lestrade, Holmes turned to Watson. "There is material here. There is scope. I am dull indeed not to have understood its possibilities."

"Even now they are dark to me," Watson replied.

"The end is dark to me also, but I have hold of one idea which may lead us far. The man met his death elsewhere, and his body was on the roof of a train carriage."

"On the roof!"

"Remarkable, is it not? But consider the facts. You told me that the body was found at the very point where the train sways as it comes round on the points. Is not that the place where an object upon the roof might be expected to fall off? Either the body fell from the roof, or a very curious coincidence has occurred. But now consider the question of the blood. Of course, there was no bleeding on the line if the body had bled elsewhere. Each fact is suggestive in itself. Together we have a cumulative force."

"And the ticket, too!"

"Exactly. We could not explain the absence of a ticket. This would explain it. Everything fits together." Holmes relapsed into a silent reverie, which lasted until the train drew up at Woolwich Station. There he called a cab and drew a piece of paper from his pocket.

"Mycroft has jotted down the more essential names upon this sheet of paper, together with a few addresses which may be of service. I think that Sir James Walter, the official guardian of the papers, claims our first attention."

When they arrived at the fine villa of Sir Walter, a butler answered their ring. "Sir James, sir!" he said with a solemn face. "Sir James died this morning. Perhaps you would care to step in, sir, and see his brother, Colonel Valentine?"

"Yes," answered Holmes. "We had best do so."

Holmes and Watson were ushered into a dimly lit drawing room and were soon joined by a very tall, light-bearded man. "It was a horrible scandal," Valentine Walter said. "My brother, Sir James, was a man of very sensitive honor, and he could not survive such an affair. It broke his heart. He was always so proud of the efficiency of his department, and this was a crushing blow. I know nothing myself save what I have read or heard."

Leaving the house empty-handed, Holmes and Watson turned their attention to the arsenal office. There, Holmes questioned the clerk and examined the safe, the room and its shutters, which hardly met in the middle, allowing anyone to see through them. Moving outside, Holmes became excited once next to the window to the office. Watson had hardly seen his friend thrilled with a keener zest when they were defiers of the law instead of its defenders. There was a laurel bush outside the window, and several of the branches had been twisted and snapped. After looking at some vague and dim marks on the earth, he turned to Watson. "I do not think that Woolwich can help us further. Let us see if we can do better in London. If Mycroft has given us the list of addresses, we may be able to pick our man."

A note awaited Holmes and Watson at Baker Street. It read, "There are numerous small fry, but few who would handle so big an affair. The only men worth considering are Adolph Mayer, of 13 George Street, Westminster; Louis La Rothiere, of Campden Mansions, Notting Hill; and Hugo Oberstein, 13 Caulfield Gardens, Kensington. The latter was known to be in town on Monday and is now reported as having left. Glad to hear you have seen some light. The Cabinet awaits your final report with the utmost anxiety. Urgent representations have arrived from the very highest quarter. The whole force of the State is at your back if you should need it. – Mycroft."

Holmes spread out his big map of London and leaned over it eagerly. "Well, well, things are turning a little in our direction at last. Why, Watson, I do honestly believe that we are going to pull it off after all." Holmes stood and slapped Watson on the shoulder. "I am going out now."

"Why not send an employee?" Watson asked.

"A matter of state importance must be handled with discretion."

"Then I will go with you."

"It is only a reconnaissance. I will do nothing serious without my trusted comrade. Do stay here, and the odds are that you will see me again in an hour or two. If time hangs heavy, get foolscap and a pen, and begin a narrative to tell future generations of how two gentlemen thieves saved the State."

Shortly after nine o'clock, a messenger arrived with a note for Watson. "Am dining at Goldini's Restaurant, Gloucester Road, Kensington. Please come at once if convenient – if inconvenient come all the same. Bring with you a jemmy, a dark lantern, a chisel, and a revolver. –S.H."

Holmes sat at a little round table near the door of the garish Italian restaurant. "Have you had something to eat? Then join me in a coffee and curacao. Try one of the proprietor's cigars. They are less poisonous than one would expect. Have you the tools?"

"They are here in my overcoat," Watson answered.

"Excellent. Now it must be evident to you, Watson, that this young man's body was placed on the roof of the train. That was

243

clear from the instant that I determined the fact that it was from the roof, and not from the carriage that he had fallen."

"But how was he placed there?"

"That was the question which we had to answer. You are aware that the Underground runs clear of tunnels at some points in the West End. Now, suppose that a train halted under a window, would there be any difficulty in laying a body upon the roof?"

"It seems most improbable," Watson said, skeptically.

"We must fall back upon the old axiom that when all other contingencies fail, whatever remains, however improbable, must be the truth. Here all other contingencies have failed. When I found that the leading international agent, who had just left London, lived in a row of houses which abutted upon the Underground, I was very pleased. Mr. Hugo Oberstein, of 13 Caulfield Gardens, had become my objective. Not only do the back windows of Caulfield Gardens open on the line but the Underground trains are frequently held motionless for some minutes at that very spot."

"Splendid, Holmes! You have got it! Should we share this information with Mycroft the officials?"

"And stop shy of our goal? Pshaw, Doctor! No, my dear fellow, we will not leave this halfway finished." Holmes sprang up. "It is nearly half a mile, but there is no hurry. Let us walk."

In short time, the men came to Caulfield Gardens. Holmes set to work upon the door and it soon flew open. He led the way up the curving, uncarpeted stair. "Here we are, Watson – this must

244

be the one." He threw open a low window as a train dashed past them in the darkness.

Noting where the soot covered window sill was rubbed, Holmes pointed out, "You can see where they rested the body. What is this? There can be no doubt that this is a blood mark. Perhaps we may find something which may still help us."

Swiftly and methodically, Holmes turned over the contents of every drawer and cupboard, but no gleam of success came to his austere face, until he came to a small tin cash box upon the writing desk.

"What's this Watson? A series of messages in the *The Daily Telegraph* agony column. No dates, but a complete conversation between Oberstein and an unknown agent. A fairly complete record, Watson! If we could only get at the man at the other end!"

Holmes sat lost in thought for some minutes before springing to his feet. "Well, perhaps it won't be so difficult after all. There is nothing more to be done here, Watson. I think we might drive round to the offices of the *Daily Telegraph*, and so bring a good day's work to a conclusion. Sometimes the press can be a most valuable institution if only you know how to use it."

The next morning found Watson sitting at the breakfast table by himself when Mrs. Hudson showed up Mycroft Holmes and Inspector Lestrade.

"Good morning, Doctor," Mycroft greeted. "Where is Sherlock? He requested we appear this morning."

Before Watson could answer, Holmes' voice echoed from the hall. "Ah, Mycroft! And Lestrade, thank you for joining us. Have you seen Pierrot's advertisement today?"

"Who is Pierrot?" Lestrade asked.

Holmes gave the two newcomers a quick overview of the previous day's activities.

"We can't do such things as burglary on the force, Mr. Holmes. No wonder your brother requested your help. Hoping you don't make a habit out of such unlawful behavior."

"Never, Lestrade! But for England, home and beauty – eh, Watson?" Turning to his brother, Holmes continued. "Here is the advertisement."

Mycroft read the advertisement out loud. "Tonight. Same hour. Same place. Two taps. Most vitally important. Your own safety at stake. –Pierrot." Mycroft lowered the paper. "Very clever, Sherlock. And what time shall we meet you tonight?"

"I think if you could both make it convenient to come with us about eight o'clock to Caulfield Gardens we might possibly get a little nearer to a solution."

By nine o'clock, the four men were sitting in Oberstein's study, waiting patiently for their man. After two hours of waiting, Holmes raised his head with a sudden jerk. "He is coming."

Two sharp taps came from the knocker. Holmes rose but motioned for the others to remain seated. The gas in the hall was dim. He opened the outer door, and then a dark figure slipped past. Holmes motioned for the man to move further into the room, and the man entered the study.

Holmes followed him closely, and as the man turned, he caught him by the collar and threw him to the ground. Before the prisoner could recover, Holmes shut and bolted the door. The man glared around, and Holmes turned the light up in the room to reveal the handsome face of Colonel Valentine Walter.

"Gentlemen," Holmes said, "this is the younger brother of the late Sir James Walter, the head of the Submarine Department."

From his horror-stricken face, Sir Walter stammered, "What is this? I came here to visit Mr. Oberstein."

"Everything is known, Colonel," said Holmes, motioning for him to move from the floor to the sofa.

The man groaned and sank his face in his hands as he sat on the sofa. Holmes and the others waited, but he remained silent.

"I can assure you," said Holmes finally, "that every essential is already known. My companions here are dangerous ruffians and together we are going to hear you confess. We know that you acquired a copy of your brother's keys; and that you entered into a correspondence with Oberstein, who answered your letters through the advertisement columns of the *Daily Telegraph*. We are aware that you went down to the office in the fog on Monday night, but that you were seen and followed by young Cadogan West. He saw your theft, and leaving all his private concerns, like the good citizen that he was, he followed you here. There he intervened, and you murdered him."

"I did not! I did not! Before God I swear that I did not!" cried the prisoner. "I confess that I did the rest. It was just as you say. A Stock Exchange debt had to be paid. Oberstein offered me five thousand. It was to save myself from ruin. But as to murder, I am as innocent as you."

Holmes stared at Walter with his cold, grey eyes.

"The young man rushed in after me when I arrived and Oberstein struck him on the head with a life preserver. The blow was a fatal one. He was dead within five minutes. Oberstein examined the papers which I had brought and said that three of them were essential. The rest he stuffed into the pockets of the young man. We waited half an hour before a train stopped outside his window and we lowered the body on to the train. That was the end of the matter as far as I was concerned."

"And your brother?" Holmes asked.

"He knew. I read it in his eyes. The shame led to his death," Walter answered with his head lowered.

"Where is Oberstein with the papers?" Mycroft asked.

"I do not know. He said that letters to the Hotel du Louvre, Paris would eventually reach him."

"Sit at this desk and write to my dictation," Holmes ordered. Walter obliged. "'Dear Sir: With regard to our transaction, you will no doubt have observed by now that one essential detail is missing. I have a tracing which will make it complete. This has involved me in extra trouble, and I must ask you for a further advance of five hundred pounds. I will not trust it to the post, nor will I take anything but gold or notes. I would come to you abroad, but it would excite remark if I left the country at present. Therefore I shall expect to meet you in the smoking room of the Charing Cross Hotel at noon on Saturday.' That will do very well. I shall be very much surprised if it does not allow Lestrade to fetch our man."

And it did.

Oberstein, eager to complete the coup of a lifetime, came and was safely engulfed for fifteen years in a British prison. In his trunk were the invaluable Bruce-Partington plans, which he had put up for auction in all the naval centers of Europe.

A few days after the Oberstein capture, a package was sent from Mycroft to Baker Street. In it lay an emerald tie-pin with a note from Mycroft saying that it was from a certain gracious lady. Holmes merely smiled and returned to his monograph on the Polyphonic Motets of Lassus.

Chapter 15: The Worst Man in London

For the next three years, Mr. Sherlock Holmes was a very busy man. It is safe to say that there was no crime of any difficulty in which he was not consulted. There were scores of private cases, some of them of the most intricate and extraordinary in character, in which he played a prominent part. Many startling successes and a few unavoidable failures were the outcome of this long period of continuous work.

Over this time, Watson had gradually been able to wean Holmes off his cocaine habit, knowing that it was not dead but sleeping. Once Holmes' artificial stimulant had been removed, Watson dutifully worked to keep his friend occupied. Operations such as the fraudulent giant rat of Sumatra and the falsified two Coptic patriarchs were unmitigated successes. Holmes' day to day operations also hummed along nicely, and some employees became captains in their fields, such as Arthur Staunton, a rising forger that Holmes took a special shine to, and Vanderbilt the safecracker.

But others, such as the Randall gang, were ordered to leave London when they did not live up to Holmes' strict code of conduct. And once, a private detective from the Surrey shore by the name of Mr. Baker began to look closely into an art forgery Holmes was behind, causing a slight stir in the organization. But contingencies were in place, and any threads the detective may have collected led nowhere, causing him to return to Surrey emptyhanded.

Holmes continued to write his monographs, but after completing his latest on the Chaldean roots in the ancient Cornish language, he sulked about the rooms at Baker Street for two days. Finally, Watson could take it no more.

"What do you say to a ramble through London?" the doctor offered.

Holmes waved away the suggestion contemptuously. "Bah! I do not see the need to take exercise for exercise's sake. No, I crave mental exaltation. My dear Watson, you know how bored I have been. My mind is like a racing engine, tearing itself to pieces because it is not connected up with the work for which it was built. Life is commonplace, the papers are sterile; audacity and romance seem to have passed forever from the criminal world.

"I while away my days writing these trifles on ancient languages and secret ciphers, but my true passion lays dormant to my pen. The thrill of a perfectly executed crime – that! That is a feat worthy of my talents. But I sit here, pretending to be some eccentric while no opportunities arise. And, so few know what I am truly capable of!"

A change had come over Holmes' manner. While working on his latest academic monograph, he had been restless. Now that he was raging against boredom, a light shone in his keen, deep-set eyes.

"You could turn your attention to the missing pearl of Borgias," Watson ventured.

"Hardly. The official force is crawling around that problem like ants at a picnic. And what they do not know is that a member of the Italian Mafia is in London pursuing the same prize. I am

251

bored, Watson, but not foolhardy enough to call the attention of the Mafia to our organization."

"Then why not put your thoughts on crime down on paper?" Watson asked.

Holmes chuckled. "That is an idea, but one I'm afraid that the case-book of Sherlock Holmes would consume me once I start. No, I am, at present, too busy with the running of my little empire to become an author. But I propose to devote my declining years to the composition of a textbook which shall focus the whole art of crime into one single volume."

Looking out the window, he continued. "But until my retirement years, I shall strive to entertain myself. In fact, I believe we may have a delightful new tool in our arsenal soon. Stoke the fire, and let me tell you about the devil's foot root which I have recently come into possession of. And after that, now that you have pulled me out of my dejected mood, perhaps we shall escape from this weary day by the side door of music. Carina sings tonight at the Albert Hall. Yes, let's plan to dress, dine, and enjoy."

But the quiet times did not last forever. Shortly after the New Year in 1899, Holmes and Watson returned home one cold, frosty evening to find a calling card waiting for them. Holmes read it, and with a swear of disgust, threw it on the floor.

Watson read the card, "Charles Augustus Milverton, Appledore Towers, Hampstead. Agent." Looking at Holmes, he asked, "Who is he?"

"The worst man in London," Holmes answered, as he sat and stretched his legs in front of the fire. "The back of the card says he will call at 6:30. He's about due. Do you feel a creeping, shrinking sensation, when you stand before the serpents in the zoo and see the slithery, gliding, venomous creatures, with their deadly eyes and wicked, flattened faces? Well, that's how Milverton impresses me. I've had to deal with the lowest men in London in my career, but the worst of them never gave me the repulsion which I have for this fellow."

"But who is he?" Watson repeated.

"He is the worst blackmailer in all of England. Heaven help the man, and still more the woman, whose secret and reputation come into the power of Milverton. With a smiling face and a heart of marble he will squeeze and squeeze until he has drained them dry. The fellow is a genius in a way, and would have made his mark in our organization – heaven knows I've sent emissaries to broker an arrangement."

"And you detest him for his competition?"

"No, Watson. It is his methods which repulse me. The few times which we have used blackmail, it has been only when needed, and even then our targets have been of the most substantial wealth. Milverton's method is as follows: He allows it to be known that he is prepared to pay very high sums for letters which compromise people of even moderate wealth or position. He receives these wares not only from treacherous valets or maids, but frequently from genteel ruffians who have gained the confidence and affection of trusting women. I happen to know that he paid seven hundred pounds to a footman for a note two lines in length, and that the ruin of a noble family was the result. Everything which is in the market goes to Milverton, and there are hundreds in this great city who turn white at his name. No one knows where his grip may fall, for he is far too rich and far too cunning to work from hand to mouth. He will hold a card back for years in order to play it at the moment when the stake is best worth winning."

"His trade cannot be that different from our own, Holmes."

"But he is, Watson. I have said that he is the worst man in London, and I would ask you how could one compare the rogues in our employ who carry out a job that is meticulously planned so that no one is hurt in the process, to one who methodically, and at his leisure, tortures the soul and wrings the nerves of anyone in society in order to add to his already swollen moneybags?"

"But surely the fellow must be within the grasp of revenge?" Watson asked.

"Technically, no doubt, but practically not. His victims dare not hit back."

"And why is he here?"

Holmes sighed as he looked into the fire. "Because the time has come for him to exert his power on me. He has, no doubt, finally found proof to link me with my crimes. Milverton must surely know of my successes and plans to take a princely sum in return for keeping the secret."

Watson's face grew as hard as stone. "Then he must be dealt with quickly and forcefully. Would you like me to call for McMurdo, or someone more permanent? Mercer, perhaps?"

"No. I have watched Milverton from afar and am aware that if he is harmed in any way that the secrets he holds will be made public immediately. You no doubt remember the row about the politician and the lighthouse?"

"That was Milverton?"

"Yes. The man landed a blow to the fiend's chin. He quickly realized his error and offered to pay more than the original price, but Milverton chose to make an example of him."

"Then we shall go to war with him. I will stand by you until we bring him to his knees."

"No, Watson. He has wisely stayed afield of my operations for years. If he is calling on me now, he must surely have enough evidence to cripple me. Although we have shared the same room for some years, I would not find it amusing if we ended by sharing the same cell."

Watson looked out the window at the stately carriage that had pulled up to their door. "Then how will you stop him?"

Holmes stared at the fire. "I won't. I have examined every alternative and the only way to continue my livelihood is to let this snake have his way and be gone."

A stillness hung in the air as Watson gaped at his friend. He had never seen such a thing: Sherlock Holmes was allowing himself to be beaten. He had seen Holmes topple whole rival organizations, gain commissions from the highest seats of governments, and even return from the dead. But this one man had broken his friend before he had even spoken a word.

A minute later that man was in the room.

Charles Augustus Milverton was a man of fifty, with a large head, a round, plump face, a perpetual frozen smile, and two keen grey eyes which gleamed from behind golden-rimmed glasses. He advanced with a plump little hand extended and murmured his regret for missing them earlier.

Holmes dismissed Milverton's hand and looked at him with a face of granite. This only caused the blackmailer's smile to broaden. He shrugged, removed his overcoat and folded it over the back of the chair.

"Good evening, gentlemen," Milverton said in a smooth and suave voice. "I come to you on a matter so very delicate… "

"Doctor Watson has already heard of it," Holmes stated flatly.

"I'm sure he has. Then we can proceed to business."

"What are your terms?"

Milverton looked at Holmes for a moment and then turned to Watson. "Doctor Watson, I am asking for seven thousand pounds per year."

Watson's face showed his puzzlement. "I am not Mister Holmes' financial advisor. But if I were …"

Milverton chuckled. "My dear doctor, I am not here to meet with Mister Holmes. He is a gentleman with protections that exceed my capabilities. I am here to conduct business with you."

For a moment, the only sound was the popping of the fire.

Realization hit Holmes, turning him grey. Through clenched teeth, he said, "What documents have you to warrant such a visit to my – our apartment?"

Milverton's insufferable smile became more complacent than ever. He regarded Holmes silently for a moment and then returned to face Watson. "You have done an admirable job in your position here, Doctor, but your recent crime in Norbury left one loose end: the telegram you sent to your man, Bradley. Normally, this wouldn't have been enough, but you had a nice conversation with the telegraph agent that day, discussing South African securities, I believe. And, as we all know, your man was eventually arrested for his crime. Even though your organization is protected through more layers than I can possibly imagine, I have a telegram sent from you which dispatched a man who was arrested and convicted of a crime you ordered."

Watson's mouth pursed into a small line. "I see. And if the payment is not made?"

"My dear sir," Milverton smiled, "it is painful for me to discuss it; but if the money is not paid there will certainly be interested parties at Scotland Yard. But if you think that it is in your best interest to let your friend here try to influence matters, then you would be foolish to pay so large a sum of money."

Milverton rose and seized his coat.

"Wait a little," Holmes said. "You go too fast. We would certainly make every effort to avoid scandal in so delicate a matter."

Milverton reseated himself on his chair. "I was sure that you would see it in that light," he purred.

"At the same time," Holmes continued, "I assure you that my organization will do what it can to help Doctor Watson, but even two thousand pounds would be a drain upon our current resources, and that sum you name is utterly beyond our power. Operating expenses of such a large organization as mine require a goodly deal of my working capital. You speak of my protections, then you must also know that they only allow me to operate under strict conditions, and creating such a large flow of money into our organization would absolutely not be tolerated. I beg, therefore, that you will moderate your demands, and that you will meet us at the price which I indicate."

If possible, Milverton's smile broadened even more. "I am aware that what you say is true about your conditions. At the same time, you must admit that someone of such renowned capabilities as yourself is a very suitable man for such a challenge. Instead of your odd writings now and then, I am presenting you with this opportunity for your talents. Consider this a favor I am doing for you."

"It is impossible," said Watson flatly.

"Dear me, dear me, how unfortunate!" cried Milverton. "I'm sure the inspectors will be interested to know about London's gentleman crime lord who has plagued the city for years. And all because you will not find a beggarly sum. It is such pity. I thought I would have a pleasant conversation with one of London's most eminent minds, and here I find you, a man of sense, boggling about terms when your friend's future and honor are at stake. You surprise me, Mister Holmes."

"What I say is true," Holmes answered, simmering. "The money cannot be found. Surely it is better for you to take the substantial sum which I offer than ruin this man, which can profit you in no way?"

"There you make a mistake, Mr. Holmes. An exposure of such a grand scale would profit me indirectly to a considerable extent. If it were circulated that I made a severe example of someone so high up in a criminal empire, I should find all of my future clients much more open to reason. You see my point?"

Holmes' building rage had reached its zenith. He sprang from his chair. "Get behind him, Watson! Don't let him out!" Holmes turned his cold, blazing grey eyes upon the blackmailer. "Now, Mr. Milverton, let us see that telegram. You speak of my organization, then you know of my power and reach. I am not a man you want to anger, and I have had enough of your petty game with my friend's good name."

Milverton had glided as quickly as a rat to the side of the room, and stood with his back against the wall. "Mr. Holmes," he said, exhibiting the butt of a large revolver from the inside pocket of his coat. "I have been expecting you to do something original. This has been done so often, and what good has ever come from it? I assure you that I am armed to the teeth. Besides, your supposition that I would bring the telegram here is entirely mistaken. Trust me, gentlemen, the doctor's telegram is safe, and will remain so as long as I remain unharmed. And now, gentlemen, I have one or two little interviews this evening."

He stepped forward, took up his coat with one hand, with the other still on his revolver, and turned towards the door. Watson picked up a chair to bash the man with, but Holmes shook his head and he laid it down again. With a bow and a smile, Milverton slid from the room, and a few minutes later, Holmes and Watson heard the slam of a carriage door and the rattle of wheels on pavement.

Holmes looked at Watson mournfully. "I give you my word, Watson, I that will turn all my mental efforts to this problem." With that, he sat motionless by the fire, his chin sunk upon his breast, and his eyes fixed upon the glowing embers for a half an hour.

Suddenly, Holmes sprang to his feet.

"You have a plan?" Watson asked eagerly.

"I do. It will take a few days, though."

"Shall I call for any employees?"

Holmes placed his hand on Watson's shoulder. "No. I would trust your predicament to no one except myself. This will be a problem that I will see to completion on my own."

With that Holmes passed into his bedroom, and a little later he reappeared. "I'll be back some time, Watson. Keep business running as usual in my stead. This matter could take some time." With that, Holmes vanished into the night.

Over the next few days, Watson hardly saw Holmes, except for fleeting glimpses at all hours, always dressed as a rakish young workman with a goatee beard and a swagger. Finally, Watson could wait no more and pressed his friend on his progress.

Holmes laughed heartily in front of the fire. "You would not call me a marrying man, Watson?"

"No, indeed. But what does that have to do with my blackmailer?"

"You will be interested to hear that I am engaged – to your blackmailer's housemaid."

Watson could only gape at this news.

"I wanted information, Watson. I am a plumber with a rising business. I have walked with the maid, Agatha, each evening, and I have talked with her. Good heavens, those talks! However, I have got all I wanted. I know Milverton's house as I know the palm of my hand."

"But the girl, Holmes. I cannot let you hurt an innocent to protect my name."

"Milverton's employees are hardly innocents. They are well aware of their master's trade. However, you will be happy to hear that I have a hated rival who will certainly cut me out the instant that my back is turned from my new fiancée. Now, Watson, for a bit of dinner, and then I am back out into the night. For tonight, I mean to burgle Milverton's house."

"For heaven's sake, Holmes, think what you are doing. You are quite out of practice. I beg of you to bring in one of your experts on this matter. If you were to be caught, your name, the organization ..."

"My dear fellow, I have given it every consideration. I would not adopt so energetic and indeed so dangerous a course if any

261

other were possible. I am in sole possession of the knowledge of the house's layout and where his papers are kept. If I were to send a confidant in my stead, there are too many variables to consider, and Agatha expects to see me, and me alone each night. That is why she puts up Milverton's beast of a dog and leaves the side gate unlocked. This is too delicate of a matter for a subordinate. My self-respect and your reputation are concerned, and for that I will fight it to a finish."

"Well, I don't like it; but I suppose it must be," Watson said. "When do we start?"

"You are not coming."

"Then you are not going. I give you my word of… "

"Watson, I appreciate your concern, but this must be handled as deliberately as possible. You have not acquainted yourself with Milverton's household and his security. You would be a liability."

Miffed, Watson sat back in his chair. Holmes quickly ate a cold supper and then slipped a burgling kit and black silk mask into his overcoat.

Holmes clasped Watson on the shoulder. "With any luck I should be back here by two with the telegram in my pocket." And with that, he departed Baker Street.

At three that night, Holmes burst through the door of Baker Street, waking Watson from his chair.

"It is done, Watson. Here is the wretched telegram," Holmes said tossing it to his friend. "Gaze upon it, and then throw it into the fire, just as I have done with every other piece of blackmail Milverton held in reserve over London's elite."

Looking at the telegram in his hands, Watson beamed. "By Jove, Holmes! You've done it!"

"And quite a sight it was, too," Holmes replied, pouring himself a glass from the tantalus. "Milverton lay dead when I left his home tonight."

"Holmes, you didn't-"

"No, my good doctor. Milverton's end came from one of his former victims who unloaded her revolver into his chest."

"But how did she get into his house? Had she scheduled an appointment with Milverton?"

"No, she scheduled her appointment with me. For a small fee, I was able to provide her safe passage into his inner sanctum. And what she did from there was her own choice. There are certain crimes which justify private revenge." Watson nodded solemnly. "Now, if you will excuse me," Holmes continued, "it has been quite a night, and I would like a few hours' sleep before our planning session in the morning on the Conk Singleton forgery. While I rest, Watson, would you make a few inquiries as to Milverton's agents? There may be one or two of use to our agency."

Chapter 16: To Avoid All Public Scandal

The turn of the century found Holmes' organization reaching new heights. Through a discreet partnership with Neil Gibson, the American Gold King, Holmes was flush with operating funds, and he used them to pull off two of the most remarkable disappearances London had ever read of.

Monty Wolder and Joshua Monken were two men Holmes employed infrequently, but when they brought a bank opportunity to Holmes that rivaled that of Holmes' score from the Red-Headed League caper, he allowed them to take up the charge, only guaranteeing protection. Holmes did not fully trust these two men's finesse with such a crime and wisely kept his distance. The crime was almost completely botched, and Holmes had to act quickly to protect them from Scotland Yard. He shuttled them onto the cutter Alicia after receiving a hefty payment and sent them off. But as far as anyone in London knew, the ship sailed into a small patch of mist and she never emerged. Nothing further was ever heard of the ship, her crew, or the two escaping criminals, except for a payment three months later with a note attached "Cargo delivered. -Alicia."

Later that year, Mr. James Phillmore came to Holmes with pressing hopes to also disappear from London. He had been challenged to a duel by the journalist Isadora Persano, and chose to flee rather than face his accuser. Persano was well known for his dueling, and Holmes agreed, but knew that Persano would be watching Phillmore closely. The next day, Mr. Phillmore stepped back into his own house to get his umbrella and was never more seen in London. Persano took to solving this disappearance himself, and he was said to have gone stark raving mad from his inability to solve this puzzle.

On the heels of these disappearances, a young man by the name of John Hopley Neligan, the son of a failed Cornwall banker, called at Baker Street. He was looking for a seaman by the name of Peter Carey. Neligan believed that Carey had murdered his father and stolen a large amount of securities from him. After cajoling the young man to turn over half of the securities to him, Holmes traced the sailor, only to find out that he had been murdered three years prior. Holmes tracked the murderer, and found that he was ignorant of the value of the securities he held. The murderer was an old shipmate of Carey's and had murdered him out of hatred. He had only taken items from Carey to make the murder seem like a robbery, and to lead the police on a false trail. Holmes easily convinced the sailor to hand over the securities, and gave young Neligan his share.

Springtime in 1901 brought another windfall to Holmes. He had just completed overseeing the forging of the Ferrers documents and clearing one of his men, Abergavenny, of murder, when a new opportunity arose.

"Watson," Holmes half sighed, "I had hoped for a slight respite to devote some time to try over the Hoffman 'Barcarole' upon my violin, but that shall have to wait. A business opportunity has presented itself."

"What is it, Holmes?"

"Shinwell Johnson has just sent word that the late Cabinet Minister, the Duke of Holdernesse, is missing his only son. He has gone missing from his room at the Priory School near Mackleton. We must act fast, for my informant says that the *Globe* has an inkling of it and is expected to be investigating soon."

"The Duke of Holdernesse is a very respected man," Watson warned.

"He is certainly one of the greatest subjects of the crown. And if word were to spread that his heir and only child had been abducted, chaos would ensue. I'm sure that we can contribute to the cause for a princely fee. Now, doctor, if you can be ready in fifteen minutes' time, I will have a four wheeler ready for us."

That evening found Holmes and Watson in the cold, bracing atmosphere of Peak County. The pair headed straight for Holdernesse Hall for an unscheduled meeting with the duke. When they arrived, they were shown into a waiting room. After a few minutes, the duke's private secretary entered. He was small, nervous and alert, with intelligent, light-blue eyes.

"I was unaware that we were to have visitors today. The Duke of Holdernesse is not used to unannounced visits," he stated.

"My apologies, my good man. We only found out about the duke's missing son this morning. Otherwise, we would have sent word ahead from London," Holmes responded.

The man was taken aback. "I'm sorry Mr.," the man paused to act if he was remembering a name, "Mr. Holmes, but if anything of the sort were true, it would not be discussed."

"Perhaps you should tell His Grace that I am here, and I intend to find his son." Holmes' demeanor changed from indifference to the stony resonance that Watson had seen chill men so many times before. "Dr. Watson and I propose to spend a few days upon your moors, and to occupy my mind as best I may. Whether I work with you or against you is, of course, for you to decide."

The young man was suddenly in a state of indecision, but was quickly rescued by the deep, sonorous voice of the red bearded duke, who entered the room. "Forgive my secretary, Mr. Holmes. Wilder is only striving to protect my interests. If you have heard of this in London, I can assume that you are a man with his ear to the ground, so to say."

"You might say that," Holmes smiled. "I know much about this from informants, and I also know that a reporter from the *Globe* will be here within a day to start his own investigation."

The last piece of information shocked both the duke and his secretary. "Tell me what you know, Mr. Holmes," the duke said.

Holmes nodded, and Dr. Watson began. "Your son was not happy at home, and the boy's sympathies were with his mother, whom you recently separated from peacefully. Which is why you enrolled him in the Priory School for the summer term, starting on May 1st.He was last seen on the night of May 13th, last Monday. His room was on the second floor, and his two roommates saw and heard nothing that night, proving that he did not leave by the door to the hall."

Holmes continued, "Your son, Lord Saltire's, window has a stout ivy plant leading to the ground. This was surely his exit. His absence was discovered the next morning. He had dressed himself before leaving. There were no signs that anyone had entered the room, nor were there signs of a struggle. Roll of the whole establishment was quickly called, and the German master was also found missing. Upon searching the master's room, it was found that he had fled from his room quickly, only partly dressed. His bicycle was also found to be missing. This cannot be a coincidence."

"How on earth could you know such things?" blurted Wilder.

"It is my business to know what other people don't know. Now if I may continue?"

The duke nodded, his lips pursed at all the information Holmes was sharing.

"Inquiry was made here at your hall, but no sign of the boy. There was an official investigation, but it has proved disappointing. Since then, investigations have all but been dropped. This affair has been most deplorably handled. Surely there were some signs by the ivy that would have yielded clues to the trained eye, but they will have been trampled over by now."

The duke harrumphed in agreement.

"Your son received a letter from you the day before he disappeared, correct?"

"That is correct."

"Was there anything in your letter which might have unbalanced him or induced him to run off?"

"No, sir, certainly not."

"Did you post that letter yourself?"

The nobleman's secretary broke in heatedly. "If you insist on these impertinent questions, I will request that you realize to whom you are speaking. His Grace is not in the habit of posting letters himself. This letter was laid with others upon the study table and I myself put them in the post-bag."

Holmes eyed the secretary coolly, conceding that his line of questioning had gone on long enough. The duke's mood clearly showed that he found this interview to be abhorrent, yet necessary.

"You will want my help, Your Grace. I promise you that having me help you is much better than the alternative of the press finding out this information."

The unspoken threat hung in the air.

"Of course we would welcome any *discreet* help you may offer us, Mr. Holmes."

Holmes flung himself into the investigation. The boy's room and that of the German master were searched and yielded no new information. A close inspection of the bicycle tire tracks were made, of which Holmes noted they were one of the 42 different impressions left by tires that he was familiar with. Holmes and Watson then pored over a map of the around the school to see which road the missing people could have taken.

"But if they had taken this road, they would have been seen," Watson offered. "It is the only road."

"A good cyclist does not need a high road," said Holmes. "The moor is intersected with paths and the moon was at the full. No, Doctor, we will have to search the moor."

It was soon reported that the missing German master had been found on the moor, dead with his head bashed in. Holmes and Watson rushed to the scene in hopes of finding sign of the duke's son, but the only sign was that of cow tracks through the grass. Upon closer examination, Holmes noticed that the cow tracks didn't show them to be walking, but *galloping* across the moor!

Holmes and Watson followed the tracks to a nearby inn where they found horses out back that had recently been shod.

"We are warm at this inn, Watson," said Holmes. "I can't possibly leave, but I don't wish to arouse suspicion from the landlord. I think we shall have another look at it in an unobtrusive way."

The two men slipped across the path and into the bush. Just moments after they had taken their spots, a cyclist came swiftly along – the duke's secretary! Wilder leaned his bicycle against the wall of the inn beside the front door. Holmes and Watson kept up their vigil as the twilight slowly crept down. After some time, Wilder poked his head out of the door and looked down the path, evidently expecting someone. Soon, a second figure walked into the inn and a lamp was lit in an upstairs window.

"Come, Watson, we must really take a risk and try to investigate this a little more closely. I must have a peep through that. If you bend your back, I think I can manage."

Holmes climbed onto Watson's shoulders and quickly returned back to the ground. "Come, my friend. Our day's work has been quite long enough. I think that we have gathered all that we can. It's a long walk, and the sooner we get started the better. I promise that before tomorrow evening we shall have reached the solution of the mystery."

At eleven o'clock the next morning, Holmes and Watson were again ushered into Holdernesse Hall.

James Wilder greeted them coolly. "You have come to see his Grace? I am sorry, but the fact is that the duke is far from well. He has been very much upset by the tragic news of the German master."

"I will see the duke, Mr. Wilder," Holmes stated.

"But he is in his room."

"Then I will go to his room. I will see him in his bed if I must," Holmes replied with a cold and inexorable manner.

Wilder surveyed the man in front of him and chose not to argue. "Very good, Mr. Holmes, I will tell him that you are here."

After a tedious wait, the duke appeared in a sorry state. As he slumped into a chair behind his desk, he seemed to be an altogether older man than he had been the day before. "Well, Mr. Holmes?" he asked.

"I think, your Grace, that Mr. Wilder should leave."

The secretary started to object, but the nobleman waved him away. After Wilder had closed the door behind him, the duke asked, "Now, Mr. Holmes, what have you to say?"

"The fact is, your Grace, that Dr. Watson and I are only interested in this problem for the reward that has been offered. I should like to have it confirmed that you are willing to pay for my information."

"Certainly. I have offered six thousand pounds to anyone who will tell me where my son is."

"I fancy that I see your Grace's checkbook upon the table," said Holmes. "I should be glad if you would make me a check. The Capital and Counties Bank, Oxford Street branch, are my agents."

The duke sat stern and upright. "Is this a joke, Mr. Holmes? Where is he?"

"He is, or was last night, at the Fighting Cock Inn, about two miles from your park gate."

Instead of looking relieved, the duke's concerned look stayed on his face. "And whom do you accuse of his kidnapping?"

Holmes stepped forward and touched the duke on the shoulder. "I accuse you. And now, your Grace, I'll trouble you for that check."

The duke's face plunged into his hands. "How much do you know? Does anyone else besides your friend know?"

"I saw you enter the Fighting Cock last night where your son was being held. I have spoken to no one."

"I shall be as good as my word, Mr. Holmes. I am about to write your check, however unwelcome the information which you have gained may be to me. I must put it plainly, Mr. Holmes. If only you two know of this incident, there is no reason why it should go any farther."

Holmes smiled and shook his head. "I fear, your Grace, that matters can hardly be arranged so easily. No, I think *twelve* thousand pounds is the sum that you owe me."

"But this is blackmail!"

Holmes sighed. "I admit that I find blackmail repulsive, but I find it more repulsive that you have exposed your innocent younger son to imminent and unnecessary danger to humor your guilty elder son, James Wilder."

The duke and Watson both looked at Holmes, astonished.

"The resemblance is most notably in the jaw," Holmes mused. "My eyes have been trained to examine faces, and not their trimmings."

"It is true," the duke confessed. "James is my son from a woman who would not marry me. He hated my young legitimate heir from the first with a persistent hatred. When James determined to kidnap Lord Saltire, he did so without my knowledge. You remember that I wrote to him that day. Well, James opened the letter and inserted a note asking Arthur to meet him in a little wood near the school. I am telling you what he has himself confessed to me …"

Holmes leaned forward and interrupted. "The check please, your Grace. Once we have concluded our business here, I will hurry back into town and escort the reporter arriving on the one o'clock train back to London. You will send a servant out to fetch your son from the inn, and no one need know the details of your deplorable behavior."

The Duke of Holdernesse solemnly wrote out the check and handed it to Holmes.

"I think that my friend and I can congratulate ourselves upon a most happy result from our little visit. There is one other small point upon which I desire some light. The horses used in the abduction were shod with shoes which counterfeited the tracks of cows. Where was this extraordinary device found?"

The Duke thought for a moment, and the led Holmes and Watson into a large room furnished as a museum and to a glass case. "These shoes were dug up in the moat of Holdernesse Hall. They were used to throw pursuers off track. They belonged to the marauding Barons of Holdernesse in the Middle Ages."

"Thank you," said Holmes. "It is the second most interesting object that I have seen in my time in the North."

"And the first?" the duke asked.

Holmes folded up his check and placed it carefully in his notebook. He patted the book affectionately, and turned to leave Holdernesse Hall without another word.

Chapter 17: As Active as Ever

On an autumn day in 1901, Holmes and Watson sat in the respective chairs, Holmes engrossed in an analysis of the documents found in the Coptic monasteries of Syria and Egypt while Watson studied a monograph on obscure nervous lesions, when the page boy delivered a calling card.

"It seems that Lord Balmoral is visiting us personally today, doctor," Holmes stated.

"I would presume it is to pay his gambling debt."

"I surmise there is more to the story than repayment of a debt. He has always paid by messenger in the past."

A middle aged man entered 221B and Holmes greeted him with the easy air of geniality which he could so readily assume.

"Lord Balmoral, it is good to see you in person. I believe it's been since McMurdo's boxing benefit all those years ago," Holmes smiled once everyone had been seated.

"Yes, I'm afraid we tend to socialize in different circles, Mr. Holmes," Lord Balmoral condescended. "Although, I admit to seeing Dr. Watson now and again at the track."

"Unfortunately, we don't cross paths very often," Holmes answered. "I tend to shy away from those unwelcome social summonses which call upon a man either to be bored or to lie. Now, what can I do for you today? Surely, it is not to accept payment of your debt to me, for those are never done in person."

"No. I will send my payment by courier as usual. I have come to you with a business proposition, Mr. Holmes."

Holmes cocked an eyebrow and motioned for his guest to continue.

"Of course, I wouldn't normally stoop to such behavior and sully my title, but my unfortunate streak with the horses lately has put me in a bit of a bind."

"Is that so? I would think the payment you received for your picture collection a few years ago would shore you up."

"It was a fine price, but the combination of my son Robert's scandal and my horse not performing in the Wessex Cup were disasters that I have not been able to fully recover from, even after these years. But I am not here to discuss my financial matters with a man such as yourself, Mr. Holmes. I am here to offer a business opportunity."

"Then please," Holmes motioned grandiosely with his arm, "let us benefit from your generosity."

"I'm sure you've heard Steve Dixie. He seems the kind of association you would have. He has an opportunity to defraud the Sultan of Turkey of a sizable sum. He needs financial backing, but I am not at liberty to fund him at this time. I agreed to act as an intermediary between you and him as he said it would not be possible to bring this opportunity to you personally."

Watson pursed his lips at the mention of Steve Dixie and waited for Holmes' response.

"He was correct in saying that it would not be possible for him to meet with me, Lord Balmoral. For Steve Dixie is a mad bull and a cowardly ruffian that I would expect a man of your exalted stature to have better sense than to be associated with. After he killed young Perkins outside the Holborn Bar a few weeks ago, he has been in my sights as someone that London should rid itself of. I will not do business with such a man, and in whatever ludicrous plan he has. My work is quite sufficiently complicated to start without the further difficulty of false information."

Lord Balmoral sprung to his feet, indignant. "How dare you accuse me of lying, Mr. Holmes!"

"Don't be noisy, Lord Balmoral. I find that after breakfast even the smallest argument is unsettling. I suggest that a stroll in the morning air and a little quiet thought will be greatly to your advantage. I am not interested in your 'opportunity,' but I will be interested in your payment that is due to me next Thursday."

With a huff of offense, Balmoral strode from the room. After he had slammed the door on his way out, Holmes and Watson looked at each other and both burst out into a roar of laughter.

"What preposterous nonsense!" Watson exclaimed.

"That was a very poor attempt," Holmes chuckled. "I'm not sure how Lord Balmoral and Steve Dixie met, but I can assure you that neither of them has any involvement with the Sultan of Turkey. What rubbish."

"Perhaps there might be a germ of an idea there, though. Could branching out to international royalty be an avenue to pursue?"

"I prefer the smaller crimes as of late, Watson. The larger crimes are apt to be the simpler, for the bigger the crime, the more obvious, as a rule, is the motive. I can use finesse in smaller dealings that don't attract as much attention. Take for instance our new endeavor with the tide-waiter. It will pay enough to be worth my time, but not large enough to cause a scandal. And as a bonus, I expect it will drive Colonel Warburton, the customs man, mad."

Still chuckling at the afternoon's entertainment, Watson returned to his monograph while Holmes scribbled out a quick message to be delivered to Merivale at the Yard in reference to the St. Pancras case, and then rose to begin brewing a product in one of his chemical vessels.

Holmes had spent several days in bed in June of 1902, but emerged one morning with a foolscap document and a twinkle of amusement in his austere grey eyes.

"I believe it is time you and I go meet with a prospective employee, doctor."

Watson looked up from his treatise on surgery quizzically.

"I have found the whereabouts of Killer Evans, of sinister and murderous reputation."

"I fear I am none the wiser," Watson replied.

"I shall enlighten you. James Winter, alias Morecroft, alias Killer Evans, native of Chicago. Known to have shot three men in the States. Escaped from prison through political influence.

Came to London in 1893. Shot a man over cards in a nightclub in the Waterloo Road in January, 1895."

"Why would we want such an aggressive man on our payroll? The roughs we employ are capable enough of their duties and handle things with the finesse you require."

Holmes nodded in agreement. "The dead man was Rodger Prescott, famous forger and coiner in Chicago. Also, a former business partner of Evans."

"Ah, so there is the angle."

"And Evans is a man of cunning. I have set eyes upon him since his release from prison last year, and he has recently been visiting a collector of oddities for an unknown reason. Upon further inspection, that collector now lives where Prescott used to reside. The collector has just left town for a few days, and I expect that we will find our man there presently."

"And the next step?"

Holmes took a revolver from the drawer and handed it to Watson. "If our Wild West friend tries to live up to his nickname, we must be ready for him. We will have a few stout men in hiding, also. But if he is as adept at counterfeiting as his former partner was, he will be a welcome addition to our organization. Come, Watson. The game is afoot!"

Holmes and Watson stationed themselves across the street from the collector's apartment. Within an hour, Holmes indicated a short, powerful man coming down the street. They watched him open the outer door of the building and go inside. The pair crossed the street to enter after him.

By the time Holmes and Watson had entered the apartment, Evans had pushed a table to one side, tore up the carpet, and was working vigorously upon the floorboard with a jemmy. Watson looked to Holmes for explanation, but saw Holmes studying the man intently, and motioned for Watson to stay silent. Evans had worked a square open in the planks, lit a stump of a candle, and vanished from view into the hole in the floor.

Holmes touched Watson's wrist as a signal, and they stole across to the open trap door. But the old floor creaked under their weight, and Evans' head emerged suddenly from the open space. He glared at them in a baffled rage, which gradually softened into a grin as he saw that Watson and Holmes both had their pistols pointed at him.

"Well, well! Mr. Sherlock Holmes!" he said coolly as he scrambled to the surface. "My old friends tol' me I might be meetin' you someday."

"Yes, Mr. Evans, I thought it time that we discussed business. I admit that I came here under the expectation of placing you in my employ, but now I am much more curious as to what is in that hole."

"I guess you would, Mr. Holmes. Always one step ahead, I suppose, and livin' up to your reputation. Well, sir, I hand it to you; you got the drop on me and-"

In an instant, Evans drew a revolver and fired two shots. Watson felt a sudden red-hot sear.

Holmes darted forward and slammed his pistol down on Evans' head, sprawling him onto the floor with blood running down his face. Holmes quickly checked Evans for other weapons and then turned his attention to Watson, only then realizing that his friend had been shot.

Holmes wrapped his wiry arms around Watson and led him to a chair. "You're not hurt, Watson? For God's sake, say that you are not hurt!"

Holmes' hard eyes dimmed and his firm lips shook. For one time only, Watson caught a glimpse of the great heart that was possessed inside of the man known for his great brain. The depth of loyalty and love which lay behind Holmes' cold mask shone through in his concern for his old friend.

"It's nothing, Holmes. It's a mere scratch," Watson grunted, indicating the flesh wound in his thigh.

Ripping Watson's trousers open with a pocketknife, Holmes sighed. "You are right. It is quite superficial."

Turning his face back to flint, Holmes faced Evans, who was sitting up dazedly. "By the Lord, it is as well for you. If you had killed Watson, you would not have gotten out of this house alive."

Holmes bound the prisoner and looked down into the small cellar which was still illuminated by Evans' candle. In it lay a mass of rusted machinery, rolls of paper, bottles, and many small bundles.

Turning back to Watson, Holmes smiled. "This is much better than a new employee. We now have another printing press – a counterfeiter's outfit."

"Yes, sir," offered Evans. "Prescott would've been the greatest counterfeiter London ever saw. That's his machine, and those bundles on the table are two thousand of Prescott's notes worth a hundred each and fit to pass anywhere. Help yourselves, gentlemen. Call it a deal, and I'm happy to join up."

Holmes laughed. "We don't operate like that, Mr. Evans. There is no bolt-hole for you in this country. You shot my friend." Holmes signaled out the window and McMurdo, Allard and Hatherly joined them. "Of course I knew of the Prescott outfit," Holmes continued, "but after the death of the man, I was never able to find out where it was. You have indeed done me a great service, Mr. Evans. I will ask my men to treat you in kind. Come Watson, we must get that leg bandaged up."

Watson spent the next month nursing his wounded leg until Holmes could stand it no longer. He had to dispatch Watson on a mission.

"You need a change, my dear Watson. Enough of your Turkish baths and lounging about our rooms. How would Lausanne do?"

"Splendid! But why?"

"Lady Frances Carfax is the sole survivor of the direct family of the late Earl of Rufton. She was left with some very remarkable old Spanish jewelry of silver and curiously cut diamonds to

283

which she was fondly attached – too attached, for she refused to leave them with her banker and always carried them about with her. A rather pathetic figure, the Lady Frances, a beautiful woman, still in fresh middle age, and yet, by a strange chance, the last derelict of what only twenty years ago was a goodly fleet."

"And I am to relieve her of these treasures? If the score is such a tempting one, why not go yourself?"

"You know that I cannot possibly leave London while old Abrahams is in such mortal terror of his life. On general principles it is best that I should not leave the country. It causes an unhealthy excitement among other criminals. Besides, Watson, the fair sex is your department."

Two days later, Watson was at the Hotel National in Lausanne, Switzerland, only to find that Lady Frances was gone. She had stayed there for several weeks and had given every indication that she intended to stay for the, paying in advance. Yet, she had disappeared with just a single day's notice. Upon further investigation, Watson learned that a bearded English savage had also been looking for Lady Frances, and some thought he was the reason for her quick departure.

After questioning the local travel agen, Watson learned that Lady Frances had fled to Baden. After dispatching a quick account to Holmes back in London, he was off.

Once in Baden, Watson quickly found the missing lady's hotel, where she made the acquaintance of a Dr. Shlessinger, a missionary from South America, and his wife. Lady Frances became smitten with the couple and helped tend to the ailing doctor as he recovered from a disease contracted during his apostolic duties. After two weeks, the doctor and his wife returned to London, with Lady Frances in tow. Watson felt a sudden tinge of jealousy at his new rivals for the lady's attention. Her readiness to join up with the pair showed that she would find company welcoming, and Watson only had to find her to woo her from her jewels.

"By the way," said the landlord, "you are not the only friend of Lady Frances Carfax who is inquiring after her just now. Only a week or so ago we had a man here upon the same errand."

"Did he give a name?" Watson asked.

"None; but he was an unusual Englishman. Almost a savage I would say, and one whom I should be sorry to offend."

Wondering if the jewels were truly worth the competition, Watson wrote to Holmes. He wrote a telegram back asking for a description of Dr. Shlessinger's left ear. Miffed at Holmes' offensive idea of humor, Watson tracked down Lady Frances' former maid in Montpellier the next day.

The maid confirmed that everything Watson had learned was true, and agreed with his intuition of the bearded man. Suddenly, she sprang from her chair, "See! The miscreant follows still! There he is!"

Through a window, Watson saw a huge, swarthy man with a bristling black beard walking slowly down the street, obviously looking for the maid's house, just as Watson had done.

Rushing out to the street, Watson accosted the man. "May I ask what your name is?"

"No, you may not," the man said with a villainous scowl.

"Where is Lady Frances Carfax?" Watson demanded.

The man stared at Watson with amazement.

"Why have you pursued her?" Watson persisted.

The savage bellowed and sprang upon Watson like a tiger. His grip of iron was on Watson's throat as he threw him to the ground in a fury. Watson had nearly passed out when he was saved by an unshaven French laborer who had been lounging in a cabaret across the street. The laborer struck the bearded man in the arm with a cudgel, and he let loose of the doctor's throat. After a moment's hesitation, the man snarled at Watson and his savior and ran off.

The French laborer leaned down to Watson. "Well, Watson, a very pretty mess you have made of it! I rather think you had better come back with me to London by the night express."

Watson blinked his eyes at the man. "Yes, Holmes, perhaps I'd better."

That night, Holmes and Watson had the carriage to themselves save for an immense litter of papers which Holmes had brought with him. After he had finished poring over them, Holmes explained his appearance. Finding that he could slip out of London undetected, and that no opportunities were on the horizon in the city, he determined to head Watson off at his next stop, the lady's former maid. Disguised as a laborer, he sat and waited.

"A singularly consistent investigation you have made," said Holmes. "I cannot at the moment recall any possible opportunity to announce yourself and your discreet inquiries which you have omitted. The total effect of your proceeding has been to give the alarm everywhere and yet to obtain nothing."

"Perhaps you would have done no better," Watson retorted bitterly.

"There is no 'perhaps' about it. I have done better. Your assailant in the street was the Hon. Philip Green, a former lover of Lady Frances, who left to find his riches in South Africa. Having done so, he is in hopes of rekindling the old flame."

"So he is more competition for Lady Frances' attention, just as I thought!"

"I concede that you stumbled upon a correct theory."

"Then you must also concede that there are too many players in contention for this matter. Surely, a larger treasure can be gotten with less work!"

"You are correct again. But you fail to notice that my name can now be associated with Lady Frances by certain parties. After your indiscreet travels across the continent, I must not allow her to evade me, lest other organizations see ours falter. We are not after her jewels now; we are after keeping our reputation. Now Watson, if you will allow me some rest, I do not plan to trouble my mind with this matter until we have breakfasted upon Mrs. Hudson's best efforts tomorrow."

When they reached Baker Street the next morning, a telegram was awaiting them. Holmes read it with an exclamation of interest and threw it across to Watson. The message read "Jagged or torn."

"What's this?" Watson asked.

"You may remember my question about Dr. Shlessinger's left ear. You did not answer it. I sent a duplicate to the hotel manager, whose answer lies here."

"What does it show?"

"It shows, my dear Watson, that we are dealing with an exceptionally astute and dangerous man. The Rev. Dr. Shlessinger is none other than Holy Peters, one of the most unscrupulous rascals that Australia has ever evolved. His particular specialty is the beguiling of lonely ladies by playing upon their religious feelings, and his so-called wife is a worthy helpmate. The nature of his tactics suggested his identity to me, and this physical peculiarity confirmed my suspicion.

"Our mark is in the hands of a most infernal couple, who will stick at nothing, Watson. All my instincts tell me that they are in London, but as we have at present no possible means of telling where, we can only possess our souls in patience. I will, of course, begin the usual lines of inquiry, and I feel that the local pawnbrokers will be of use in this matter, for Peters will surely be looking to unload some of his ill-gotten gains soon enough."

After a week of suspense, a flash of light finally came. Just as Holmes had predicted, a silver-and-brilliant pendant of old Spanish design had been pawned in Westminster Road. The pawner matched the description of Peters, and Holmes immediately threw himself upon the scent. Three days later, Holmes' man Archie Ross sent word to 221B. "We have him. No. 36 Poultney Square, Brixton."

"There we have it, Watson. Now, to set eyes on Poultney Square-"

But before Holmes could flesh out his plan, another note arrived from an out-of-breath messenger. Holmes read it aloud. "Two men delivered a coffin to house under watch."

"We must take our own line of action now. The situation strikes me as so desperate that the most extreme measures are justified. I would have preferred to have handled this from a distance, but not a moment is to be lost. There's nothing for it now but a direct frontal attack. Are you armed?"

The two men arrived by cab at 36 Poultney Square and rang loudly at the door of a great dark house. The door opened immediately, and a tall woman stood in front of them.

"Well, what do you want?" she asked sharply.

"I want to speak to Dr. Shlessinger," said Holmes.

"There is no such person here," she answered and tried to close the door, but Watson jammed it with his foot.

"Then we will see the man that lives here, whatever he may call himself," Watson said firmly.

After a moment's hesitation, the woman threw open the door. "My husband is not afraid to face any man in the world. He will be with you in an instant."

Holmes lit a cigarette and Watson hardly had time to look around the dusty sitting room before a big, bald-headed man stepped into the room. "There is some mistake here gentlemen. Possibly if you tried further down the street-"

"That will do; we have no time to waste," said Holmes firmly. "You are Henry Peters of Adelaide, late the Rev. Dr. Shlessinger, of Baden and South America. I am as sure of that as that my own name is Sherlock Holmes."

Peters stared hard at Holmes. "Your name does not frighten me, Mr. Holmes. What is your business?"

"I want to know what you have done with the Lady Frances Carfax, whom you brought away with you from Baden."

"I'd be very glad if you could tell me where that lady may be," Peters answered coolly. "I'd plans for her but she gave us the slip, and all I could get out of her was a couple of trumpery pendants that the dealer would hardly look at."

"Enough of this," Holmes sighed. "I would not sit here smoking with you if I thought that you were a common criminal, you may be sure of that. Be frank with me and we may do some good. Play tricks with me, and I'll crush you. You have something that I want, something hardly worth my efforts, but it has become a matter of pride at this point and I will not be turned away. My quarrel is not with you, Mr. Peters, and you accommodate me, I can see that you are set up comfortably in Prague."

Peters considered his options and nodded in assent. "You're not a man I wish to trifle with, Mr. Holmes. I'll accept your offer."

"Good. An agent will meet you at noon at the Manes Pavilion five days from today. Now, where are Lady Frances' jewels?"

"And Lady Frances?" Watson added.

"The jewels are upstairs. My wife will fetch them. Lady Frances is in the coffin in the next room."

"Of course you murdered her," Watson sighed.

"No, I couldn't bring myself to it. Her head's been wrapped in chloroform and left in the coffin to be buried tomorrow."

Mortified, Holmes and Watson looked at the man for only a moment, before rushing out of the room. They both grabbed screwdrivers from a nearby table and with a united effort, they tore off the coffin lid to reveal Lady Frances Carfax. In an instant, Holmes had raised her to a sitting position.

"Is she gone Watson? Is there a spark left?"

Watson worked furiously at artificial respiration, injected ether and worked with every device that science could suggest. Finally a quiver of the eyelids spoke of slowly returning life.

Holmes turned to face the couple watching from the doorway. "I am a man of my word, and my offer is still available. See that the jewelry is delivered to a man by the name of Redmond at the Waterloo station at nine tonight. I don't ever want to lay eyes on you two wretched souls again. Now go!"

Peters and his wife exited quickly and Holmes turned back to Watson. "How is she, doctor?"

"She will recover, but will require someone to nurse her back to health."

"Of course, but it would not do for you and I to be here when she awakes. It could lead to uncomfortable questioning. Can she be left alone for an hour?"

"She is safe for the short term. But her long-term recovery will need to be overseen," Watson answered.

"Then let us go then. On our way back, we will dispatch a telegram to Mr. Philip Green and let him know that although Lady Frances has been burgled by a villain who has fled London, she is alive and can be found at this address."

"And of Peters?"

"I have given him my word, but I shall expect to hear of their capture soon in their future career. Now that we have finished our adventure with Lady Frances Carfax, I think that something nutritious at Simpson's would not be out of place."

Chapter 18: The End of the Path

In September of 1902, Holmes was hired by Colonel Sir James Damery to persuade a friend's daughter out of marrying the murderous Baron Adelbert Gruner, with whom she had become entranced. After using Shinwell Johnson's underworld contacts and a street fight with two of Gruner's men, Holmes was able to acquire proof of the baron's evil dealings and convince his bride-to-be to abandon her plans. Holmes' client turned out to have an even higher rank than Colonel Sir Damery, and Holmes was rewarded very well for his adventure.

As 1902 wound to a close and 1903 loomed on the horizon, Sherlock Holmes began to contemplate his retirement. Looking out the window at the passersby below one morning, he commented to Watson, "I think that I may go so far as to say, Watson that I have not lived wholly in vain."

Watson looked up from the Clark Russell sea story he was reading and nodded in acknowledgement.

"If my record were to close soon, I could still survey it with equanimity. In over a thousand crimes I am not aware that I have ever given less than my personal best. Of late I have been tempted to look into the problems furnished by nature rather than those more superficial ones for which our artificial state of society is responsible. Perhaps, it is time to draw to an end the time of the most capable criminal in Europe and I disappear into that little farm of my dreams."

"What has brought on this introspection, Holmes?"

"From the point of view of the expert criminal, London has become a singularly uninteresting city since the death of the late-lamented Professor Moriarty. With that man in the field, one's morning paper presented infinite possibilities against which to test my organization. Often it was only the smallest trace, the faintest indication, and yet it was enough to tell me that the great malignant brain was there. To the scientific criminal no capital in Europe offered the advantages which London then possessed. But now..." Holmes shrugged his shoulders and returned to his chair after this whimsical protest.

"It has been over ten years since Moriarty perished. You can't mean to say that there has been nothing to stimulate your interests in that time."

"Of course, the occasional challenge would arise; certainly, Baron Gruner is a most recent example. Small summons from Mycroft and our bout with Mr. Milverton were also high points, but they have become few and far between in the memoirs of Sherlock Holmes. Colonel Moran continues to make threats against me, but I am hardly interested in him as long as he is imprisoned. I am perhaps to blame for the state of things, for I have done so much to produce them myself. Our unrivaled history of unsolved crimes has caused law enforcement to advance to such a degree that the reward for a well-planned crime is hardly worth the risk. Increased scrutiny on suspicious figures has caused me to cut my ties with the Spencer John gang. And just last week the Pinkerton agency was in London, hot on the trail of a member of the Italian Red Circle syndicate. Why would I risk calling attention to myself when such an organization is in our midst?"

"But your consulting business has picked up quite nicely in the past years. The Hammersmith and James Saunders commissions were both lengthy and engaging. Why, the Fairdale Hobbs matter …"

"A simple matter. Hardly worth my time; although the payment was sufficient. My own little practice seems to be degenerating into an agency for recovering lost pencils and giving advice to young ladies from boarding-schools. And even you, Watson, my old friend, cannot say that our enterprises fully entertain your attention."

"Holmes! How can you say that?"

"Watson, I'm sure it is no surprise to you that I am aware of your liaisons."

Watson blushed. "But I hadn't said anything yet…"

"You need not, my friend. It is evident. You have stopped playing billiards with Thurston and are spending much less time in your club, yet you are spending money at the same rate, if not more so, than before."

"How on earth did you know that?"

"Your checkbook is locked in my drawer, and you continue to ask for the key on a steady basis. Clearly, something else has taken your time. You have twice returned with some splashes on the left sleeve and shoulder of your coat. Had you sat in the center of a hansom you would probably have had no splashes, and if you had they would certainly have been symmetrical. Therefore it is clear that you sat at the side. Therefore it is equally clear that you had a companion. These times, I also noticed a faint smell of white jessamine. After my studies in Montpellier, I am familiar with seventy-five perfumes, and this scent suggested the presence of a lady, and the other points, along with seven others too trivial to mention, pointed me to my conclusion."

"Splendid! It's true, I have met a young lady."

And soon enough, the good Watson had deserted Holmes for a wife, leaving behind Baker Street with the scientific diagrams on the wall, the acid-stained bench of chemicals, the violin case leaning in the corner, the starting point of so many remarkable adventures.

Sherlock Holmes was alone.

But Holmes' solitude did not last long. Although he lived alone, his time was soon taken up with one man: Colonel Sebastian Moran. Just days after Watson's nuptials, Moran had escaped from prison, and Holmes knew that it was only a matter of time before they met again. Holmes spent the following weeks in fear of air guns, and exhumed the wax bust of himself that had worked so well in their previous meeting.

He fully expected the tiger hunter to take up chase immediately, but when news of the theft of the great yellow Crown Diamond appeared, Holmes knew that Moran was the only man who could pull off such a heist without word of it leaking to Holmes through his informants. Apparently, Moran was not interested in just the death of Sherlock Holmes, as he had threatened over the years, but in resurrecting Moriarty's crime syndicate that Holmes had thwarted so many years before.

Once the underworld heard of the theft and that it was not orchestrated by Holmes, stirrings amongst its members began that he could not allow. Even though Holmes had resigned himself to retirement within the year, his pride would not let him tolerate a new criminal organization rising up while he still resided in London. And an organization headed by anyone associated with the Moriarty gang was deplorable.

Knowing full well that this would be his last bow as the crime lord of London, Holmes decided that he would take down Moran on his own. Through low level contacts, Holmes was able to find out that Moran had been recruiting, and was quickly able to locate him. Dressed as an old woman, he spent the next day following Moran from his lodgings to the workshop of old Strubenzee, where the colonel exited with a very pretty air-gun. Holmes rushed back to Baker Street, knowing that a showdown was eminent. He had just exhumed himself from his disguise when Billy the page boy appeared, announcing that Colonel Sebastian Moran was in the waiting room with another man.

"Ah yes, Sam Merton, the boxer. Not a bad fellow, but the colonel will not hesitate to use him," Holmes mused. After scribbling a short note, he turned to the page. "Show him up when I ring, Billy. And deliver this note to Mercer immediately afterwards."

"Yes sir," the boy responded.

"Oh, by the way, Billy, if I am not in the room show him in just the same."

Holmes moved to his bedroom, and Billy brought in Moran. After the page left, Moran advanced slowly into the room, jumping when he saw the dummy sitting with its back towards him. Thinking it to be Holmes, Moran advanced on tip toe and raised his heavy stick above his head for a strike.

"Don't break it Colonel, don't break it!" Holmes greeted in a sardonic voice from the bedroom door.

Moran staggered back, shocked.

"It's such a pretty little thing. Tavernier, the French modeler, made it. He is as good at waxwork as Straubenzee is at air-guns. You'd be surprised the history it has," Holmes said coolly. "Pray, take a seat. Put your hat and stick on the side table. Would you care to put your revolver out also?"

As Holmes drew a curtain around the statue, Moran sat down. "I wanted to have five minutes' chat with you, Holmes. I won't deny that I intended to assault you just now."

Holmes sat near Moran and crossed his legs. "It struck me that some idea of that sort had crossed your mind. But why this attention?"

"You have gone out of your way to annoy me. You've put your creatures on my track. Yesterday there was an old sporting man. Today it was an elderly lady. They had me in view all day."

"Keeping an eye on the man who has repeatedly threatened my life is not necessarily out of line. But really sir, you compliment me! You give my little impersonations your kindly praise."

"It was you! You aren't dogging me because of my threats from prison. Why are you doing this?"

"I want that yellow Crown Diamond," Holmes said matter-of-factly. "You knew that I was after you for that, and that was your intention when you stole it. The theft would not only shake my aging organization and make a name for yourself, but it would force us to face one another. And you are here tonight to find out how much I know about the matter. Well, you can take it that I know all about it, save one thing, which you are about to tell me."

Moran sneered at Holmes. "And, pray, what is that?"

"Where the diamond is."

Moran barked out a short, ferocious laugh in reply.

Holmes sighed and continued. "Now, Colonel, if you will be reasonable we can do business together. If not, you may get hurt. Do you know what I keep inside this book sitting next to me?"

"No, sir, I do not."

"You. You're all here. Every action of your vile and dangerous life. The real facts as to the death of Miss Minnie Warrender of Laburnum Grove. The story of young Arbothnot, who was found drowned in the Regents Canal just before his intended exposure of you for cheating at cards, not unlike Ronald Adair I might add. How about the robbery in the train deluxe to the Rivera? How about the forged check on the Credit Lyonnais the same year?"

"No, you're wrong there."

"Then I'm right on the others. Now, Colonel, you are a card player. Also a cheat, but a card player, still. When the other fellow holds all the trumps it saves time to throw down your hand. These crimes have all gone unreported because they never interfered with my organization and many were protected by Professor Moriarty. But he is dead and you are impinging on my territory. Now, if I touch this bell it means the police, and from that instant the matter is out of my hands. You are a wanted man, Colonel. Do you dare risk it?"

Moran stared at his opponent, hatred burning in his eyes, but Holmes could also see that his words had had an effect on the man.

"Now, consider. You're going to be locked back up. So is Sam Merton. What good are you going to get out of your diamond? None in the world. But if you let me know where it is... Well, I'll grant you and Mr. Merton time to leave London for good."

"And if I refuse? I'm supposed to trust you? You murdered Moriarty."

"Come now, Colonel. It could hardly be called murder. It was self-defense. Perhaps I am growing soft in my old age, but I am willing you to go your way and I shall go mine. But if you make another peep or are seen anywhere near London or myself, then God help you."

Holmes rang the bell and Billy stepped in.

"Billy, show up the large gentleman from the waiting room." Turning back to Moran, he continued, "I think we had better have your friend at this conference. No good fingering your revolver. No, it didn't go unnoticed that you sat on it earlier. Nasty, noisy things, revolvers. Better stick to air-guns."

Billy soon returned and showed Sam Merton in.

"Good day, Mr. Merton. I should say it is all up."

Merton looked at Moran. "Is this cove tryin' to be funny or what? I'm not in the funny mood."

"You'll feel even less humorous as the evening advances, I can promise that. Now look here, Colonel, I'm a busy man and I can't waste time. I'm going into the bedroom. Pray make yourselves at home. You can explain to your friend how the matter lies. I shall try over a piece on my violin. In five minutes I shall return for your final answer. You quite grasp the alternative, don't you? Give up the stone, sir."

With that, Holmes disappeared into his bedroom.

Merton spun towards Moran. "What's that? He knows about the stone?"

Music began to play from behind the closed door to the bedroom as the Colonel and the boxer talked over their plight, Moran telling all the details of his conversation with Holmes.

After looking at the shadow of the wax statue for a minute, Moran turned back to Merton. "Look, I've got the stone in my secret pocket. It can be out of England tonight, cut into four pieces in Amsterdam before Saturday. Holmes won't do anything to us until he knows where the stone is, which will give us enough time to get it out of the country. You run off to Van

Seddor and give him the stone. I'll fill up Holmes with a bogus confession. Here's the diamond."

Moran took a small leather box from his pocket and extended his arm towards Merton.

As if by magic, Holmes stood up quickly from the chair where the statue had been earlier. "I thank you." Quickly, he snatched the box from Moran and stepped back. "No violence gentlemen, I beg of you. Consider the furniture! It must be very clear to you that your position is an impossible one."

"You devil!" Moran cried. "How did you get there?"

"You are not aware that a second door from my room leads behind the curtain. And as for the music, these modern gramophones are a wonderful invention. No, Colonel, no. Don't try anything. I am covering you with a .450 Derringer through the pocket of my dressing gown."

Holmes rang the bell for Billy again. When the boy entered, Holmes simply said, "Send them up."

A cadre of tough men came through the door moments later. Mercer, Holmes' general utility man, led Hatherly, Redmond, McMurdo and Allard into the room.

"Ready, Mr. Holmes?" Mercer asked.

Holmes toyed with the box in his hand. "Yes, Mercer. Make sure that Colonel Moran is no longer a threat to me. Billy, will you show these gentlemen out and tell Mrs. Hudson that I should be glad if she would send up dinner as soon as possible?"

After the group had shut the door behind them, Holmes settled into his chair, lit his pipe with a burning coal from the fireplace, and decided once and for all that his time in Baker Street had come to an end.

Chapter 19: A Life Led Far from the Fogs of Baker Street

Sherlock Holmes did indeed retire after more than twenty years in criminal practice in London. Refusing to become like one of those popular tenors that are still tempted to make repeated farewell bows even though they had outlived their time, Holmes said farewell to his rooms on Baker Street at the end of 1903. Five miles from Eastbourne upon the Sussex downs, he settled into a little villa with his housekeeper. After completing one last monograph upon the similarities between dogs and their owners, Holmes withdrew from public life. During this period of rest, some ambitious folk offered princely offers for him to plan or just consult on their schemes, but he always refused, determining that his retirement was to be a permanent one.

Holmes had given himself entirely up to a soothing life of nature after years amid the gloom of London. He continued his studies in chemistry and took a passing interest in philosophy, but beekeeping became his passion. Holmes had become an omnivorous reader in his retirement of all things natural, and his book collection on bee culture boasted the most renowned and obscure volumes.

Holmes, the housekeeper and his bees had the estate all to themselves. From his position upon the southern slope of the downs, his villa commanded a great view of the Channel. He found himself at the mercy of occasional attacks or rheumatism, but strolls among the chalk cliffs and the admirable beach in the exquisite air were a welcome relief to his aging body.

Now that he was married again, Watson had passed almost beyond Holmes' ken. An occasional weekend visit from

Watson was all that Holmes ever saw of his old friend anymore. Watson had found a new career as an author of some fame. From his years of experience, Watson was able to take capers he had been privy to and turn them into stories of the consulting detective, Sheridan Hope. These stories proved to be wildly popular, and using the pseudonym Ormond Sacker, Watson published a number of them in the Strand magazine. Although Holmes chided Watson for his romantic flourishes and complained that Watson had degraded what should have been a course of lectures into a series of tales, he secretly enjoyed seeing his life's work being shared with the public in a guarded manner.

Upon seeing Watson's talent, Holmes took to writing himself. In fact, it was said that he had become a hermit among his bees and books. But Holmes, with his strangely retentive memory for trifles, was working on his magnum opus. After many pensive nights and laborious days watching the little working gangs among their hives as he once watched over the criminal world of London, Holmes spent time in the great garret of his little house stuffed with books to produce the fruit of his leisure years, *The Practical Handbook of Bee Culture, with Some Observations upon the Segregation of the Queen.*

But Holmes' quiet retirement was too good to last. World events were conspiring against his quiet lifestyle. Germany was flexing its muscles and making all of Europe nervous. The Balkan War loomed on the horizon. Holmes, just like the rest of England, followed these world events with a sense of foreboding. And one day, he received a telegram from his brother Mycroft. "Be at home at noon tomorrow."

Knowing that Mycroft did not issue orders such as these lightly, and typically being at home during this hour of the day anyhow, Holmes awaited his expected guest. He planned to see some government official, or possibly his brother if the issue was a serious matter. Holmes was even prepared to beg off activity if the Foreign Minister arrived at his home. But Holmes was completely surprised when the Prime Minister crossed his threshold and seated himself upon the sofa.

"Mr. Holmes," the Premier began, "we are aware of your past history as both a rogue and an accomplice to our covert operations. Germany is currently collecting great amounts of intelligence on mother England. The fact is, things are going wrong and no one can understand why they are. Agents have been suspected and even caught, but there is evidence of some strong and secret central force. It is absolutely necessary to expose it. I know that you are leading a retired life and have turned away offers of great value, but I implore you to take this task on for the greatest value, that of the security of your nation. Mr. Holmes, will you use your remarkable combination of intellectual and practical activity to help your government?"

Holmes paused for only a moment before responding. "Mr. Prime Minister, you have my word that I will do what I can to be of service. If you would send all relevant materials to my humble home, I will spend my time poring over them. I would prefer to work from my own quarters, but if I must return to London, I will do so."

306

Scores of documents soon arrived and Holmes could quickly see that this was a most serious matter. Although he had hoped to be able to consult from his home, strong pressure was brought upon him to use his every resource, and he soon did. Holmes sent a plan for someone to infiltrate Germany's organization of spies and thieves to deduce the head of the spy ring, starting in America, instead of the European countries where new faces would face tougher scrutiny. Of course, word was sent back from the Prime Minister's office that they wished Holmes himself to be their agent, bringing him out of retirement for one last bow.

Returning to his old resources of disguise, Holmes found himself in Chicago, Illinois in 1912. There, he met with agents from the Foreign Office, who assisted him as he acquired the correct American accent and wardrobe. When the time was right, Holmes posed as an out-of-work auto mechanic from Altamont, Illinois and took to hanging around garages throughout the city. After many conversations about Teddy Roosevelt and Comiskey Park, Holmes was able to use a few tricks picked up from Birdy Edwards' experience infiltrating a secret society in Pennsylvania more than two decades before, and joined an Irish secret society of bitter Irish Americans, full of hatred for England. There, he was quickly dubbed "Altamont" by the regulars, and his infiltration of the spy ring began in earnest.

After months in Chicago, Holmes' handlers informed him that his next step would take him to Buffalo, New York. The Foreign Office created a family member for him to visit out east, and Holmes left Chicago for Buffalo. Knowing that he would need to be accepted by the new group more quickly than he had been in Chicago, Holmes requested letters vouching for his character from the head of Chicago's Irish society. Using this inroad, Holmes was not only welcomed as a fellow brother-in-arms, but was able to find employment at a local garage, where he whiled away time discussing his hatred for America and Britain with the other Irish idlers.

Altamont's well-known hatred for English and Americans led him to be recruited for a mission in Skibbareen, Ireland, where he and a few select others gave serious trouble to the constabulary. While in Ireland, Altamont became involved in gun-running against Britain. From these activities, he eventually caught the eye of a subordinate for the German agent, Von Bork. The agent recommended Altamont to his superior as a likely spy, and Holmes was soon hired as a British mole. Over the next few months, Holmes earned the utmost confidence of Von Bork, and was able to subtly undo most of his plans and lead five of the German's best agents to prison.

Through the two years Holmes spent as a double-agent, his quiet life had been filled with excitement. His only regret was the horrible goatee he grew as part of his disguise. All of Holmes' hard work came to an end on August 2, 1914.

That morning, Holmes had sent a message to Von Bork. "Will come without fail tonight and bring new spark plugs. – Altamont"

Von Bork waited in the study of his stately manor with baited breath for the gem of his collection, secret British naval signals. Once this item was in his possession, Von Bork would be received back in Berlin in the highest quarters for all of his work. The rest of his family had fled back to Germany, and he was alone with only his old British housekeeper left to keep him company. The agent began to pack his papers in a valise for his early morning departure when he heard the sound of a distant car. When it arrived, a passenger sprang out and advanced swiftly, while the heavily built, elderly chauffer settled down like one who was resigning himself to a long vigil.

"Well?" asked Von Bork as he greeted his visitor.

Holmes, under the guise of Altamont, waved a small brown paper bag above his head. "You can give me the glad hand tonight, mister. I'm bringing home the bacon at last!"

"The naval signals?"

"Same as I said in my cable," said Holmes around a half-smoked, sodden cigar. "Every last one of them, semaphore, lamp code, Marconi - a copy, mind you, not the original. Too dangerous." Holmes slapped Von Bork with a rough familiarity.

The German winced at the touch. "Come in. I'm all alone in the house. I was only waiting for this."

Holmes followed Von Bork into the study and stretched his long legs as he settled into an armchair as the German continued. "I'm shutting down tomorrow morning now that I have this," he smiled as he indicated Holmes' delivery.

"Well, I guess you'll have to fix me up also. I'm not staying in this gol-darned country all on my lonesome. In a week or less, from what I see, John Bull will be on his hind legs and fair ramping. I'd rather watch him from over the water."

"You've done splendid work and taken risks. By all means go to Holland, and you can get a boat from Rotterdam to New York. No other line will be safe in a week from now. I'll take that book and pack it with the rest."

"What about the dough?" Holmes asked in his accent.

Von Bork smiled with some bitterness. "You don't seem to have a very high opinion of my honor. You want the money before you give up the book."

"Well, mister, it is a business proposition."

"All right. Have it your way. I don't see why I should trust you any more than you trust me. Your check is upon the table over there. I claim the right to examine the parcel before you pick the money up."

Holmes passed the parcel to Von Bork and he undid the string and two wrappers of paper. He sat for a moment in stunned silence as he stared at the title which read *The Practical Handbook of Bee Culture*.

The master spy had only an instant to glare at this title before Holmes' iron grasp gripped the back of his neck and a chloroform sponge was placed against his face.

When Von Bork awoke, he found Altamont and the chauffer enjoying his wine while he lay bound on the sofa with a strap around his upper arms and another around his legs. Holmes had quickly gathered every dossier available and had Von Bork's valise sitting at his feet.

"We need not hurry ourselves, Watson," Holmes stated. "We are safe from interruption. There is no one in the house except old Martha, Von Bork's maid, who has played her part to admiration. She has collected the addresses of all of Von Bork's letters and will meet with me at Claridge's Hotel in London tomorrow. Ah, I see our friend is awake!"

Von Bork broke out into a furious stream of German invective, his face convulsed with passion.

"Though unmusical," Holmes observed, "German is the most expressive of all the languages. As I look through your files, Mister Von Bork, I realize that you have a great deal to answer for!"

"I shall get level with you, Altamont. If it takes me all my life I shall get level with you!"

"The old sweet song," answered Holmes. "It was a favorite ditty of the late lamented Professor Moriarty. Colonel Sebastian Moran has also been known to warble it. And yet I live and keep bees upon the South Downs still."

"Who are you?" Von Bork cried.

"It is really immaterial who I am, but since the matter seems to interest you, Mr. Von Bork, I may say that this is not my first acquaintance with the members of your family. I have done a good deal of business in Germany in the past, and my name is probably familiar to you. It was I who brought about the separation between Miss Irene Adler and the late King of Bohemia when your cousin was the Imperial Envoy. It was I who saved from murder Count Von und ZuGrafenstein by the Nihilist Klopman. It was I ..."

Von Bork groaned and sank back into the sofa. "There is only one man. And most of my information came through you!" he cried.

"It is certainly untrustworthy. Your admiral may find the new guns rather larger than he expects, and the cruisers perhaps a trifle faster. You have at last been outwitted. You have done your best for your country and I have done my best for mine." Holmes turned to his other companion. "The papers are now ready, Watson. If you will help me with our prisoner, I think that we may get started for London at once."

Holmes and Watson hoisted the bound Von Bork into the spare seat of their little car with his precious valise wedged beside him. Soon enough he would be in custody in Scotland Yard.

Holmes turned back to his old friend. "Stand with me here upon the terrace, for it may be the last quiet talk we shall ever have."

The two friends chatted in intimate converse for a few minutes, recalling once again the days of the past and the adventures that they had shared together. As they turned to the car, Holmes pointed back to the moonlit sea and shook a thoughtful head.

"There's an east wind coming, Watson."

"I think not, Holmes. It is very warm."

"Good old Watson! You are the one fixed point in a changing age. There's an east wind coming all the same, such a wind as never blew over England yet. It will be cold and bitter, Watson, and a good many of us may wither before its blast. But it's God's own wind none the less, and a cleaner, better, stronger land will lie in the sunshine when the storm has cleared." Holmes paused for a moment in his reverie.

"Start her up, Watson, for it's time that we were on our way."

Acknowledgements

This project started out as a simple article I'd hoped to submit to *The Baker Street Journal*, but soon ballooned into the book you hold in your hands. Without the help and support of the following people, *The Criminal Mastermind of Baker Street* would have probably never been completed. I would first and foremost like to thank my amazing wife and daughter, Amy and Savannah, who were understanding about the many days when I would hide myself away to research and write. Josh Monken for the seemingly never-ending edits and continuity suggestions. Chris Redmond for the great guidance in helping mold my original ideas and advice on the publishing process. Brad Keefauver for the encouragement and advice on the submission process. Scott Monty and *I Hear of Sherlock Everywhere* for giving me my first chances to write seriously about Sherlock Holmes. Sonia Featherson for unwittingly inspiring me with her Canonical quotes on Twitter. Steve Emecz and Rich Ryan for how welcome they made me feel through the whole publishing process. And finally, to the Parallel Case of St. Louis, the Noble Bachelors of St. Louis and the Harpooners of the Sea Unicorn for giving me a place to really dig into the Canon and bounce ideas off other Sherlockians.

My blog can be found at:

http://interestingthoughelementary.blogspot.com/

Bibliography

Baring-Gould, W. S. (1962). *Sherlock Holmes of Baker Street: The life of the world's first consulting detective.* New York: Clarkson N. Potter.

Bell, H. W. (1995). *Baker Street studies.* New York: Otto Penzler Books.

Bower, H. (1894). *Diary of a journey across Tibet.* London: Livington, Percival and Co.

Bunson, M. (1997). *Encyclopedia Sherlockiana: an A-to-Z guide to the world of the great detective.* New York: Macmillan.

Clarkson, S. (1999). *The canonical compendium.* Ashcroft, B.C.: Calabash Press.

Cochran, W. R., & Speck, G. R. (1996). *Commanding views from the Empty House: collected writings.* Indianapolis, IN: Gasogene Books.

Cordially Invited to the Wedding of Irene Adler and Godfrey Norton. (2012, November 03). Retrieved March 26, 2017, from https://lisagordon1138.wordpress.com/2012/11/03/cordially-invited-to-the-wedding-of-irene-adler-and-godfrey-norton/

Davies, D. S., Forshaw, B., & Klinger, L. S. (2015). *The Sherlock Holmes book.* NY, NY: DK Publishing.

Doyle, A. C. (n.d.). *A study in scarlet.* New York: A.L. Burt Co., Pub.

Doyle, A. C. (1920). *The sign of the four. A scandal in Bohemia, and other stories.* New York: A.L. Burt.

Doyle, A. C. (1923). *The valley of fear*. London: Butler & Tanner Ltd.

Doyle, A. C. (1977). *The complete original illustrated Sherlock Holmes*. Castle Books.

Doyle, A. C., & Baring-Gould, W. S. (1967). *The annotated Sherlock Holmes*. New York: C.N. Potter; Distributed by Crown .

Doyle, A. C., & Tracy, J. (1980). *Sherlock Holmes: the published apocrypha*. Boston: Houghton Mifflin.

Doyle, A. C. (1994). *His last bow: a reminiscence of Sherlock Holmes*. New York: Book-of-the-Month Club.

Doyle, A. C., & Klinger, L. S. (1999). *The memoirs of Sherlock Holmes*. Indianapolis: Gasogene Books.

Doyle, A. C., & Klinger, L. (2001). *A study in scarlet*. Indianapolis: Gasogene Books.

Doyle, A. C., & Klinger, L. S. (2002). *The hound of the Baskervilles*. Indianapolis: Gasogene Books.

Doyle, A. C., & Klinger, L. S. (2004). *The sign of four*. Indianapolis: Gasogene Books.

Doyle, A. C., Klinger, L. S., & Chui, P. J. (2005). *The new annotated Sherlock Holmes*. New York: Norton.

Doyle, A. C., & Robson, W. W. (2009). *The case-book of Sherlock Holmes*. Oxford: Oxford University Press.

Great French Wine Blight.(n.d.). Retrieved April 11, 2017, from http://wineportfolio.com/sectionLearn-Great-French-Wine-Blight.html

Guinn, L., & Mahoney, J. N. (2016). *A curious collection of dates: through the year with Sherlock Holmes*. Indianapolis: Gasogene Books.

Hardwick, M. (1992). *The complete guide to Sherlock Holmes*. New York: St. Martin's Press.

Hardwick, M., Hardwick, M., & Paget, S. (1999). *The Sherlock Holmes companion*. Twickenham: Senate.

Harrison, M. (1975). *The world of Sherlock Holmes*. New York: E. P. Dutton.

History of Boxing.(n.d.). Retrieved April 11, 2017, from http://fightclubamerica.com/about/history-of-boxing/

Peck, A. J., & Klinger, L. (1996). *"The date being--?": a compendium of chronological data*. New York, NY: Magico magazine.

Redmond, C. (2009). *Sherlock Holmes handbook*. Toronto: Dundurn Pr.

Redmond, C., &Wilmunen, J. V. (1994). *The tin dispatch-box: a compendium of the unpublished cases of Mr. Sherlock Holmes*. Waterloo, Ont.: Privately published.

Redmond, D. A. (2002). *Sherlock Holmes: a study in sources*. Shelbourne, Ont: Battered Silicon Dispatch Box.

Roberts, S. C. (1994). *Holmes & Watson: a miscellany*. New York: O. Penzler.

Rockhill, W. (1894). *Diary of a journey through Mongolia and Tibet in 1891 and 1892*. Washington D.C.: Smithsonian Institution.

Sherlock Holmes And Chicago 1912. (n.d.). Retrieved March 26, 2017, from

http://www.sherlockpeoria.net/Who_is_Sherlock/SherlockHistory2009/Chicago1912.html

Smith, E. W. (1944). *Profile by gaslight*. Simon.

Starrett, V. (1994). *221 B: studies in Sherlock Holmes*. New York: O. Penzler Books.

"The Empty House" (The Strand Magazine, October 1903).(n.d.). Retrieved April 11, 2017, from

http://sherlockholmes.stanford.edu/2007/notes1_1.html

Tracy, J. (1977). *The encyclopedia Sherlockiana*. Doubleday.

Also from MX Publishing

MX Publishing is the world's largest specialist Sherlock Holmes publisher, with over a hundred titles and fifty authors creating the latest in Sherlock Holmes fiction and non-fiction.

From traditional short stories and novels to travel guides and quiz books, MX Publishing cater for all Holmes fans.

The collection includes leading titles such as *Benedict Cumberbatch In Transition* and *The Norwood Author* which won the 2011 Howlett Award (Sherlock Holmes Book of the Year).

MX Publishing also has one of the largest communities of Holmes fans on Facebook with regular contributions from dozens of authors.

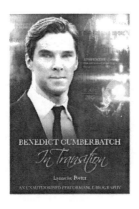

www.mxpublishing.com

Also from MX Publishing

Our bestselling books are our short story collections;

'Lost Stories of Sherlock Holmes', 'The Outstanding Mysteries of Sherlock Holmes', The Papers of Sherlock Holmes Volume 1 and 2, 'Untold Adventures of Sherlock Holmes' (and the sequel 'Studies in Legacy) and 'Sherlock Holmes in Pursuit', 'The Cotswold Werewolf and Other Stories of Sherlock Holmes' – and many more......

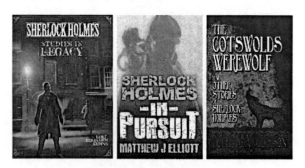

www.mxpublishing.com

Also from MX Publishing

"Phil Growick's, 'The Secret Journal of Dr Watson', is an adventure which takes place in the latter part of Holmes and Watson's lives. They are entrusted by HM Government (although not officially) and the King no less to undertake a rescue mission to save the Romanovs, Russia's Royal family from a grisly end at the hand of the Bolsheviks. There is a wealth of detail in the story but not so much as would detract us from the enjoyment of the story. Espionage, counter-espionage, the ace of spies himself, double-agents, double-crossers...all these flit across the pages in a realistic and exciting way. All the characters are extremely well-drawn and Mr Growick, most importantly, does not falter with a very good ear for Holmesian dialogue indeed. Highly recommended. A five-star effort."
The Baker Street Society

www.mxpublishing.com

Also from MX Publishing

The Missing Authors Series

Sherlock Holmes and The Adventure of The Grinning Cat
Sherlock Holmes and The Nautilus Adventure
Sherlock Holmes and The Round Table Adventure

"Joseph Svec, III is brilliant in entwining two endearing and enduring classics of literature, blending the factual with the fantastical; the playful with the pensive; and the mischievous with the mysterious. We shall, all of us young and old, benefit with a cup of tea, a tranquil afternoon, and a copy of Sherlock Holmes, The Adventure of the Grinning Cat."
Amador County Holmes Hounds Sherlockian Society

Also from MX Publishing

The American Literati Series

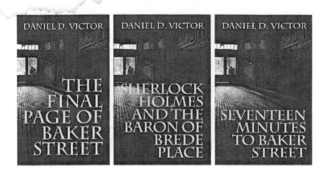

The Final Page of Baker Street
The Baron of Brede Place
Seventeen Minutes To Baker Street

"The really amazing thing about this book is the author's ability to call up the 'essence' of both the Baker Street 'digs' of Holmes and Watson as well as that of the 'mean streets' of Marlowe's Los Angeles. Although none of the action takes place in either place, Holmes and Watson share a sense of camaraderie and self-confidence in facing threats and problems that also pervades many of the later tales in the Canon. Following their conversations and banter is a return to Edwardian England and its certainties and hope for the future. This is definitely the world before The Great War."
Philip K Jones

www.mxpublishing.com

Also from MX Publishing

The Detective and The Woman Series

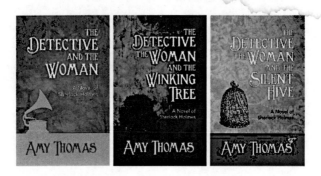

The Detective and The Woman
The Detective, The Woman and The Winking Tree
The Detective, The Woman and The Silent Hive

"The book is entertaining, puzzling and a lot of fun. I believe the author has hit on the only type of long-term relationship possible for Sherlock Holmes and Irene Adler. The details of the narrative only add force to the romantic defects we expect in both of them and their growth and development are truly marvelous to watch. This is not a love story. Instead, it is a coming-of-age tale starring two of our favorite characters."
Philip K Jones

www.mxpublishing.com

Also from MX Publishing

The Sherlock Holmes and Enoch Hale Series

The Amateur Executioner
The Poisoned Penman
The Egyptian Curse

"The Amateur Executioner: Enoch Hale Meets Sherlock Holmes", the first collaboration between Dan Andriacco and Kieran McMullen, concerns the possibility of a Fenian attack in London. Hale, a native Bostonian, is a reporter for London's Central News Syndicate - where, in 1920, Horace Harker is still a familiar figure, though far from revered. "The Amateur Executioner" takes us into an ambiguous and murky world where right and wrong aren't always distinguishable. I look forward to reading more about Enoch Hale."
Sherlock Holmes Society of London

www.mxpublishing.com

Also from MX Publishing

Sherlock Holmes novellas in verse

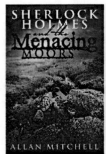  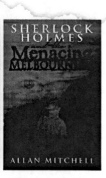

All four novellas
have been
released also in
audio format
with narration
by Steve White

Sherlock Holmes and The Menacing Moors
Sherlock Holmes and The Menacing Metropolis
Sherlock Holmes and The Menacing Melbournian
Sherlock Holmes and The Menacing Monk

"The story is really good and the Herculean effort it must have been to write it all in verse—well, my hat is off to you, Mr. Allan Mitchell! I wouldn't dream of seeing such work get less than five plus stars from me..." **The Raven**

Also from MX Publishing

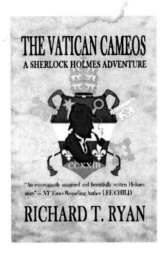

THE VATICAN CAMEOS

A SHERLOCK HOLMES ADVENTURE

"An extravagantly imagined and beautifully written Holmes story" – NY Times Bestselling Author LEE CHILD

RICHARD T. RYAN

When the papal apartments are burgled in 1901, Sherlock Holmes is summoned to Rome by Pope Leo XII. After learning from the pontiff that several priceless cameos that could prove compromising to the church, and perhaps determine the future of the newly unified Italy, have been stolen, Holmes is asked to recover them. In a parallel story, Michelangelo, the toast of Rome in 1501 after the unveiling of his Pieta, is commissioned by Pope Alexander VI, the last of the Borgia pontiffs, with creating the cameos that will bedevil Holmes and the papacy four centuries later. For fans of Conan Doyle's immortal detective, the game is always afoot. However, the great detective has never encountered an adversary quite like the one with whom he crosses swords in "The Vatican Cameos.."

"An extravagantly imagined and beautifully written Holmes story"
(**Lee Child**, NY Times Bestselling author, Jack Reacher series)

CPSIA information can be obtained
at www.ICGtesting.com
Printed in the USA
LVOW10s1327161117
556549LV00021B/138/P